Amberlin
Awakening
Book 2 of the Amberlin Series
W. Bradford Swift

AMBERLIN: AWAKENING

First edition. May 23, 2018.

Written by W. Bradford Swift.

Part One

Mountain Haven

Amberlin Gentry watched the dishwater as it spiraled down the drain. It reminded her of another time several years ago when she'd been young and innocent and found it fun to play with water funnels. Then grandmother Rose had intervened. She paused a moment with her right hand poised over the water, her index finger pointing at the funnel, but then stopped. She recalled the angry reaction of her grandmother as she had played with the water spout of her draining tub when she'd been six or seven. She could still feel the crisp slap across her hand and the harsh words that accompanied it. It was the only time she could remember either of her grandparents using any form of physical force to correct her.

She relaxed her hand and drew it away from the sink, reaching instead for a hand towel. Using the special powers that had been passed on through the generations of the Gentry women had only led to trouble—had, in fact, eventually led to her dearly beloved Papa Herb's death. It would be best to follow her grandmother Rose's advice and leave such abilities alone.

She turned away from the kitchen sink and gazed around the spacious kitchen that was, in many ways, the focal point of her family now. It had been almost four years since she had arrived at Canyon Green's homestead. It was tucked away at the end of a winding mountain road, miles from the closest town of Little Switzerland. She'd arrived with Miriam and her mother, Evelyn. Amberlin had spent most of her childhood thinking her mother had died in childbirth delivering her. She later learned that had been a lie perpetrated by her grandmother and Missy Stover, the minister's wife of the Golden Acre Christian Community where they all lived. That lie had also been a product of the Gentry women's special powers and had shaped much of Amberlin's childhood. Papa Herb had insisted such powers could and should be viewed as a blessing from God, but Rose had insisted they were a curse from Satan. After what had happened to Papa Herb, Amberlin tended to agree with her grandmother.

The three of them had arrived at the Green's homestead as fugitives from justice. Evelyn had been shot by Missy Stover at the same time that Reverend Stover had shot and killed Papa Herb. The Stovers had then turned the story around, convincing the police that it had been Evelyn who'd shot her father in retaliation for his condoning her being admitted to Western Carolina Sanitarium. There she'd met Miriam Mason, one of the nurses who had befriended Evelyn and eventually helped her to escape.

The three of them had fled from the asylum seeking someone who could doctor Evelyn's gunshot wound without turning them into the authorities. Canyon Green had been a godsend. A friend and Army buddy of Miriam's deceased husband, Canyon had been a medic in the service. He had no love lost for the police even though he was a staunch patriot at heart. They hadn't planned to stay long; just long enough for Evelyn to receive the help she needed, but days had turned into weeks and weeks into months. Before anyone knew it, those months had turned into a year, and then two. Somewhere along the way, Miriam had returned to her mother's home to reclaim her son, Matthew or Matty as everyone called him. She had then returned to the Green's homestead and to the man with whom she'd fallen in love.

Amberlin sat down at the round oak kitchen table with the carved lion feet around where they all sat for their meals. The sprawling log cabin had been in Canyon's family for generations. It had stood abandoned for a few years, but when Canyon had returned from the Army with an honorable discharge, he'd reclaimed his heritage. He had spent years repairing the cabin that sat in the middle of about twenty acres of rolling farmland mixed with woods. It had become not only a haven from the law but, over time, a home complete with a new family.

While she still missed Papa Herb and yes, her grandmother Rose as well, Amberlin had finally released them to recede into the past. The only fragment retained was old Ruffian, Papa Herb's Australian sheepdog. She had found him wandering in the woods behind their burned-out home where Rose had lost her life, the only time Amberlin had dared to return to Golden Acres.

Now, she had Miriam and Canyon. On most days, she thought of them as her aunt and uncle, even though she thought of Matty as her younger brother. Then, there was Evelyn, her true mother with whom she'd reunited after so many years of thinking her dead. Some days she thought of her as her mom, but on other days when Evelyn was having one of her 'off days,' she felt more like an older sister. On the awful days, Evelyn seemed like a much younger sister that needed protection, compassion, and more than a little forgiveness.

Amberlin hung the towel up and walked into the foyer area where she pulled on her heaviest coat. The weather in mid-January in the North Carolina mountains could be brutal, but chickens still needed to be fed, and their nests checked for eggs that would make up the bulk of the next day's breakfast. Luckily, Canyon insisted on taking care of the small herd of goats and cows himself, though from time to time he called upon her to help with the milking. She wrapped the new scarf that Miriam had given to her for Christmas around her neck and donned a wool cap over her blonde curls before picking up the egg basket. She took a last look around at the myriad of coats, boots and other winter paraphernalia. There'd been no new snow for close to a month so the well-worn path to the chicken coop wouldn't require boots.

"Matty, I'm going to check on the chickens. I'll be back in a few minutes, and we can play that game of checkers I promised you."

"Hurry back," the young boy called from the other room. "I'll set the board up. Can we play the best two games out of three?"

"Sure, I guess so," Amberlin replied. "I've completed my homeschool work for today."

She took a deep breath, preparing herself for the assault of cold air as she opened the front door. As she trudged to the coop, she smiled. Life on the farm wasn't always easy, but she'd grown to love it. She felt blessed that they'd truly found a haven here.

Amateur Night Practice

It had started as a fluke and a dare. Not long after they had settled in Canyon's homestead, he'd invited them to accompany him to the Rock Inn Mountain Tavern in nearby Little Switzerland. The Tavern was run by one of Canyon's old Army buddies and weekly hosted an amateur night on Thursdays that had grown in popularity among the locals.

The Rock Inn had been around for ages and had grown to be one of the most popular night spots for locals as well as tourists. The tavern's rustic look of rough-hewn logs and rock exterior seemed to draw people in with a *welcome, stay awhile* atmosphere.

Evelyn declined the invitation, feeling it too risky to be seen in public just yet, but Miriam and Amberlin had graciously accepted.

"I think we could use a little fun in our life," Miriam had said, and Amberlin agreed.

It was on their third amateur night when Canyon leaned over to Amberlin who had been quietly singing along with the music.

"You have a beautiful voice. Why not get up there and share it with everyone else?"

"Up there?" Amberlin said pointing to the stage where the latest amateur duo was finishing up. "I couldn't do that. I'd be too scared."

"Come on," Canyon had insisted. "I'll borrow Mike's guitar and accompany you. It'll be fun."

They continued to banter back and forth about it during the next two songs with Miriam joining in to encourage Amberlin to give it a try.

She finally conceded as much to shut the two up as anything. It turned out that Canyon was more than a passable guitarist, and had a pleasant tenor voice of his own, but it was Amberlin's angelic soprano that had captured the crowd, and much to her surprise, Amberlin enjoyed singing for the enthusiastic throng of neighbors mixed in with a few out-of-towners.

Now, six months later, Amberlin and Canyon had become regulars to amateur night, and she looked forward to spending most Thursday nights at the

Tavern and on stage. She spent much of her time during the week listening to Canyon's old radio that sat in the corner of the great room. She found she particularly enjoyed the stations that played a combination of country music and folk songs. She particularly liked the Kingston Trio and the songs of the Weavers.

Each week she would pick out two or three songs she liked and practice singing them as she did her chores in preparation for trying them out at Amateur Night. Even Evelyn had started joining them, though she insisted on wearing a disguise of dark sunglasses, one of Canyon's hats with her hair tucked up in it, and an old Army jacket of his that made it hard to tell if she was a man or a woman. Amberlin had grown to accept such paranoid antics from her mother. After all, as Miriam had explained to her, Evelyn had had a rough go of it imprisoned for so many years in the mental institution. She might have entered Western Carolina Sanitarium of sound mind, but she certainly hadn't left that way.

On Monday morning as everyone sat around the kitchen table finishing breakfast, Canyon reached into his back pocket and pulled out a crumpled letter. Opening it, he straightened the pages before sliding one of them over to Amberlin.

"Would you do me a favor for Amateur Night this week?" he started.

Amberlin glanced down at the sheet in front of her and started reading what appeared to be a poem. She instantly recognized many of the lines as coming from the Bible.

"Sure," she replied. "What's this?"

"It's the lyrics to a song an old friend of mine wrote. I thought we could practice it so we could sing it on Thursday. Kinda my way to acknowledge and celebrate what will be happening on Friday."

"Okay, I'm game." She paused for a moment before adding. "What's happening on Friday?"

Canyon stared at her for a moment. "You're kidding, right?"

Amberlin racked her brain trying to remember but came up empty a second time. She shrugged. "Give me a hint?" she asked.

"It happens every four years," Canyon replied.

Amberlin shook her head again. "Sorry."

"John Kennedy will be sworn in as our thirty-fifth president," Canyon replied, a hint of agitation seeping into his voice.

"Oh, yeah, that," Amberlin replied blushing. She knew Canyon was a huge fan of Kennedy, one of the few in this part of the country. "Are you sure we won't be hooted off stage?"

"No, I'm not, but I'm willing to take that chance. How about you?"

Amberlin wasn't quite so quick to reply this time. Finally, she said, "Yeah, I guess so, as long as you promise to protect me if we start a riot."

Canyon chuckled. "Not a problem. I'm hoping for just the opposite effect." He pointed down to the paper in front of her. "The song is all about peace, so I'm hoping it'll be well received."

"Do you know the melody?" Amberlin asked after reading over the lyrics again.

"Yeah, pretty sure. We can practice it later this afternoon when I get back from grocery shopping."

"Okay," Amberlin replied. "Can I go with you to the Piggly Wiggly? I'd like to take my skates. It's been cold enough the last couple of weeks that the pond behind the store should be frozen."

"Me too! Can I go?" Matty chimed in.

"Sure, as long as you have at least half your homeschool work finished. I'll be heading out around ten."

"Okay, let's get to it," Amberlin said as she and Matty rose from their chairs.

"Will you pull me around on the ice?" Matty asked.

"I don't see why not?" Amberlin replied.

"Dishes to the sink," Miriam reminded them. "It's Evelyn's and my turn to clean."

As Amberlin settled in the overstuffed chair in the living room near the large stone fireplace, her favorite place to study during the wintertime, she read over the lyrics again, humming softly to herself what she thought the melody might be. She decided she liked the song and wondered who had written it. She was often surprised by the many people Canyon knew, especially other musicians. Before he'd joined the Army, he'd been a part of a small band that had traveled around the country playing small gigs wherever they could find work. Unfortunately, the group disbanded in its second year due to a number of disagreements among its members, made worse by the lack of money. Canyon had kicked around playing backup guitar with some other bands before finally deciding to join the service to see the world. After his training, he became part of the American forces sent into Vietnam as "advisors" to help the Republic of Vietnam fight Communist insurgents known as "Viet Cong." That's where he met Angus Eisen, the owner of the Rock Inn Tavern.

Showtime

An hour before they were scheduled to leave for Amateur Night, the babysitter called to let Miriam know that she'd not be able to sit for her because her mom had come down with the flu. As Miriam walked into Amberlin's bedroom to share the news, she ran into a heated conversation between Evelyn and Amberlin that was rapidly growing into an argument, one that had become a regular part of the Thursday evening routine. On the bed lay a navy blue wool jumper next to a white blouse.

"I do like the jumper you made, Mom," Amberlin said with a note of impatience in her voice. She stood next to the bed dressed in a pair of bell-bottom jeans and a white peasant blouse. "I've told you that before. It's just not something to wear at the Tavern."

"Why not?" Evelyn asked.

Seeing Miriam come into the room, an exasperated Amberlin turned to her for support. "Miriam, tell her. You've been to the Tavern. Isn't what I'm wearing okay?"

Miriam, who'd been drawn into similar arguments between the two Gentrys smiled and answered diplomatically. "Well, I think either outfit would be fine, but since you're going to be singing tonight, I think what you're wearing will do. However, I've just heard from the babysitter that she won't be able to make it tonight."

There was a long silence, the subject of which outfit to wear forgotten. The news meant someone would have to stay home with Matty. Before Evelyn could offer to stay, Miriam spoke up.

"Y'all go on. I'm not feeling in a very festive mood anyway. I'd enjoy a quiet evening at home with Matty. Besides, he owes me a rematch in checkers."

"Are you sure?" Evelyn asked. "I think it's really my turn to stay home."

"No, no, you go on and cheer for your daughter," Miriam replied then added. "Just not too loudly. We don't want to draw too much attention."

Amberlin felt a queasy sensation begin to build just below her solar plexus. She felt better when Miriam could be with them. She seemed to know just how to respond to keep Evelyn on an even keel. Still, she did want her mom to hear her sing the new song, so she kept her mouth shut.

By the time they arrived a little after nine, the Mountain Tavern was jammed with a standing room only crowd. It was one of the few spots open at night in the wintertime. Luckily, Angus made it a point to save them a table near the stage. It was the least he could do for his old friend and one of his most popular acts. Amateur Night had already begun, so the three of them had to wait at the bar for a duo that Amber didn't recognize to finish their off key rendition of an old southern Gospel song. As the crowd applauded politely, Canyon led the way to their table in time for the next act. Minutes later, one of the waitresses dressed up in jeans, a cowboy shirt and hat arrived with their drinks—a draft beer for Canyon and two iced teas for Amberlin and Evelyn.

As the evening unfolded, Amberlin felt her anxiety building. She always felt nervous before performing, but this night seemed worse. She glanced around at the rowdy crowd that grew louder as the evening progressed and the beer and wine poured forth. She estimated there were probably two men for every woman. Many of the men wore sweaty ball caps with their bills turned in various directions while others sported their favorite cowboy hats. I know these people, she told herself. I've grown up around folks like this. Good hardworking men and women who came out at night to tip a few mugs of beer and blow off a little steam. Nothing to worry about, right? Besides, every time she'd sung before, these same people had given her a warm reception, often clapping for another song or two.

She was still trying to calm herself when she felt Canyon's hand on her own.

"It's our turn. You ready?" Canyon asked as he stood up and reached for his guitar.

Amberlin nodded.

They made their way to the stage with a warm round of applause and several of Canyon's friends exhorting him on. "Give 'em hell, Canyon...'bout time, real singers...show 'em how it's done." Amberlin noticed that Canyon also wore a pair of bluejeans minus the bellbottoms and a white shirt. She made a mental note of this. Next time Evelyn tried to persuade her to wear the wool dress, she'd point out that Canyon and she had to wear a matching outfit as part of their routine.

Canyon took a moment to tune his guitar before looking over to Amberlin with a reassuring smile and a nod. They began with a crowd favorite, *Ebony Eyes*, followed with *Crazy* that allowed Amberlin to sing solo while Canyon accompanied her on his guitar. They finished both to loud rounds of applause with hoots and whistles mixed in. Amberlin was ready to walk off the stage but knew they still had one more song to sing.

"Angus has given us the go-ahead to finish tonight's amateur hour with a new song that hasn't even hit the airwaves yet. I'd like to dedicate it to our new President of the United States, John Kennedy, who will be sworn in tomorrow," Canyon said as he lightly strummed his guitar.

The crowd reaction was mixed with several men apparently taking issue with the dedication.

"I hear Kennedy is going to have the Pope in his Cabinet," yelled one man from the back of the room.

"Going to sell us out to the Commies," another shouted.

Canyon chose to ignore the comments. Instead, he smiled at Amberlin again and gave a nod to start the song.

As they sang, the crowd grew quiet. The music flowed serenely as Canyon plucked out the various chords. By the time they reached the last verse, the crowd became mesmerized by Amberlin's melodic rendition of the song that suggested that everyone has a divine purpose while also encouraging peace throughout the world.

There was a long pause as the final notes slipped into the night. The applause that followed lacked the normal hoots and whistles but seemed more respectful and dignified to Amberlin's ears. As she started to rise to leave the stage, Canyon reached over and patted her on the back, whispering, "Well done, my angel."

Disruption

1

As the three of them left the Tavern to make their way home, Amberlin felt proud of their performance and was thrilled how well the last song had been received, though she didn't understand a few of the comments she'd heard from the crowd before the song. She intended to ask Canyon about them when they got home.

Approaching Canyon's '55 Chevy pickup truck, she noticed five or six men around another pickup truck laughing and joking with each other as they passed around a bottle. She recognized one of the men as Josh Jenkins and remembered that he and Canyon had had words once or twice before. Canyon had explained to her that he and Josh had gone to the same school years ago, though he didn't think Josh had ever graduated.

They were almost to Canyon's truck when she heard Josh yell out, "Hey Canyon, what's up with you? You turn into some kinda commie pinko?"

Canyon ignored the comment as he opened the door to the truck and started to help Amberlin into the cab, but before she had a chance to climb in, Josh strolled over to them, wavering from side to side a bit.

"Hey, I'm talking to you, Canyon. Don't you try and run away."

Canyon slowly turned to him. "You're feeling no pain tonight, huh Josh. Why don't you boys just get on back to your moonshine, and we'll call it a night?"

"You were in the army, weren't you?" Josh asked, taking another long pull from the bottle before passing it to one of his comrades behind him. He cocked the ratty looking cowboy hat back on his head. "Tell me, did the commies get to you while you were overseas? Vietnam, wasn't it?"

Canyon nodded but didn't say anything. He was about to turn back to help Amberlin when around the back of the truck stormed a red-faced Evelyn.

"How dare you talk like that to a veteran?" Evelyn inserted herself between the two men. She yanked her cap off her head, loosening a cascade of blond hair. She used her index finger to poke Josh in the chest. "Were you ever in the service? Huh, were you?"

Josh stepped back, a confused look growing on his face, unsure what to make of this counter-offensive. "Who the hell are you?"

"Well, were you?" Evelyn asked again, ignoring his question.

"No," Josh finally answered. "Got flat feet. They wouldn't take me."

"Flat feet to go with your fat head," Evelyn stayed on the offensive. "Then you've no right to question Canyon's loyalty to his country," she said, her voice growing in volume with every word.

Amberlin had seen this a few times before, had even been the recipient more than once. She knew her mom was about to lose it big time. On previous occasions, Miriam had been available to calm her down and avoid a serious blowup, but Miriam wasn't here this time. It would have to be up to her to try to ease the mounting tension, but how?

She took her foot off the running board of the truck and eased herself around Canyon who appeared to be unsure what to do himself. Amberlin walked slowly over to her mother who was now standing less than a foot from the larger man, her face stuck forward only a few inches from his.

What am I going to do? Amberlin thought hard for a solution. Any second someone was likely to take a swing at the other person; then all hell would break loose. She took a deep breath and prayed for guidance. Suddenly, she remembered a couple of lines from their closing song:

A time of war, a time of peace
A time you may embrace...

She quickly closed the few feet between her and her mom, and before she had time to reconsider her actions, she reached out and hugged her mother with all her might and whispered in her ear, "I love you, Mom." She repeated the words three times. As she did so, she felt a wave of love radiate from her heart like the ripples of water after a pebble is dropped in. She felt the tightness of her mother's muscles slowly relax and her breathing ease.

Evelyn finally replied, "I love you too, sweetie." She turned to her daughter and returned the hug. As they held each other, Amberlin glanced first to Canyon then to Josh. She was surprised and perplexed to see similar peaceful looks on both men's faces, when just seconds ago, there had been anger. She was even more shocked to see the identical look on Josh's companions' faces.

Finally, Josh spoke up. "The young lady is right. We'll finish this discussion another time. Y'all be careful driving home, ya hear?" And with that, he turned to his friends. "Let's go fellas. We need to find us another bottle. This one's empty." He returned to his truck, tossing the bottle into the truck's bed where it shattered. His friends piled into his vehicle and drove off with tires screeching and shouts about the South rising again.

2

MISSY STOVER SAT ALONE in the front pew of the Golden Acres Church sanctuary where she was accustomed to sitting whenever her husband, Reverend Stover, delivered the Sunday message. She held her Bible in her lap gently caressing its leather cover as was her habit whenever she prayed. She could feel the difference in its texture from where she'd slowly worn through the outer layer through the years. She had miscalculated the morning temperature when she'd donned the flowery frock, forgetting that the deacons had decided to keep the sanctuary temperature much colder during the week. Luckily, she kept a wool sweater in her office that she could put on once she was through talking with God.

She sat in silence for another minute organizing her thoughts and getting herself in the right frame of mind. She'd known for the last few days that there was something she needed to ask God and now she was clear what it was. Three years ago, she'd finally persuaded her husband to extend their work beyond Golden Acres with a series of spring and summer revivals, mostly around the Southeast. They'd done well, converting hundreds of lost souls and raising contributions well beyond anything they'd been able to do in Golden Acres. But over this last year, their work for God had grown stale and uninspiring.

Holding the Bible to her chest, she started, "Dear Lord, I come to you as your humble servant, thankful for your Son and your grace. I know I'm just a sinner in your eyes, but I also feel called to perform greater works in your name. The world is so filled with evil and non-believers. The task is great but I know you expect much from your flock, and I am here for your guidance. Please, Lord, direct me to how I can better serve you."

She paused to wipe a tear from her cheek before continuing. "Please instill in my husband, Reverend Stover, your blessings and the passion and backbone so needed in our work. I realize he is weak and has his faults, but you have joined us together so that I might give him the strength he needs to do your work. I will not fail you. Just let me know what you want from me next. I await your sign. In Jesus' precious name, Amen."

"Okay, that's done," she whispered. "Now on with the day." She arose, straightened her dress, and with her Bible still pressed against her chest, strode out of the sanctuary and down the hall to her office. She went immediately to the closet and put on the wool sweater even though the spare heater had kept her office temperature several degrees warmer. Walking over to her desk, she set her Bible on it and glanced down to the stack of mail and the newspaper next to the mail. She nonchalantly glanced through the paper as she waited for the chill to pass. She flipped from the front back to the entertainment section where there was already a feature story on the upcoming Academy Awards. Next to it was a second story about the surge of Hollywood divorces, unwanted pregnancies, and extramarital affairs.

What a den of iniquity, she thought. She felt a shiver run through her body that was not connected to how warm or cold she was. She closed her eyes and bowed her head. "Thank you, God, for delivering the sign so promptly and clearly. Amen."

She stared at the paper again. That's where we're meant to take our revival this year, straight into the Devil's den, Missy thought. Of course, persuading Reverend Stover wouldn't be easy. He was always much more conservative when it came to such matters, but she wasn't really worried. After all, she had God on her side, and he'd given her plenty of tools to work such miracles.

Visitation

1

Later that evening after the close call in the parking lot with Josh and his gang, Amberlin found it difficult to shut her mind off and go to sleep. The looks on the men's faces kept flashing in her mind. What had happened to them, especially to Josh and Evelyn who were on the edge of fighting? Or had it all just been her imagination? Maybe no one really wanted to fight and were looking for a way out. Maybe, but Amberlin didn't think so. She'd felt something powerful emanate from her as well.

She tossed and turned for hours, replaying the incident in her dreams. She finally fell asleep still wondering about the episode. Around three or four in the morning, she found herself once more in the parking lot, but this time there was a mysterious blue haze around everything that hadn't been there before, even though the scene played out exactly as she recalled it...until she reached out to hug her mother. Suddenly, everything froze in place. She pulled away from her mother and glanced around to find Papa Herb sitting on the bed of Canyon's truck with a second figure Amberlin didn't recognize sitting next to him. Papa Herb was dressed in the same khaki pants and long sleeve blue shirt she remembered him wearing on that fateful day he'd been shot and killed by Reverend Stover in the parking lot of the asylum. The other man, several years younger looking than her grandpa, wore loose-fitting black pants, a flowing white shirt, and sandals, even though the temperature of the evening was in the low thirties.

A gasp caught in Amberlin's throat at seeing her grandpa after so much time, but she was also mystified by his appearance. She took several steps in his direction but stopped when he held his hand up to her. "Where have you been?" she asked. "You said you'd always be with me."

"Oh, I have," Papa Herb replied with a fatherly smile that never failed to melt Amberlin's heart. "Just not so you would know it...until now."

"Why now?" Amberlin shot back.

"Because it's time."

"Time? Time for what?"

"Time for you to get on with it," Papa Herb replied with a light wave of his hand.

"What are you talking about?" Amberlin asked, feeling a ripple of impatience beginning to grow within her.

"It's time for you to get on with fulfilling your Divine Destiny," the man sitting next to Papa Herb replied in a soft voice bordering on a whisper.

"What? Wait a minute. Who are you, anyway?"

"I'm Mo," the man replied simply.

"Who? Mo who...wait a minute." The name sounded vaguely familiar. "Are you Mo Zoloff, the spiritual sage Papa Herb used to tell me about?"

"Yes, that's right," the man replied with a slight bow. "So kind of you to remember."

"But you look so young."

"Well age is irrelevant where we come from, but this is how your grandpa remembers me, so I'm happy to oblige him."

Amberlin shook her head to gather her thoughts. She finally asked, "What do you mean it's time for me to get on with my Divine Destiny? I don't have a clue what that even means anymore. I don't think I ever did."

"I know," Papa Herb replied.

After a long pause during which Amberlin glanced from one man and then the other, she finally continued. "Well, aren't one of you going to tell me what it means?"

The two men looked at each other before turning back to her. "No, it doesn't work that way," Mo replied, "but I can give you a hint."

"Oh great, a Cosmic guessing game. Just what I need."

"Something like that." Mo chuckled.

Another long pause passed before Amberlin finally blurted out. "Well, okay. What's the hint?"

Mo turned to Papa Herb. "You're right. She is feisty."

Papa Herb nodded. "You haven't seen anything yet."

"Remember the story your granddad told you about the time he and I first met? He asked me before he left if there was a third word starting with P that went with protect and prepare?"

"Yes, I remember. The word was purpose, right?"

Mo nodded. "Yes, well, there was actually a fourth word he didn't ask about."

"And it has something to do with my Divine Destiny?"

"Exactly...precisely," Mo said.

"Well, what is it?" Amberlin replied when he didn't continue.

Mo didn't reply at first but glanced over to Papa Herb who gave him a slight nod. As he did so, Amberlin noticed the two figures becoming less substantial. She could see through them. Finally, Mo turned back to her and said, "Peace."

Amberlin felt a shiver run up and down her back as the word resonated with her soul. But the word elicited as many questions as it answered. She opened her mouth to ask one of them to elaborate, but before she could, she noticed the fading continuing.

"Wait a minute. Where are you going? You can't just zip back into my life, lay a word like *peace* on me and then fade away into the night."

But evidently, they could because they were.

"I love you, my dear," Papa Herb said. "Never forget it. Oh, and one more thing." His body was just an ethereal illusion by this time, and his words were growing fainter as well.

"Well, what is it?" Amberlin said as she stepped closer to the truck to hear him.

"Watch...Ken..." The last word faded into nothingness.

"What? Say that again?" But it was too late. Her two visitors had disappeared. She stood there for several seconds, a perplexed look on her face. "Who the hell is Ken?"

2

AS MIRIAM FINISHED saying the morning blessing, Amberlin raised her head and reached for the mug of coffee she'd fixed herself in an effort to wake up.

"You don't look so good," Miriam commented as she reached for the butter. "And is that coffee you're drinking?"

"Yes," Amberlin replied. "I didn't sleep well last night."

"I'm sorry to hear that," Evelyn said. She reached over to grasp her daughter's hand. "Was it because of what happened last night? If so, I'm sorry."

"No, it wasn't that...well, maybe it was a little." Amberlin corrected herself. "I did dream about being in the Tavern's parking lot, but that wasn't the most disturbing part of the night."

"Oh? What was?"

"I had two visitors last night."

"You what?" Evelyn asked. "Who? How?"

"In my dream. Papa Herb and a spiritual sage named Mo Zoloff came to me in a dream. Papa Herb used to tell me stories about Mo."

Evelyn gasped. "You're kidding. I dreamt about father as well. How strange."

"You did? I guess he was making the rounds last night," Amberlin quipped. "What did he want?"

"He asked for my forgiveness for leaving me in the asylum for so many years," Evelyn said. "I told him it wasn't his fault, so there really wasn't anything to forgive. It was Missy Stover and mother who instigated that."

"What did he tell you?" Evelyn asked.

Suddenly, Amberlin wasn't sure she was ready to tell anyone about the conversation they'd had. "Well, not much really. He just told me that he loved me and was looking over me." She paused before continuing. "There was one thing he said as he was leaving that didn't make any sense."

"What was that, sweetie?"

"Something about watching Ken."

"Who's Ken?" Miriam asked.

"That's the thing. I don't know anyone by that name."

"I think I know what he was referring to." Canyon spoke up for the first time. "You said he told you this as he was leaving?"

"Yeah, kinda just fading away."

"I bet he was asking you to watch John Kennedy's inauguration today."

"Maybe," Amberlin replied, "but how am I supposed to do that? Isn't that taking place in Washington D. C.?"

"That's right, but it's going to be televised today. You'll be able to watch history being made since it's the first inauguration of a U.S. president covered on television."

"But why in the world would Papa Herb want me to watch that? My grandpa had the least interest in politics of anyone I ever met."

"I don't know," Canyon replied as he reached for the coffee pot to pour himself another cup. "I guess you'll need to watch to find out. We can watch it together. Consider it part of your homeschool work."

Amberlin groaned. "That's what you always say when you want me to do something that's either boring or unpleasant."

"Well, actually I'm not telling you to watch it," Canyon countered. "It was your grandpa that made that request."

Inauguration

1

A little bit before 1 p.m. everyone moved from the kitchen where they had been eating lunch into the living room. Canyon had turned on the TV earlier, so it could warm up, and so he could adjust the rabbit ears to bring in the station as clearly as possible. Even so, there was a fair amount of snow appearing on the screen, and the sound faded in and out. As the rest of them took their customary seats around the set, Canyon adjusted the antenna to improve the quality of the picture and sound including turning the two strips of aluminum foil that had been added for this special occasion.

When he was satisfied that he had the best picture possible, he joined Miriam on the overstuffed couch, stepping over Amberlin and Matty where they sat on the floor.

"Okay, they're about to start," Canyon said. "Matty, please limit the squirming for the next few minutes. Can you do that?"

"Yes, sir," Matty replied. "I'll do my best."

"And Amberlin, I would encourage you to listen closely to our new President's acceptance speech. Imagine that your grandpa knew that there was something in the speech that's meant especially for you. Will you listen in that way?"

"Sure thing," Amberlin replied," though I can't imagine what the President of the United States would have to say to me."

"Well, we're about to find out," Miriam said as she reached over to grasp Canyon's hand.

The ceremony started off slowly with a stodgy looking man in a black robe asking Kennedy to repeat after him the oath of office.

"So that's Kennedy," Amberlin said. "He's handsome."

"You can say that again," Miriam and Evelyn both said at the same time, then giggled.

"Listen up," Canyon said, but he was chuckling at the women's responses as well.

"Look at those men behind him with those funny looking hats," Matty said as he pointed to the TV screen.

"Those are called top hats," Miriam said. "Now, shh."

The first line that caught Amberlin's attention came early in the speech. "For man holds in his mortal hands the power to abolish all forms of human poverty and all forms of human life."

She'd never thought of that before. We could end poverty or end the world. For the first time, she began to have an inkling of the power and responsibility of being the President of the United States. It certainly wasn't something in which she'd normally be interested.

As Kennedy continued to speak, Amberlin felt moved and inspired by his words. Evidently, the crowd was inspired as well for the new President had to stop often and wait for them to stop applauding. She also noticed that he referred to peace several times. Each time he did, Amberlin felt a shiver run through her, recalling Mo's words from last night. She pulled a pen from her jean pocket and started writing notes on her palm.

But it wasn't until the end of the speech that Amberlin finally heard what she felt sure Papa Herb wanted her to hear:

"And so, my fellow Americans: ask not what your country can do for you—ask what you can do for your country.

"My fellow citizens of the world: ask not what America will do for you, but what together we can do for the freedom of man."

As Kennedy concluded his speech, Amberlin heard Papa Herb's voice. "He's talking to you, my little one, for you are both an American and a citizen of the world."

2

EVERYONE CONTINUED to sit around the TV without talking. Matty lay on his back using the small of Amberlin's back as a pillow as he played with two of the toy soldiers from the collection Canyon had given him for his birthday.

"Is it finally over?" he asked. "Can we go out and play now?"

"In a little while," Amberlin replied. "Just be patient a little longer."

Matty groaned but then went back to playing with the toy soldiers.

"What did you think?" Canyon asked. "Did you hear anything that spoke to you?"

Amberlin turned a bit to look at him. "Yes, I think so. You remember how I told you that Papa Herb often talked to me about Divine Destiny and how he felt I had an especially important one to fulfill?"

"Yes," Canyon replied.

"But he never told me what he thought it was."

"Right."

"Well, last night Mo gave me a hint about it."

"What was that?" Canyon asked.

"Just one word: peace."

"Really? Well, peace is certainly important. We could all surely benefit from more of it."

"But you're a soldier," Matty spoke up as he pretended to shoot one of the toy soldiers with the other one. "I thought you were for war, not peace."

"Not at all, Matty, my boy. Sometimes soldiers need to fight wars so we can have peace."

Matty paused his play for a moment as he considered what Canyon had said. Finally, he replied, "Well, that seems kinda dumb. War just makes people madder and wanting to fight more. How does that bring peace?"

"You make a good point, son. It's one of the reasons I'm no longer a soldier," Canyon replied.

Having said his piece, Matty sat up. "Can I go out and play now?"

"Yes you may," Miriam answered. "You've done quite well. Just be sure to put on a coat and your mittens. It's cold out there."

"Aww, Mom," Matty groaned, but on the way to the front door, he paused long enough to get his coat and mittens.

"And a hat," Miriam yelled from the living room which elicited another groan before the door slammed shut.

"So, peace," Canyon said, returning to the conversation. "What about it?"

"I don't know exactly, but Kennedy talked about it several times in his speech. I wrote them down on my hand." She looked at her palm. "He talked about a 'peaceful revolution of hope.' Later he mentioned the 'instruments of peace,' and a 'quest for peace.'

"Wow, you were really paying attention."

Amberlin nodded as she moved to sit cross-legged. "But I don't get it. How can I possibly have anything to do with bringing world peace? I'm just a kid, and I'll sure never be in a position of power like Kennedy. I know at the end he said, 'ask not what your country can do for you—ask what you can do for your country,' but come on. Let's be realistic. There has never been a woman President, and I'm sure not going to be the first."

"Well, what would your Papa Herb have to say about that?" Canyon asked.

"He'd probably tell me to trust in God and to let my life unfold."

"Sounds like pretty good advice to me."

Amberlin nodded. "Yeah, I guess so."

Canyon stood up and stretched. "There's one other thing you might want to keep in mind."

"What's that?"

"Last night, you brought peace to a very tense situation in that parking lot. Any second it could have broken out into a big fight, but you stepped in even though you didn't know what to do at first, right?"

"Yeah?" Amberlin said cautiously. "Yeah! You're right."

"So, I wouldn't get overly worried about fulfilling your Divine Destiny just yet. You seem to be doing just fine," Canyon said. "Now, I have a list of chores to get to."

3

IN MANY WAYS, GROCERY Day was the highlight of the week since it was one of the few occasions that Canyon took time to drive into town, even if it was only to the Piggly Wiggly. Today, Evelyn, Amberlin, Matty, and he were squeezed into the cab of his pickup truck. Matty had tried to sit in the back in the truck's bed, but Canyon had nixed that.

"I know we've had a bit of a warm spell especially for late February, but it's still not that warm," Canyon had replied.

"Yeah, I'm not even taking my skates this time," Amberlin added to support Canyon's decision.

It was rare for Evelyn to be included in such trips, but she'd begged and pleaded to be allowed to join the group, promising to stay in the truck upon their arrival.

"I just need to get out of the house for awhile," she claimed. "I have a bad case of cabin fever."

Arriving at the grocery store, Canyon reminded Evelyn of her promise. "We won't be too long. I'll leave the keys in the ignition. In case you get cold, you can turn it on for the heater."

Evelyn nodded. She opened her mouth as though to speak, then shut it again.

As the three of them entered the front entrance to the Piggly Wiggly, they heard a pleasant greeting from Ellie Crane who ran the store. "Welcome to Piggly Wiggly. Thanks for shopping with us. Oh, hi, Canyon and company. Good to see you again. Welcome to the madhouse."

Amberlin looked around, realizing that the store was more crowded than usual.

"This almost springlike weather has brought folks out by the droves," Ellie said. "Not that I'm complaining, mind you. It's great for business though not so great for my sanity."

"Grab a cart," Canyon instructed Amberlin as he watched Matty tear off for the candy section. "You can pick five pieces of the penny candy, young man. No more, you hear?"

"Yes, sir," Matty replied over his shoulder.

As Amberlin returned with the cart, Canyon pulled the grocery list Miriam had given him earlier in the morning from his flannel shirt pocket. The two of them wove their way through the crowd of other shoppers as they strolled up and down the aisle. They were coming down the third row approaching the front of the store when Canyon asked, "Where's Matty? He's not in the candy section."

Amberlin shrugged her shoulders. "I don't know."

"Ellie, have you seen Matty?" Canyon asked.

"I think I saw him heading to the back. I figured he needed to use the restroom, but that was several minutes ago," Ellie replied.

"I better go check on him," Canyon said. He handed Amberlin the list. "You keep shopping. I'll only be a minute."

Canyon walked back to where the bathrooms were but was surprised to find no Matty. Growing a little more worried, he exited the men's room and looked around to find the backdoor cracked open. He walked over and opened it in time to see Matty down on the pond pretending to skate. As he did so, the young boy moved farther and farther from the edge.

Canyon opened his mouth to yell at him, but before he could say anything, he heard the cracking of ice, and a second later Matty disappeared.

"Matty!" Canyon yelled as he ran towards the pond. "Ellie, someone—help! Matty's fallen into the pond."

Matty

Amberlin was in the process of asking Ellie where she could find the next item on the grocery list when she heard a muffled yell from the rear of the store.

"What was that?" Ellie asked turning her attention to the commotion.

"It sounded like Canyon," Amberlin replied, "but I couldn't make out what he said." But it didn't sound good, she thought as they both started running towards the sound. As they ran, Ellie called out to several of the men she passed.

"Allan, follow me. Jake, you and Pete, help me out for a minute, will ya?" By the time they reached the back door, a small crowd of close to a dozen men and women trailed behind them. Ellie threw the door open with Amberlin close behind her. The two women saw Canyon down at the frozen lake but no sign of Matty. Amberlin noticed the break in the ice and her body froze in fear as she realized what must have happened to him.

"Matty fell through the ice," Canyon yelled, confirming Amberlin's fears. "I'm going in." As he made that last statement, he kicked his shoes off and ran onto the ice. As he neared the opening, he lunged out and slid the last few yards, disappearing into the chilling waters which promptly devoured him like a hungry beast.

"Jake, fetch the rope next to the door," Ellie ordered. "The rest of you follow me but stay away from the ice." Everyone jumped into action. Within moments of reaching the edge of the pond, Jake returned with a long length of rope neatly coiled. He handed it to Ellie.

"I'm light enough to be able to get closer to the break. Take this other end and be prepared to pull on my command." Without hesitating, Ellie made her way out onto the ice, getting within a few yards of the opening before she heard the crisp sound of new cracks. She promptly stopped and threw the end of the rope into the black hole where Canyon had disappeared moments before. Several feet of the rope disappeared into the water as Ellie played out more of it. Then nothing. Several seconds passed as everyone held their breath hoping and praying.

This was a stupid idea, Evelyn thought as she reached over to try to find a new station on the truck's radio. Why had she promised Canyon she would stay in the truck? It had been years since the incident at the asylum when she'd been falsely accused of shooting her father. Surely no one was looking for her by now. Still, the idea of being apprehended and returned to the institution, or worse, hauled off to jail, had kept her overly cautious. Cautious and free, she thought. She was between radio stations when she heard the distant yelling of a man's voice. While she couldn't make out the words, she could tell someone was in urgent need of help.

She hesitated for just a moment as she considered what to do. I better check it out, she thought, as she turned off the truck's engine and opened the door. As she started around the rear of the truck in the direction she thought the sound had come from, she noticed a foot long length of pipe left over from a recent plumbing job lying in the back. If someone were being mugged, she'd need a little help to balance out the situation, she thought. She grabbed the pipe from the truck bed and stuck it into her waistband. She heard a second shout and recognized Canyon's voice and ran in its direction.

Amberlin stared at the length of rope lying motionless in the black water of the hole. Please, God, let them be okay. She felt powerless as she stood there frozen by fear and uncertainty. What could she do? Two of the people she dearly loved were lost under the ice, and there was nothing she could do about it.

Stay calm. Your time will come.

It had been ages since she'd heard that inner voice but recognized it instantly as the voice of Papa Herb. He'd been right. He hadn't abandoned her. But what did he mean, her time would come?

She was still pondering the question when she noticed the rope quiver slightly followed a second later by a length of it disappearing under the water.

"We've got ourselves a nibble," Ellie shouted to the crowd behind her. "Okay, men. Pull slow and steady. Let's see what we've caught."

The line of men did as they were told and within seconds Canyon's head broke the surface of the water as he took a loud gasp of air. He held the rope wrapped around one arm, and a limp Matty held securely in the other. "Get me out of here," he pleaded between chattering teeth.

"Keep pulling men. We've almost got them," Ellie instructed. She knelt down and reached out her arms. "Just a little further. I've got you. Just a little more." Without turning her attention away from the two people in front of her, she yelled. "Someone get some blankets."

"They're on their way," someone in the crowded yelled back. "They'll be here in just a second."

Amberlin looked around to see a couple of women running down the hill from the store with blankets in their arms. She was moved to see how everyone joined forces in a crisis like this. As she started to turn back to the rescue scene at the pond, she noticed another familiar figure—her mother running towards her from around the building. She started to yell to her mom to go back to the truck but then stopped. It felt good to see her mother coming down the hill even as she worried that someone might recognize her.

Evelyn ran to her and gave her a big hug as she took in what was happening. Amberlin felt something in her mother's coat poke her but didn't think much of it. It felt so good to be hugged. The two of them clung to each other as the men finished pulling Canyon and Matty to safety. Everything would be okay now, Amberlin thought with a sigh of relief... that caught in her throat as she heard, "He's not breathing. The boy's not breathing."

It couldn't be, Amberlin thought as she looked on to confirm that, indeed, Matty showed no signs of life. Someone threw a blanket around Canyon's shivering shoulders as he lay Matty's still form down on a second blanket.

"You've got to help him," Evelyn whispered in her ear. "It's up to you."

"What can I do?" Amberlin asked. She'd recently read about a technique developed by the American Heart Association called CPR that was advocated to help people in such emergency situations, but she had no idea how to perform it.

"Does anyone know CPR," she called out to the crowd, but everyone only looked at her with blank stares.

"You have to help him," Evelyn repeated. "Remember how you saved me in the asylum," Evelyn continued, referring to when Papa Herb and Amberlin had found Evelyn in the midst of hanging herself. Amberlin had somehow managed to bring her mother back from the brink of death, but that had been years ago. Truth be known, she'd questioned whether she'd really done anything or if her mother had simply woken on her own.

It's time, Papa Herb added. *Trust yourself and remember, as you pray, move your feet.*

It had been one of Papa Herb's favorite sayings and most important lessons, the need to be in action as one asked for help from God.

Amberlin felt Evelyn relax her grip and gently push her towards Matty. *What am I to do? What am I to do?* Amberlin kept asking herself, but even as she did so, she kept moving toward the little boy who she'd grown to think of as her younger brother.

She heard several people in the crowd speak out. "What's she doing? Shouldn't we get help? Where's the sheriff? He's on his way."

Then a large man in bib overalls wearing a bulky coat that made it him even larger, stepped between her and Matty. "Stop, little girl. Let the adults handle this."

Before she could say anything, she felt Evelyn pushing her way between Amberlin and the man. Her mom held a length of pipe in one hand, waving it at the intruder. "Step out of the way," she ordered, "or you'll be lying there next to Matty. Let her do her thing."

A hush grew over the crowd as the man stared at the little woman who threatened to take him out. Tense seconds passed, then the man shrugged and stepped aside. "It's on you if the boy doesn't make it."

Her pathway cleared again, Amberlin rushed to Matty where she promptly lay down beside him. She grasped his frozen body in her own and hugged him. As she did so, she closed her eyes and envisioned entering his body with her spirit. *Come back to me, Matty,* she pleaded. *There are people here who love you and would miss you if you left us so soon. Please, come back.*

She wasn't sure how long she lay there with Matty in her arms. Someone had placed a couple of additional blankets over them creating a warm nest as the crowd of people huddled around them keeping a safe distance as Evelyn stood guard. Amberlin continued to call to Matty. *Remember how much fun we had last summer picking blueberries near our home? And how about those trips down to the creek fishing for crawdads? Just think how much you'll miss if you leave us now. Please, come back to us. We all love you so much, and you have such a great life awaiting you.*

She continued like this for an indeterminate amount of time. Finally, Amberlin felt Matty move. She glanced down at his angelic face as his eyelids fluttered. "Welcome back, little man."

"It's a miracle," a young woman still holding a bag of groceries in one arm shouted. She held the hand of her daughter with her free hand. "How did she do it?"

Evelyn turned to her and replied proudly, "My daughter is a healer."

"Really?" the woman asked.

Canyon, still shivering despite the blankets wrapped around him, stepped between the two women. "Evelyn, what are you doing here? You need to return to the truck, immediately." He turned to the other woman. "Hello, Maybelle. Good to see you again. Please, don't pay Evelyn any mind. She has a vivid imagination especially when it comes to her daughter. You have a good day now, you hear?"

Before Maybelle could reply, he turned back to Evelyn. "It's time for us to go. Help Amberlin. I'll carry Matty..." Leaning closer to her, he whispered, "...before Sheriff Bailey arrives."

As Evelyn helped her daughter to the truck, Canyon bent over to pick up Matty, keeping the boy wrapped in a blanket.

"Come on up to the store," Ellie said. "We need to get you out of those wet clothes."

"I'll be okay," Canyon replied as he started walking towards the parking lot. "It's more important to get Matty home where he belongs." He stopped and turned to Ellie. "Thank you for pulling us out. I owe you."

Healing

1

Upon returning home, Miriam took control over Matty's care, confining him to bed rest for the next two days despite his protesting that he was fine and wanted to go outside and play. She also took Canyon aside and thanked him profusely for saving her son's life, then later that night, thanked him again in her own special way.

It appeared everything was returning to normal when, on the third morning after the incident at the pond, there was a knocking at the door. Matty had been allowed out of bed so he could join the family at the breakfast table. Everyone stared at each other, unsure what the sound meant at first. Canyon's homestead was so far off the beaten track that it was rare for anyone to find there way there.

Finally, on the second round of knocking, Miriam stood up. "Someone's at the door. I'll go see who it is. Go ahead and finish eating." As she passed through the living room, she looked out its window and saw a rust-colored pickup truck that made Canyon's vehicle look like a showroom model. Not recognizing the truck, she approached the front door with caution and stared out its window to see a frumpy looking woman in a black overcoat that appeared to be three sizes too large with a small girl also clad in a wintry outfit, even though the warm spell had continued for the past several days.

She opened the door with a warm, yet cautious smile. "May I help you?"

"Yes," the woman replied. "At least I pray so. I'm Maybelle Winslow, and this is my daughter, Tandy. May we come in?"

"Sure, I guess so," Miriam replied, opening the door wider and escorting the two visitors to the living room.

"I'm sorry to intrude on you like this unannounced," Maybelle said as she unbuttoned her coat but kept it on. She turned and loosened her daughter's coat as well. As the two women talked, Evelyn and Amberlin came into the room.

"You were at the pond, weren't you? What are you doing here?" Evelyn asked bluntly, immediately on the defensive.

Miriam frowned but didn't say anything but waited for the woman to answer Evelyn's question.

"It's my daughter," Maybelle said, apologetically. "She's...well, she ain't right?"

"So?" Evelyn replied. "What do you expect us to do about it?"

"Evelyn, enough," Miriam spoke up. "Maybelle's a guest in our home." She turned to the woman. "Please, continue."

"I thought she could help her," Maybelle said pointing a finger at Amberlin.

"Well, you thought wrong," Evelyn blurted out.

"What's wrong with your daughter?" Amberlin asked, stepping in front of her mother and putting a hand on her shoulder in an attempt to calm her.

Maybelle hesitated, a worried look growing on her face. Finally, she said, "She's a sweet girl, don't get me wrong. She's one of the kindest little girls you'd ever want to meet."

Amberlin bent down to Tandy and smiled at her. She figured the girl was probably no more than three or four. Her light brown hair was tied in a short ponytail with a pink ribbon that matched her dress and socks. As she gazed at her, Tandy returned her smile revealing two small dimples. Such a pretty girl, Ambelin thought. When she smiles, she looks like one of those cherubs you see on Valentine Day cards.

After another long pause, Maybelle continued. "But sometimes, she...well, she has these spells. She turns mean and violent."

"Maybe she just needs a good spanking," Evelyn suggested.

"Mother, really," Amberlin chastised her before turning her gaze back to the little girl, feeling a growing connection between them. She remembered what it was like to be misunderstood at such a young age.

"It's not that, really it's not," Maybelle continued. "Like I said, most of the time she's as sweet and well behaved as she can be, but it's like she becomes..." The words hung in the air, the thought too painful for Maybelle to finish. "Problem is it's getting worse. She's having spells three or four times a week now. They're lasting longer, and are more difficult to control. I'm at my wit's end."

"I'm sorry to hear that," Miriam said as she gave Evelyn a warning look. "But why bring her here. It sounds like she needs to see a doctor."

"She's already been to Dr. Pruitt. He put her on some medicine, but all it did was knock her out. She walked around like some zombie, but she still had the spells." She turned to Evelyn. "At the pond the other day, you said your daughter was a healer, so I thought..."

"She what?" Amberlin interrupted, shooting her mother an angry look. "I'm sorry, but she made a mistake. I'm nothing special. I just managed to keep Matty warm until he woke up."

"I'm sorry we can't help," Miriam said stepping in. "I can give you the name of some doctors over in Asheville who may be able to help your daughter. Let me get some paper and something to write with."

As Miriam left the room, there was an awkward silence. Amberlin was about to speak up when she heard Maybelle gasp.

"Oh no," Maybelle said, staring at her daughter. Tandy was no longer looking at Amberlin but now gazed beyond her with a blank look on her face, her eyelids fluttering like the wings of a butterfly. "It's happening."

2

AS AMBERLIN STUDIED the little girl before her, she tried to ignore Papa Herb's voice that had started talking to her shortly after she claimed to not be special. *You know that's not true. This girl needs help. Reach out to her. Trust yourself.*

As Tandy's focus shifted away from Amberlin, she heard Maybelle's warning. "It's happening."

Instinctively, Amberlin reached out her hand to lightly caress the young girl's cheek. She thought she felt a connection for just an instant, but it faded away before she could be sure, only to be replaced with a new feeling...a much more forceful, even angry sensation. Suddenly, Tandy's eyes shifted back to her, but the angelic smile had been replaced with a look of such pure hate and anger it took Amberlin's breath away. She snapped her hand away as though she'd just touched a hot stove. Something, indeed, was happening within Tandy; something beyond Amberlin's experience or expertise.

Amberlin straightened up and stepped away but continued to study the girl whose attention now shifted to her mother standing a few feet away. She sneered at the woman, and Amberlin thought she heard a low guttural snarl reverberate from deep within Tandy's chest. The girl crouched like a cornered animal before leaping at her mother with such speed; it looked like to Amberlin that everything had been sped up for just a second or two. One second she was looking at the girl on the floor in front of her. The next moment, she was flying through the air towards her mother, her arms outstretched, her tiny fingers like claws.

Evidently, Maybelle had grown accustomed to such antics since she had thrown her arms in front of her face to fight off the attack from her daughter. "Oh, please, Tandy. Not again, not now," Maybelle pleaded even as she moved to defend herself. "Oh, my poor little girl."

But as far as Amberlin could tell, the small girl that had been standing before her seconds ago was no longer to be found, having been replaced with a Tasmanian devil intent on tearing Maybelle's eyes out. Before Amberlin could move, Evelyn had reached out and grabbed Tandy's shoulders in an effort to pull the girl away from her mother, but Tandy turned on her with blinding speed and went for Evelyn's face next.

Evelyn fell back to avoid having her eyes clawed out, shrieking in a mixture of terror and anger. "I told your mom you needed a good spanking. Guess I'll have to be the one...to...give..." She struggled to finish the thought.

Momentarily frozen to the spot, Amberlin watched her mother being attacked by a little girl who moments before she'd compared to a cherub, but who now wreaked of evil. "Tandy, no. You mustn't do that. Please, Tandy, calm yourself." Amberlin reached out to pull her away from Evelyn, grabbing her in a bear hug, trapping her arms against her body. Tandy kicked and screamed, throwing her head side to side, her teeth gnashing in thin air. As Amberlin held her, she felt a surge of energy course from the girl and into her body, but she held on until she'd pulled Tandy off her mother. She heard Maybelle continuing to implore her daughter to stop just before the back of Tandy's head struck her in the face with the force of a jackhammer. She fell into the blackness of an abyss.

Peace Corps

1

Amberlin awoke to the sound of a screech owl outside her bedroom window. Her mouth felt dry from needing to breathe through it, and her nose was swollen and painful to the touch. Even in the dark, the shadows of her bedroom looked familiar, but as she tried to sit up, the pain in her head forced her back on the pillow where she watched the light show that only grew more vivid upon closing her eyes.

She felt rather than saw the movement beside her bed, followed seconds later with the gentle touch of someone's hand upon her own. "Welcome back, dear heart," Miriam said gently rubbing her hand.

Amberlin groaned. "My head is killing me. What happened? How did I get here?"

"Canyon carried you," Miriam replied, answering the last question first. "I heard the commotion in the living room and rushed back just in time to see Tandy's head butt you. I shouted to Canyon who was already on the way to see what all the noise was about. Canyon, Maybelle, and I were finally able to subdue Tandy while Evelyn checked on you. Let me tell you; your mother was fit to be tied. She was ready to take Tandy out to the woodshed and teach her a lesson she'd never forget, but by then the spell had passed. When Tandy saw you laid out on the floor with a bloody nose, she started crying inconsolably which melted even Evelyn's heart. Maybelle was on the verge of crying as well. I think we all were."

"How long have I been out?" Amberlin asked, not daring to open her eyes just yet for fear the fireworks would begin again.

"You lost most of a day," Miriam replied. "It's close to dawn."

"And you've been sitting there all that time?"

"No, we've been taking turns." Miriam patted her hand again before removing her hand and stretching. "You rest easy. I'm going to let the others know you're awake and then start on breakfast."

"Before you go, could you help me to the bathroom?" Amberlin asked. "I really need to pee."

"Sure," Miriam said. "Take it slow and easy."

After relieving herself, Amberlin gazed into the mirror as she washed her hands and was shocked to find her nose twice its normal size and the skin around both eyes were black and blue. I look like a damn raccoon with a bad nose job, she thought. So much for Amateur Night this week. There's no way I'm going to be seen in public looking like this.

2

MIRIAM INSISTED AMBERLIN remain in bed for another day before finally relinquishing to her insistence that she was fine and didn't need to be treated like an invalid. Still, the headaches remained with her for a couple more days reminding her of the traumatic incident.

Close to a week had passed and everything appeared to have returned to normal when the next visitor found her way to Canyon's homestead. Amberlin and Matty were in the midst of a ferocious game of checkers when they heard the knocking at the door. Miriam passed through the living room where the two were playing on her way to answering the knock. Amberlin heard a muffled conversation take place followed with the closing of the door. As Miriam passed through the living room again on the way to resuming her tasks in the kitchen, Amberlin stopped her.

"Who was that at the door?"

"Oh, no one, really. Nothing for you to be concerned about." Miriam replied.

"Really?" Amberlin asked as she jumped two of Matty's checker pieces with one of her own. "I could have sworn I heard a woman's voice mention my name."

"Yes, that's true," Miriam replied, her face reddening a bit. "If you must know, she said she was a friend of Maybelle's."

"Oh?" When Miriam didn't continue, Amberlin added, "And?"

"She wanted us to know that Tandy is doing well."

"Really? Is that all? She came all the way out here just to tell us that?" Amberlin turned away from the game of checkers and looked straight at Miriam. "What else did she say that you don't want me to know?"

Miriam's eyes flitted around the room trying to avoid Amberlin's gaze but finally returned to look straight at her. She took a deep breath before continuing. "She said that Tandy hasn't had any more spells since visiting 'the healer,' and she wanted to know if you could cure her arthritis."

Amberlin groaned, a bad feeling beginning to grow in her gut. "What did you tell her?" she finally asked.

"I told her that you weren't available and that if she needed help with her arthritis, she should make an appointment with Dr. Pruitt."

"And she accepted that?"

"Yes. Well, I guess so. I don't really know," Miriam stammered. "I shut the door in her face. I'm pretty sure she left after that."

Amberlin watched as Matty jumped three of her checkers ending up with his piece at her end ready to be kinged.

"This isn't good," Amberlin said.

"Yes, it is," Matty replied exuberantly. "I'm beating the snot out of you."

"What are we going to do?" Amberlin asked, ignoring his comment and directing the question to Miriam.

"We're not going to panic," Miriam replied. "I'll give Maybelle a call and ask her to keep what happened here to herself...and to not send any more of her friends to you. I'm sure this will blow over in a day or two."

Unfortunately, Miriam was wrong. By the time she reached Maybelle, the news of the miraculous healing had already spread all over town. Over the next week, three more people visited the homestead, each one more adamant about seeing the healer than the last. When Evelyn heard about the visits, her motherly protective instincts took over. She fabricated several "No Trespassing" signs and posted them around the homestead. When Canyon came home from a grocery run, he discovered Evelyn sitting on the porch in a rocking chair with one of his shotguns cradled in her lap.

"You know that gun isn't loaded," Canyon said as he climbed the stairs with two bags of groceries in his arms.

"Yeah, I know," Evelyn replied as she slowly rocked back and forth, "but anyone else coming down that road won't."

3

The first day in March brought springlike weather to the North Carolina mountains, and the promise of even warmer weather on the way. Amberlin set the large platter of scrambled eggs and bacon on the table as Canyon arrived from the front porch where he'd retrieved the morning paper. The teenage boy and his mother who delivered the newspaper were the only ones allowed beyond Evelyn's "No Trespassing" signs.

As Miriam finished saying the blessing, Canyon opened up the paper and read the headline:

President Kennedy Establishes Peace Corps

Canyon continued reading: "According to President Kennedy, the people of undeveloped nations are struggling for economic and social progress. Our own freedom and the future of freedom around the world, depend, in a very real sense, on their ability to build growing and independent nations where men can live in dignity, liberated from the bonds of hunger, ignorance, and poverty."

"Now, there's a man taking a stand for what he believes," Canyon said, a note of pride in his voice.

As Amberlin sat there eating her eggs and bacon, his words reminded her of the recent dream and what Mo Lozoff had told her about the connection between her divine destiny and peace. Did this mean she was supposed to join Kennedy's "peaceful army" of volunteers? She didn't know for sure, but the thought didn't feel right. But it also didn't feel right to stay hidden away on Canyon's homestead with no contact with anyone but her immediate family. She decided it was time to take a stand herself.

"I just want to let everyone know that I'll be going to Amateur Night next time they have it. I believe that's in two weeks." She stood up as she made the announcement. After all, it felt right to stand up when taking a stand. She gazed around the table at the surprised faces, all but Matty's whose face sported a large milk mustache and didn't appear to care one way or the other.

"Do you think that's wise?" Miriam asked in her customary calm voice.

"Why, of course, it's not wise," Evelyn spouted before Amberlin could reply. "It's not wise at all. It's downright stupid...and dangerous I might add. I won't hear of it."

"Now, now, Evelyn," Miriam continued, maintaining a calmness to her voice with some effort. "We've spoken about this before. Amberlin is old enough to make her own decisions, and if she feels this is right for..."

"I don't care what she feels," Evelyn interrupted. "I'm her mother, and it's my job to be sure she's safe and unharmed."

"It would have helped if you hadn't spoken up about me being a healer," Amberlin replied. "Besides, I can't stay hidden out here for the rest of my life."

Evelyn opened her mouth to reply, then closed it again. "Well, that was an error on my part, and I'm sorry for that," she finally consented. "But I still think it's too early to take such a risk."

Amberlin and Evelyn glared at each other, neither one ready to give up her point of view, as Miriam looked on, unsure what to say. Finally, Canyon broke the silence by clearing his voice. He folded the newspaper and stuck it under his arm as he stood up. He picked up his plate to take it over to the sink. "I'll be sure to have my guitar well tuned," he finally said in a soft voice of authority. "It'll be fun singing with you again, Amberlin. I look forward to our next Amateur Night." With that, he walked over to the sink and placed his dirty plate in it before exiting out the back door.

Old Friends

1

I t had been weeks since Canyon and Amberlin had made an appearance at Mountain Haven's Amateur Night, so when they strolled in on Thursday evening, it caused quite a stir. Canyon had the forethought to alert Angus ahead of time, who made it a point to have many of Canyon's most loyal friends in the house. Even so, as the two of them made their way to the stage, Amberlin heard several less than positive comments among the applause and cheers.

"Well if it ain't the witch showing her face again," one lady shouted from the bar. "Yeah, along with the cult leader himself," a man standing next to her with a nearly empty beer mug added. But the comments seemed to only spur the rest of the crowd to cheer and applaud that much louder in an attempt to drown out the jeers.

They started with a rousing rendition of a Mountain Haven's favorite, "Working Man's Blues" with Canyon leading the way, then moved on to Amberlin singing "Everybody's Somebody's Fool." Both songs were well received even by the few patrons that had started out as hecklers. Canyon then took the microphone from Amberlin, to introduce their last song.

"This past week our newly elected President announced the formation of the Peace Corp,' so, in honor of this bold step, we'd like to finish up our time with you tonight with a song we sang a few weeks ago. And with that, he strummed the opening chords of "Turn, Turn, Turn."

As the crowd applauded and the two of them returned to their seats, a young man with jet black hair and an outfit to match followed them to their table. "I heard there was a healer in these parts, so I had to check to see if it was you," he said directing this strange introduction to Amberlin. Fearing that the man was about to cause trouble, Canyon began to rise to put himself between the man and Amberlin, but something in the man's voice sounded familiar, so Amberlin put her hand on Canyon's arm. "It's okay," she said. He froze half out of his chair. Amberlin stared at the slender man. He appeared to be in his late teens or early twenties, though it was hard to tell because of his long hair and scruffy beard that hid much of his face. He held a half-empty mug of beer in one hand.

"Never thought I'd run into you here, though," the man continued, flashing a quick smile that lit up his face.

"Ben? Ben Stover? Is that you under all that hair?"

The man laughed. "Yes, indeed it is. How ya been, Amberlin?

2

"YOU KNOW THIS GUY?" Canyon asked, visibly relaxing as he sat back in his chair.

"Yeah," Amberlin replied, then turning back to Ben said, "Sit down." She pointed to one of the few empty chairs in the bar. As Ben sat down, she studied his face. She could now recognize through the mass of hair her old friend from Golden Acres. Well, she guessed Ben had been her friend. They'd sure hung out together enough.

"What are you doing in these parts?" Amberlin asked.

"Looking for you," Ben replied. "Like I said, I'd heard a rumor that someone around here was mysteriously healing people so I just had to check it out to see if by chance it could be you. I really didn't think it would be, but..." he paused and looked around... "but from what I heard I'm guessing it was you."

"But how did you find me here at Mountain Haven?"

"Well, I wasn't really looking for you tonight. I just came here to check out the local talent." He waved one hand in front of himself. "All this is the new me, you could say."

"What's that supposed to mean?" Amberlin asked. "All what?"

"The hair, the beard, the clothes," Ben said pointing to each part of him. "I've been traveling around the last year or two trying to make ends meet with my music. You know, waiting for that special break."

"I had no idea," Amberlin replied.

"Yeah, no one did." Ben smiled. "After all, I was the preacher's son, and you know my folks. They would have skinned me alive if they'd found out I was practicing the guitar and singing songs that weren't about being saved and going to heaven."

"So they don't know?" Amberlin asked. She'd not thought about Reverend Stover or his wife, Missy, for over a year, and she wasn't sure she wanted to start thinking about them now.

"I don't know what they know," Ben answered. "Nor do I care. I left Golden Acres over a year ago and don't plan to return anytime soon...like never."

The two sat looking at each other, suddenly uncomfortable as they thought about the past which included Ben's father shooting and killing Amberlin's grandfather, Papa Herb.

"So, how are you doing?" Amberlin finally asked, deciding it was best to change the subject.

Ben shrugged as he took a long draught of his beer, almost emptying the mug. "Doing okay, I guess. Still waiting for that call from Ed Sullivan, but working pretty steady. Sometimes music gigs, sometimes just odd jobs. Had a pretty good thing going with a country band...until they broke up. Hey, let me ask you. What was that last song you sang?"

"Oh, just one that a friend of Canyon's wrote and sent to him," Amberlin replied nodding to Canyon who was sitting quietly across from her still studying Ben as though studying a snake, trying to determine if it was a poisonous one or harmless.

"Yeah? Well, I liked it. It's the kind of music I want to do more of. The band I was in did mostly country. You know, Johnny Cash, Earl Scruggs, a little Roger Miller, but I think folk music is what's up and coming, at least for me."

The next amateur group was tuning up in preparation to play.

"It's about to get noisy in here again," Amberlin said, leaning across the table and raising her voice to be heard. "Why don't you come out to the homestead tomorrow night for dinner?" She turned to Canyon. "Will that be all right?"

Canyon shrugged. "Don't matter to me. It's Miriam's and your turn to cook."

"You cook?" Ben asked, a skeptical look on his face.

"Not as well as I sing," Amberlin replied, "But Miriam will be doing most of it, and she's a good cook." She gave him directions. "We eat around six, but you can come earlier if you like and we'll catch up."

Friday Night Dinner

As Ben walked up the path to Canyon's front door, he studied the fourth "No Trespassing" sign he'd seen in the last five minutes, this one nailed to one of the porch's posts. Underneath this one, the hand-written message read, "Just in case you missed the other ones."

He smiled, but at the same time, the signs gave him a creepy feeling even though he'd been invited by Amberlin, and it had been approved by the big dude she sang with. He paused at the front door with his fist a few inches from it and took a couple of deep breaths before rapping on the door with a crisp knock that he hoped sounded more confident than he felt.

It had been good to see Amberlin after so much time, and the time had sure been good to her. She was no longer the cute, precocious little girl he'd grown up with at Golden Acres. She'd transformed into a beautiful young woman with a mane of golden hair that highlighted the high cheekbones and slightly turned up nose and full lips, all of which was capped off by an amazing voice that seemed to come from heaven itself.

And she asked me to dinner, he thought, so buck up and relax. You've got this. He knocked on the door a second time. A moment later the door opened and there before him stood the vision of youthful beauty that he'd imagined in his mind. Damn, she's even prettier than I'd remembered, he thought as he smiled at her.

"I hope I'm not too early."

"No, not at all. You're right on time," Amberlin replied returning his smile. "Come on in."

"What's with the signs?" Ben asked as he followed her into the living room.

"Oh, those," Amberlin said with a touch of embarrassment. "Those were my mom's idea. They've kinda worked. We were getting people coming out wanting me to...well, you know..."

"So the rumors I heard were true?"

Amberlin waved him to a chair and sat down across from him on the mismatched couch. "I don't know. Things have gotten a bit out of hand here lately."

She told him about Matty's accident falling through the ice and the subsequent visit by Maybelle.

As Amberlin talked, Ben heard other voices coming from the next room—what sounded like a conversation that was becoming more heated by the minute even though he couldn't quite make out the words.

Amberlin looked in the direction of the voices. "I'm sorry. I need to let you know..." but before she could get any further, Ben heard from the next room a very clear and loud woman's voice, "...I just don't understand why we should be feeding the kid of the preacher who murdered my father."

"That's my mom," Amberlin said turning back to Ben. "I'm sorry. This may have been a bad idea. She's pretty upset..."

"No, that's okay," Ben replied. "I understand. Maybe I should go."

But before he could move, the door behind Amberlin flew open and in walked a red-faced Evelyn. She stood in the middle of the room and looked around.

"Well, where is he? Where's the snot-nosed little punk?" She directed the question to Amberlin.

Ben stood up as Amberlin waved a hand in his direction. He stood as tall as he could to show Evelyn that at over six feet, he was no longer a snot-nosed anything. "Hello, Mrs. Gentry. I'm Ben. It's good to see you again under hopefully better circumstances."

Evelyn stared up at him. At just a little over five feet, he half expected, even hoped his larger size would calm her down a bit, but then he really didn't know this lady.

"So you're that rat-faced Reverend Stover's son, the one that lied to the cops and framed me for my father's murder?"

"Well, I'm sorry about that," Ben replied, suddenly feeling more like a snot-nosed little punk than he had a moment before. "I didn't really tell the police anything." He paused and took a deep swallow. "I just didn't correct what my folks told them."

"Oh, well, then that makes it all peachy keen, doesn't it?" Evelyn countered, taking a step towards him. "Why, I should..."

"Evelyn, that's enough. Behave yourself." Ben heard the authoritative voice of another woman. He looked over Evelyn's shoulder as another woman Ben didn't recognize entered the room from the same door Evelyn had come through.

"Yeah, Mom, calm down," Amberlin added as she stepped between him and her mother. "Ben is here as a friend. It's not his fault what happened. Besides, that's all in the past now."

"Hello, Ben, I'm Miriam. I was one of Evelyn's nurses at the asylum. It's good of you to come over. I think this is a perfect time for us all to sit down and sort these matters out...in a calm way as four adults," she said, staring directly at Evelyn. "Please, sit down." She motioned Ben back to his chair, then waited until Evelyn joined Amberlin on the couch before sitting down on the straight back chair next to it.

"Now, I understand from Amberlin that you play the guitar and sing as well," Miriam said, smiling warmly at him.

"Yes, ma'am. My guitaring is better than my singing, but I can carry a tune okay."

Ben heard a groan come from Evelyn. Miriam glowered at her.

"I apologize, but Evelyn was confined to the asylum for so many years that her social skills need a little polishing."

"Yeah, thanks to Missy Stover...oh, hey, that's your mother isn't it?" Evelyn snarled. "And I'm expected to sit here and play nice with her kid...the only one who could have spoken up and cleared my name?"

"I'm sorry about that," Ben said, growing more uncomfortable by the second. "I was much younger then and my mother warned me to keep my mouth shut, or I'd end up with social services taking me away from them. They're far from perfect parents, but at least I knew what to expect from them. Ending up in some orphanage or being raised by a foster family was just too much to think about with all that was going on."

"I understand, Ben, really I do," Miriam said before Evelyn had a chance to react. "But maybe now is the time for you to come forward and clear matters up. We can all go to the police and..."

"No way!" Evelyn shouted, rising to her feet and glaring at her. "I've spent most of my adult life a prisoner in that damn asylum, and now I've tasted freedom. There's no way I'm going to go back to being a prisoner. Turning myself in and placing my freedom at the mercy of some judge and this kid's testimony is way too risky. Bad idea. Not happening. No way."

A long pause ensued while everyone stared at each other unsure what to say that could relieve the tension. They were still staring at each other when Ben heard someone knocking on the front door.

"Holy hell, if that's one of those damn townsfolk..." Evelyn started.

But Miriam interrupted. "Calm down, Evelyn. Let Canyon take care of it." As she spoke, Canyon walked into the room on his way to the front door, a look of concern on his face.

"Everyone keep your voices down. That's Sheriff Otis. I saw him driving up while I was coming in from the barn."

As he spoke, Ben noticed Evelyn's face blanche from a reddened look of anger to a pale look of fear. Despite how she'd been treating him, he felt sorry for her and understood where much of her anger came from. She'd been mistreated by life and had suffered for years at Missy Stover's hands. So have I, Ben thought. Not in the same way, but still she'd made his life hell for many years, as well. They had at least that much in common.

Guess Who Came to Dinner

1

"Okay, everyone, stay calm. We've practiced for something like this happening plenty of times," Canyon said, then noticed Ben. "Oh, hey, that's right. You're here for dinner, aren't you? Just hang loose for a bit. Miriam, take Evelyn to our special spot, just in case." As Miriam escorted a much meeker Evelyn out of the room, he turned to Amberlin. "You two stay here. This won't take long." He hoped that turned out to be true.

He strolled to the front door and paused long enough to take a couple deep breaths before opening it. "Why, Sheriff Otis, what are you doing way out here?" As he spoke, he stepped out onto the porch and closed the door behind him.

Sheriff Otis had been in charge of keeping the peace for close to thirty years. His closely cropped hair had turned gray over ten years ago, and his mustache was mostly gray as well, but despite being in his early sixties, the sheriff maintained a well-trimmed body and a deep tan that exuded good health, all of which was highlighted by a well-tailored and maintained uniform.

"Can we sit for just a minute?" Otis asked pointing to the two white rocking chairs.

"Sure, I guess," Canyon replied.

The two of them rocked back and forth for close to a minute before Otis finally spoke up. "You know, before your pappy passed away several years ago, he made me promise to keep an eye out for his son. That's been a pretty easy promise to keep. You've been a good boy...well, man now." He stopped rocking and turned to look at Canyon. "Think of this as a social call, if anyone asks. What I'm about to tell you, well, this conversation never happened." He paused for a moment and chewed on the edge of his mustache.

"You see, I have a new deputy, a transplant from Raleigh—a real go-getter. He's looking to make a name for himself in these parts, so he's been investigating some of the cold cases. You know where I'm going with this, right?"

Canyon shrugged but didn't say anything. He fought to keep his face as deadpan as he could.

"I've heard reports from a few concerned citizens that you have someone staying with you. Is that right?"

"Yes, that's correct," Canyon answered. "You've met both of them, Amberlin and Miriam."

"Yes, both are very nice, but they're not who I'm referring to," the sheriff continued. "Another woman. She threatened Charlie Thompson with a pipe the other day at the pond behind the Piggly Wiggly. I also heard she had words with Josh Jenkins a few weeks ago. Know anything about that?" Otis asked as he gave Canyon a stern look.

Canyon shrugged again.

"Look, you know my approach to law enforcement has been to let quiet, peaceful people be, but when someone starts to cause a disruption, well, it's my duty to investigate. On top of which I now have this eager beaver deputy..." It was Otis' turn to shrug.

"Listen, Canyon. My deputy and I will be back in a day or two with a search warrant. I'd suggest your guest not be here by then. Harboring a fugitive from justice...well, it's a serious offense. 'Nough said for now."

Sheriff Otis stood up, and Canyon followed suit a moment later. The sheriff held out his hand, and the two of them shook. "Thanks, Sheriff," Canyon said. "I appreciate the heads up."

As the sheriff started towards the stairs, he turned and pointed to a brightly colored VW bus sitting in the driveway with the words, "Flower Child" written on the side.

"That yours?" he asked.

Canyon shook his head. "Nope. A friend of Amberlin's here for dinner."

Sheriff Otis nodded. "Probably be best this friend not be around either. I can only imagine what I'd find if I checked inside that hippie-mobile."

"I understand," Canyon replied, feeling the hackles on the back of his neck rising for the first time.

"Beautiful place you have here," Otis said gazing out over the fields. "Nice and quiet, just like the rest of the county. Sure would like it to stay that way." And with that, he strolled down off the porch, climbed in his patrol car and drove away.

2

AS CANYON ENTERED THE living room without the sheriff accompanying him, Amberlin breathed a sigh of relief until she noticed the worried look on Canyon's normally placid face.

"Trouble?" Amberlin asked.

"Afraid so," Canyon replied. As Miriam and Evelyn re-entered the room, he filled everyone in about the sheriff's warning.

"Holy hell!" Evelyn exclaimed jumping up from the couch. "What the hell am I going to do? I can't let him find me here, but where can I go?"

"Calm down," Miriam said. She walked over to Evelyn and took one of her hands. "We're all in this together. We'll figure out something."

"Yeah," Amberlin added. "At least Sheriff Otis was kind enough to warn us."

"I should have known better than to go out in public," Evelyn said, the fear growing on her face. She began to hyperventilate.

"Please, sit down," Miriam asked. "You're getting yourself all worked up."

"You bet I'm getting worked up. They're coming for me which means I'm heading either back to that damn asylum or, even worse, to jail."

"We're not going to let that happen," Amberlin replied, though she was growing more concerned by the minute as well. Evelyn's panic was contagious. "Maybe we can hide you somewhere until after the sheriff and his deputy leave..."

"I don't think that's going to work," Ben spoke up for the first time. Amberlin turned to him with a surprised look on her face. She'd forgotten he was there.

"Why?"

"You stay out of this!" Evelyn shouted. "If it weren't for your family, I wouldn't be in this mess here."

"Mother, please, let him talk," Amberlin pleaded. "Please, sit down and stay calm." Evelyn glared at her daughter but finally did as she asked.

After a moment, Ben continued. "As I told you, I came here because I'd heard a rumor that there was a healer around here, and I thought it might be you."

"Yeah, I remember. So?"

"Well, it's just a matter of time before my folks hear the same rumors and come to investigate. I'm sorry to have to say this, but the truth is my parents hate both of you. They believe the Gentry women are Satan's disciples."

Amberlin groaned, and Evelyn leaped up from her seat a second time and started pacing, muttering a long litany of profanity as she did so. Miriam frowned but didn't say anything, letting her former patient walk off her anger and frustration.

Amberlin watched her mother pace back and forth, occasionally glancing to first Miriam and then Canyon. What were they going to do? She knew her mother was right. There was no way she could survive being imprisoned again. Her sanity was borderline even now. Being confined would undoubtedly send her over the edge.

Finally, Miriam's calm voice brought Amberlin back to the present. "There's a big pot of chili simmering on the stove. It'll take me only a minute to finish preparing the bread. Amberlin, if you'll help me, I suggest we go ahead and eat. Sometimes, the best way to solve a problem like this is to step away from it for a while."

Evelyn stopped pacing and stared at Miriam for a long couple of seconds before finally replying, "Yeah, why not? We've all got to eat." She turned and led the way to the dining room.

Moving Target

1

After Miriam finished saying the blessing, Amberlin passed around the large platter of French bread that had been sliced, buttered, and toasted to golden perfection. Everyone sat quietly eating as they each stared into their bowl of chili. Finally, after several minutes of silence, Canyon spoke up.

"Once again, outstanding chili, Miriam, my dear."

"Thanks, Canyon, but I know how easy you are to please. I honestly think I could put down a bowl of canned dog food and if it were heated and had a little cheese and diced onions on it, you'd say the same thing."

"Not true," Canyon replied, then studied the chili more closely. "That's not how you prepared this, is it?"

"Oh, stop," Miriam laughed. "You're incorrigible."

Several more minutes of silence elapsed before once again Canyon spoke up. "Well, are we going to discuss the elephant in the room?"

"And what would that be?" Miriam asked. "You want to know the source of my dog food supply?"

"No, I'll let you keep your secret," Canyon replied with a chuckle. "What are we going to do with the situation with Evelyn and the authorities?"

"Oh, that," Miriam said, suddenly serious again. "Yes, I guess we better talk about it. Anyone have any ideas?" She looked around the table at the collection of worried looks; all except Ben who looked hopeful.

"Ben, do you have something to say?" Miriam prompted him.

After a moment of hesitation, during which Ben finished swallowing his food and wiped his mouth, he spoke up. "Well, this may sound like a crazy idea, but since no one else seems to have any other ideas, I have a suggestion...if you want to hear it."

Miriam noticed Evelyn opening her mouth to say something, so she reached out and touched Evelyn's hand. "Sure, let's hear what you have."

Ben hesitated again before finally taking a deep swallow. "Well, you know the old saying 'it's hard to hit a moving target?'"

Everyone around the table nodded except Evelyn. Miriam squeezed her hand tighter to keep her from blurting anything out.

"Yes, go on."

"As I told Amberlin the other night, I was at the bar looking for my next gig. There was a fella up from Atlanta checking out the talent. His name is Grenwald. I know him from his setting up a couple other bands I've played with so we sat down and talked. He helps find new talent for several of the night spots down in Atlanta and the surrounding area. We got to talking about how rare the actual talent was at Amateur Night..."

"What the hell does this have to do with my problem?" Evelyn asked as she yanked her hand away from Miriam.

"I'm getting to that," Ben replied calmly. "He said the only exception was that young woman who sang 'Everybody's Somebody's Fool.'"

"Why that was my song," Amberlin said.

"Exactly," Ben replied. "He was quite taken with you. I happened to mention that I knew you and would be having dinner..."

"Again, what does any of that have to do with the law and me?" Evelyn interrupted again.

"My point is that it's hard to hit a moving target," Ben continued with a sly smile on his face. "It's also hard to find someone who's constantly on the move. Just ask my folks if you don't believe it. My idea is that we hit the road, the three of us, starting with Atlanta. I'll play the guitar, be Amberlin's back up singer, and Amberlin will be our lead singer."

"And what am I supposed to do?" Evelyn asked, the tone of her voice a little less belligerent.

"I don't know," Ben replied. "What are you good at?"

"She could be our manager," Amberlin jumped in before Evelyn could reply. "She can help organize the gigs, collect the money, keep the books, stuff like that. She can do all those things far better than either one of us."

"I kinda like the idea of keeping track of the money," Evelyn said, a smile appearing on her face for the first time.

"And our main job is to stay a step or two in front of the long arm of the law," Ben added. He picked up a slice of French bread and took a large bite. "Delicious bread," he added as he gazed around the table at everyone.

No one spoke for almost a minute. Finally, Miriam broke the silence. "You know, it's a crazy idea, but it might be just crazy enough that it'll work."

Amberlin nodded. "Yeah, it would give us a way to make enough money to live on while still staying on the move, at least for a while until things quiet down here," but as she spoke she felt a wave of fear course through her. What was she thinking? Going on the road with Ben Stover, who she'd been out of touch with for the last four years, accompanied with her mother, who had her own inner demons with which she had to contend. Miriam was right. This was crazy and far too risky to make a snap decision even though there wasn't much time left.

"I've got to take a walk," Amberlin said as she rose from the table and started towards the front door.

"Now?" Miriam asked. "It's almost dark outside and will be in a few more minutes."

"I won't be long. I just need to clear my head."

"What about my idea?" Ben asked a note of concern in his voice.

"I'll let you know when I get back," Amberlin replied, then left the room. At the door, she shrugged on a jacket then spied the backpack that had laid forgotten on the hook under the coat for months. She suddenly knew where she needed to go—to seek counsel from a friend. Which friend, she didn't know but trusted she would recognize him upon their meeting.

2

MISSY STOVER STARED out the window of the dilapidated RV she'd rented to serve as the revival's headquarters. The gaudy sign of the Brotherhood of Christ Church blinked back at her. Whoever heard of using orange neon for a church sign? But then again, they were in Los Angeles, California, where, as far as she could tell, all bets were off, especially when it came to taste and decency.

She moved her gaze to the window behind her so she could admire the large tent that was in the final stages of being erected. There, in just a few hours, God's work would begin anew, here in the den of iniquity known as Hollywood. Missy took a minute to cross herself. Even though she was far from

Catholic, there were times in one's life when a little extra of God's protection was called for, and this was one of those times.

After all, she'd had to dig deep into the Golden Acres coffers to pull this revival together so far from home. When that money ran out, she had dug into their family savings. So she was betting everything on the *Reborn in Hollywood Revival* being a success, not only in the number of lost souls brought back into the fold, but also economically. If it didn't work out, Golden Acres would have to declare bankruptcy, and the two of them were likely to end up in jail for misappropriation of funds.

But like her mama always used to say, "Go big or go home," even though she seldom followed her own advice and died a pauper married to the town drunk. Yeah, and when Rev. Stover finds out how much money I've had to spend to kick this revival off, he's likely to go big—as in ballistic. So be it, Missy thought. I've had to deal with his angry outbursts for most of our married life. She was prepared to deal with him once again. She already had her "gun loaded for bear" with all his transgressions that forced her into making such a bold move. She was also prepared to remind him of the many passages in the Bible where a follower of Jesus Christ had to take risks in the name of the Lord.

But none of that will be necessary as soon as six thousand sinners find their way to God's canvas cathedral out there later tonight, Missy thought. She was prepared for that outcome with a bottle of champagne chilling in the fridge. Surely God would forgive them for partaking of alcohol after the divine work of tonight. "Bring 'em on Lord Jesus. We're ready to do your work."

Turtle Time

Amberlin strolled around Canyon's farm that had become her home for the past four years. While it had started out as a temporary first aid station where Evelyn's gunshot wound could be attended to, it had become their sanctuary away from the dangers of the outside world. But now the world was threatening to invade their safe haven.

But going on the road as a small troupe of misfit musicians seemed dangerous in its own way, Amberlin thought as she wandered aimlessly around the grounds before finally finding herself approaching the small watering hole intended for the farm animals. It had also become one of her favorite places to visit, but she couldn't remember ever coming to it so late in the day. At the same time, she knew it was an ideal place to meet some of her *friends*. Unfortunately, on this particular visit, there were none of the customary ducks, geese, or other birds around, and no deer or other furry creatures.

Amberlin sat down on a log on the edge of the pond and gazed across the water at the remnants of the sunset in the west. Her mind began to wander back to earlier days when Ben, Hannah, and she had hung out. She remembered the time Hannah, and she had set up an arm wrestling match as a way for Amberlin to get a better read on Ben using her special intuitive power that grew stronger with contact. She had learned that the young Ben had a crush on her and wondered if the older Ben still felt that way. Hard to say, she thought, but that might explain why he'd made the suggestion to go on the road together.

She also remembered how Ben had often gone out of his way to act out to convince people he was bad, but then she'd caught him feeding the ducks when no one was around. Then there'd been the explosion of emotions she'd felt while arm wrestling him—a wave of shame and guilt that had literally knocked her out of her chair. Ben Stover was indeed a complicated person. And now I'm thinking of traveling around the country in his van with my nutsy mother? Who's the crazy one here? Maybe all of them.

As the sun dipped below the horizon, the temperature began to drop. About time to get back, she thought, but she hadn't yet made a decision. Glancing down at the knapsack at her feet, she remembered why she'd brought it and why she'd taken a walk in the first place. As she bent down to pick it up, she paused, a flicker of movement to her side catching her attention. Sitting next to her was a small Painted turtle about five or six inches in size, its yellow eyes studying her intently.

"Why, hello, friend," Amberlin said, surprised that she'd not noticed its arrival on the log. "How are you this fine evening?"

Had the turtle nodded its head in recognition to the question? Surely not. She began to reach for the book of animal lore she kept in the knapsack, her favorite possession given to her years ago by Papa Herb, but stopped suddenly when she heard, "That really won't be necessary. Why don't we talk instead?" Her eyes flashed to the turtle who nodded again and appeared to smile. "Yes, that's me. I always love it when humans first hear my voice."

"I bet you do," Amberlin finally replied. "I had no idea turtles could talk."

"Oh, for sure, most don't, but you said you needed to talk to a friend, so they sent me. Something about time being of the essence."

"Yes, it truly is," Amberlin agreed. "I've got to make a decision, and I don't have much time."

"I understand," the turtle said. "Well, if you were to open that book there, you'd find that the appearance of a Painted turtle, that's me, indicates that a new world is about to open up and with it new opportunities. Does that help?"

"Yes, if that means I'm supposed to follow those opportunities?"

"Well, what do you feel would be the right move? Close your eyes for a moment and get in touch with your inner guidance to answer that question."

Amberlin closed her eyes and took a couple deep breaths. New opportunities were often scary, she realized, but that didn't mean they weren't worth pursuing, especially if they also felt exciting as did this one. She opened her eyes and nodded to the turtle who continued to stare at her.

"Well?" the turtle asked. "What did you get?"

"That just because an opportunity is scary doesn't mean it's not worth doing especially if it's also exciting."

"Good. We turtles also mean it's time to get in touch with your primal senses. What does that say to you?"

Primal senses? Amberlin wondered. "Could that mean it's time for me to get back in touch with the special gifts from God that I've been ignoring for so long?" Gifts like the ability to talk to a turtle, she almost added but didn't want to take a chance of insulting her little friend.

"Very good," the turtle replied. "Have a good evening," he added before slipping off the log and into the water.

"You too," Amberlin said as she waved goodbye to him.

Revival: Night Four

1

For the fourth night, Missy stood at the rear of the tent and counted the number of filled seats. For the seventh time, the number was less than a thousand and with that number of people scattered out in a tent with a seating capacity of six thousand...well, the optics looked bad by anyone's standards. Despite that, her husband had been undaunted by the turnout. At the end of each night, he spent hours unwinding while Missy did everything she could to hide her disappointment and worry as the unpaid bills continued to mount.

After Rev. Stover would finally retire to bed, Missy stayed up to pray to God, then she'd pull out the day's tithe and proceed to pay whatever bills she could. Even so, the mound of unpaid bills continued to grow as did her prayer time. It wasn't unusual for her to finally join her husband in bed around three or four in the morning only to lie awake worrying until dawn finally broke.

As she finished tonight's count, she watched an elderly man in a wheelchair being pushed by his valet up the center aisle. Missy groaned. Oh no, her one ace in the hole and he was already leaving. She'd been so sure that he was her answer to the hours of prayers. Hadn't his name appeared the very next day after she'd pleaded with God for help? There it had been right on the front of the L. A. Times, picture and all. She couldn't remember the content of the article, only how influential the old codger was. She'd hounded his office for days with over a dozen calls inviting him to the revival, and he'd finally come, but now he was leaving early. This would not do.

Missy rushed over to intercept him at the rear of the tent. As she walked she plastered on her most gracious "southern nice" smile as she placed herself in the wheelchair's direct path making it impossible for the valet to continue his way to the exit.

"Why Mr. Hearst, it's such a pleasure to meet you. I'm thrilled that you were able to make it tonight. Isn't the Lord's work of my husband's truly inspiring? Surely, you can stay a little longer. I know tonight's crowd is, well, a little sparser than we're accustomed to, but believe me there will be many souls saved tonight. Just wait until the alter call, you'll see."

"That won't be necessary," Hearst replied in a gravelly voice of an old man unaccustomed to speaking. "You're his wife, aren't you? The one that's been calling my office every fifteen minutes?"

"Why, yes, I'm Missy Stover. I apologize for all the phone calls. I just didn't want you to miss this opportunity to hear the word of God."

Hearst, dressed in a black suit with a dark gray blanket over his legs despite the warm night temperature, frowned at Missy's remarks. He cleared his throat with a guttural cough that sounded like he'd cough up half a lung, before continuing. "I've heard all I need to hear. I particularly wanted to hear what your husband had to say about the state of the world and particularly those pesky Commies, or should I say 'godless Communists'?" He reached out and patted Missy's hand. "Don't fret, my girl. You've done your job. Now, if you'll excuse me, move aside and let me do mine."

Missy stepped aside. What had her husband said about the world's affairs? Had Hearst reference to "godless Communist" come directly from Rev. Stover's message? Despite hearing him deliver more or less the same sermon for the past several nights, she couldn't remember. Had she just inadvertently made their task even more difficult? Would there be even fewer people tomorrow night? After all, Californians were known for their crazy, liberal views, but what about Hearst's views? She really had no idea, but she suspected she was about to find out.

2

IT HAD BEEN THE WORST night so far. Not only was the attendance even less than the previous nights but most of this crowd seemed to have left their wallets and purses home. There was no question about it, Missy thought as she finished counting the money and tried her best to avoid looking at the mounting pile of bills. The revival was quickly driving them into bankruptcy. It was time to come clean with her husband, but how?

Missy started by bringing out the bottle of champagne that had languished in the back of the refrigerator for the past week. She had failed to remember glasses so they'd have to drink out of paper cups, but the point wasn't so much to create a festive mood as it was to try to mellow her husband out a bit before breaking the bad news to him.

"What's this?" Reverend Stover asked as he entered the RV, wiping the perspiration from his face with a towel, his suit jacket draped over one arm, his long sleeve white shirt stained with sweat. "Surely we're not celebrating tonight's turnout. It was the sparsest one yet."

"True," Missy agreed, "but you're doing such good work for the Lord. I figured it was time to break out the bubbly." She popped the cork which bounced off the low ceiling almost hitting him.

Stover dropped his coat over the back of a chair and sat down in it. "What's really going on, Missy?"

"My, what a suspicious mind you have," Missy replied playfully as she poured the champagne into a paper cup and handed it to him.

"I've been married to you long enough to know when something is wrong," Stover replied, taking the cup from her and taking several deep swallows.

Missy finished pouring herself a cup of champagne, moved to make a toast but then, noticing he was already downing his cup, so took a swallow of her own. Finally, she squared her shoulders and took a deep breath. "As you know, so far the turnout hasn't been quite as good as we'd expected."

"That's an understatement if I ever heard one," Reverend Stover said as he finished off his champagne and reached for the bottle. "Not half bad stuff."

"Well, yes," Missy continued. "I'm afraid it's put a bit of a kink in our cash flow."

"How much of a kink?"

"Well, that's a little hard to say," Missy started, but Stover interrupted her.

"Oh, come now, Missy. I know you better than that. No doubt you have it figured out within a few cents. How bad is it?"

Missy groaned and pointed to the stack of bills on the table. "Those are the bills we can't pay with more on the way." She downed the rest of her champagne and braced herself.

"You're kidding," Reverend Stover said, then seeing the distressed look on his wife's face added, "You're not kidding." He took a deep breath. "How in the name of Saint Pete did we run up so many bills?"

"Well, it takes a lot to run a revival," Missy started, then added in a softer voice, "and everything costs more out here."

Reverend Stover sat in his chair staring at the mound of bills, fuming with anger. Finally, he looked up at her. "Well, we'll have to close it down. Cut our losses. Damn, I knew this was a bad idea from the start, but no, you insisted. You swore this was all part of God's plan. I should have listened to my own gut."

"It is part of God's plan," Missy replied, her own hackles beginning to rise. "It's our opportunity to have faith and trust in the Lord."

"Yeah, but there's also a lot to say about 'trusting in God *and* tying your camel,'" Reverend Stover retorted. "In this case, that means being able to pay our bills...which we can't."

"We've just got to give it time for the word to get out," Missy said. "Let's give it one more week. If the crowds haven't improved..."

"Hell, by then we truly will be bankrupt. No, I say we cut our losses now." He finished off his second cup of champagne and poured the rest of the bottle in his cup.

"The weekend is just three days away," Missy finally said after a long pause. "Saturdays have always been one of our best days. Let's, at least, finish out the weekend so we can pay for the space we've been renting from the church. Please? I have a feeling that tomorrow is going to be a better day."

"You and your damn feelings are what got us in this fix in the first place," Stover countered, but then paused to catch his breath. After a moment, he continued. "Okay, we'll keep it open through Saturday, but then we get the hell out of Dodge before our creditors come to tar and feather us."

Discovered

1

The next morning, Missy felt her husband rise from bed and a couple minutes later heard the door to the RV open and close. She groaned, remembering the to-do list that awaited, but then recalled that item number one on the list was to call the dozen or so people to whom they owed money. She turned over, placing the pillow over her head and fell back to sleep.

She didn't stir again until hours later when the loud honk of an eighteen wheeler awoke her. She sat up and glanced at the clock to find it was almost eleven. She was still in the process of dressing when she heard Reverend Stover return.

"Where have you been?" She asked trying unsuccessfully to keep the accusatory tone out of her voice.

"Oh, just talking to some folks that happened by asking about the revival," her husband answered in a much more chipper voice than she'd expected given last night's bad news. Was he happy that the revival that had been scheduled to run at least a month would be closing after the first week? Surely not.

"You seem to be in a good mood this morning," Missy said as she moved into the small kitchenette to fix herself some coffee.

"Yes, I am," Stover replied. "It's a wonderful day out there. One thing about California, it has beautiful weather. Can you fix me a cup as well?"

Missy dropped in another scoop of coffee in the percolator and plugged it in. She stood there staring at the top of the lid as the coffee began to steep. After a minute, she felt her husband's arms encircle her waist.

"It's all going to work out," he said. "Like you said last night, this is a test of faith. If this revival is meant to be the way we serve God, then so be it. If not, we'll simply head on back to Golden Acres and serve him there."

She felt the tears begin to burn her eyes. She didn't have the heart to tell him how deep in debt their mountain community was from this failed attempt. Time enough for him to find out about that later.

She turned towards him and placed her head on his shoulder. At first, she tried to stifle the sobs, but he only patted her back and whispered in her ear. "It's okay. Let it out." So, she did.

2

THURSDAY NIGHT'S CROWD was only slightly larger than the previous evening which was unfortunate, Missy thought. She'd never heard her husband speak with more power or authority. She wasn't surprised when the altar call brought substantially more people to be saved than other nights. Well, we might be going bankrupt, Missy mused, but at least we've made a difference with those folks who now had a ticket to heaven rather than hell.

So it was with low expectations that Missy entered the tent the following evening only to find a buzz of activity from a crowd that already appeared larger than any previous nights. She glanced down at her wristwatch. Still, an hour before Reverend Stover was scheduled to start speaking. How could this be? She watched in amazement for the next hour as the tent continued to fill. As Reverend Stover stepped onto the stage, she estimated the crowd to be more than five thousand people.

Praise the Lord! Missy thought ecstatically, a little ashamed that she'd ever doubted the power of God. But Missy also had a practical side to her religion, realizing that many if not most of God's miracles could be traced back to human intervention. So, what had happened? She was still contemplating this line of inquiry when Reverend Stover stepped onto the platform and surveyed an almost capacity crowd. He'd already shed his suit coat and rolled up the sleeves of his white dress shirt. Clearly, he's ready to kick ass and take names, Missy thought. Her chest swelled with pride as he opened his arms wide and said, "Welcome to you all on this glorious day that the Lord has made. May we all rejoice and be glad in it!" His voice boomed over the crowd, and for the first time, Missy was thankful she'd spent the extra money for the top of the line PA system.

Missy stood at the back of the tent and finally heard her husband's message. Damn, he's good! she thought as he expounded on the evils that were overtaking the world and the role those godless commies played. So it had been her husband's words that Hearst had quoted. She suddenly realized that they were coming up to the collection time. She looked around frantically for one of the volunteers. Seeing a young girl she recognized from a previous evening holding one of the collection baskets, she rushed over to her.

"Quick, run back to the service tent and get everyone out here with a basket in their hand. We're about to take part in one of God's miracles."

The girl nodded as she handed her basket to Missy and rushed away. "The extra baskets are in the other tent," Missy called after her. She turned back to gaze at the crowd. Time to count heads, then realized it would be far easier this evening to count empty chairs, and in the next moment realized there weren't any. In fact, she noticed dozens of people standing at the rear of the tent with still others trying to enter from the outside. My Lord, it's a standing room only crowd!

The next several minutes rushed by frenetically as the collection was taken up and the second half began. It took Missy a minute to realize that her husband was calling her to join him on the stage. What's he doing? That's not part of the schedule. She quickly glanced down at the flowered dress she wore and wished she'd chosen the red one instead. Too late now. As she started up the aisle to a round of polite applause, she tried to straighten her hair. I'll kill you for this, she thought but smiled despite herself. Reverend Stover met her at the stairs and helped her up.

"My good friends of California, let me introduce you to my wife who has been instrumental in making this glorious evening of God possible. Missy Stover, the love of my life." The applause increased as Missy felt her face flush with embarrassment and pride. "Would you like to say a word to this fine flock of God's children?"

Missy stared at her husband with a look of amazement and fear. She realized for the first time in her life, she didn't know what to say, so she simply shook her head and pointed back to him. "You're the speaker of the family, not me," she said.

"Ever so humble, my dear wife," Stover proclaimed as he escorted her to the stairs so she could make her escape. As she stepped off the stage, her heart still fluttering at breakneck speed, a young man wearing a snazzy looking Fedora with a pad and pen in hand approached her.

"May I ask you a few questions, Mrs. Stover?"

"I guess," Missy answered still trying to recover from the last few minutes. "Who are you?"

"I'm Randy Donning with the *San Francisco Chronicle*," he replied as the two of them strolled to the back of the tent.

"Really?" Missy responded. "San Francisco. You had quite a drive didn't you?"

"Well, if my office were in San Francisco, I would have, but I work out of the L. A. office."

"Oh, I see," Missy replied. "Well, before I answer your questions, maybe you can answer one of mine."

"Sure...shoot."

"Why are you covering the revival tonight? I mean we've been here most of the week."

Randy leaned over close to her. "To tell you the truth, my editor-in-chief received a telegram from the newspaper's owner a couple days ago, so he sent me out yesterday. Several other reporters and I met with your husband. I'm just following up."

"What did the telegram say?"

"According to my editor it was the shortest telegram he'd ever received," Randy answered. "It said, 'Puff Stover,' and it was signed 'Hearst.'"

Part Two

Hit the Road

1

By mid-afternoon the following day, Amberlin and Evelyn had their clothes packed in suitcases and duffle bags and loaded on top of Ben's VW bus. Lunch had been quieter than normal with no one wanting to talk about the pending departure, but now the time for goodbyes had arrived.

As Ben checked to be sure the luggage was securely tied to the rack, Amberlin and Evelyn hugged first Canyon, and then little Matty. The little boy seemed confused by what was happening but, noticing everyone else was crying, joined in as well. Last of all the two Gentry women came to Miriam.

"This is all so sudden," Miriam said as she hugged the two of them, "but if you know it's the right thing to do, I'll trust it's all in divine order. It's just so sudden," she repeated.

"Relax," Evelyn said as the three of them stood to hug each other next to the van. "We have it on the best of authority that this is a grand opportunity. If you doubt it, just go down to the pond and ask the turtle. It was a turtle, right, Amberlin?"

"Give me a break. I wish I'd never told you about that." Amberlin said as she snuffled and wiped her eyes with one of Canyon's handkerchiefs he'd given her earlier.

"That's right," Miriam added sniffling back the tears as well. "God works in mysterious ways. You of all people must know that, Evelyn."

"True enough," Evelyn relented, "but a turtle? Couldn't it have been something more dramatic like an albatross or an eagle...or maybe a lavender unicorn?"

Amberlin laughed despite how she was feeling inside. "I'll keep an open mind about getting advice from a unicorn in the future. Until then, we'll just have to make do with the messengers sent to us."

"Hold on," Canyon said as he rushed back to the house. "I packed some food for you to eat on the trip. At least it'll get you started eating well," he said over his shoulder, returning a minute later with a picnic basket filled with food.

"No one had much of an appetite during lunch," he explained, "so there was plenty of leftovers. You know Miriam makes the best fried chicken around, warm or cold."

Evelyn took the basket and gave him another hug as Amberlin opened the side door of the van. The first thing she noticed was the back area filled with an old mattress with blankets and pillows strung about on top of it. "You sleep in this?" she asked, turning to look at Ben.

"Sure thing," Ben replied. "It's quite comfortable."

"What's that smell?" Evelyn asked as she opened the passenger door.

"Ahh, that's just some herbs I use to help me sleep," Ben replied, his face suddenly growing red.

"Well, you're sure as hell going to have to find a different sleep aid," Evelyn bit back. "There'll be no pot smoking while I'm part of this troupe. You hear?"

"Yes, ma'am," Ben replied.

"And don't call me ma'am," Evelyn shot back. "My name is Evelyn, or if you prefer, Spooks." She glanced back to where Miriam was standing next to Canyon. "It was good enough for the asylum, and I have a feeling this trip will be just as crazy. So, no more Evelyn Gentry. Never heard of her. Right?" Everyone nodded.

"Okay, Spooks it is from now on," Ben said. He walked around to the driver's side of the van, whistling the tune, "We're Off to See the Wizard," as he climbed in.

2

"I KNOW OF A PLACE A few miles down the road where we can stop," Ben said from the driver's seat.

"No, I think we should keep on going," Spooks countered from the passenger's seat. "We've been on the road for less than two hours. Besides, we have the food Canyon packed for us.

"Well, I know but..." Ben started to say, but Spooks interrupted, ..."I said we'll keep driving."

"Who the hell made you boss?" Ben countered back.

"Why, of course, I'm in charge," Spooks replied, turning towards him. "After all, I'm the adult here, and besides, that's the job of a band's manager."

"No it's not," Ben shot back. "It was my idea to form a band to start with, it's my set of wheels, and I'm the one with the connections, so it only makes sense that I'm in charge. So, I say we stop when..."

"Now wait just a minute," Spooks interrupted again.

"Hey, guys, stop arguing," Amberlin said from the rear of the van where she'd been rearranging the pillows and blankets. "Besides, you're both wrong."

"We are?" Ben and Spooks asked simultaneously.

"That's right," Amberlin replied. "Neither of you are in charge because I am."

"What?" Ben asked looking at Amberlin in the rearview mirror. "You?"

"Why you?" Spooks asked as she turned and stared at her daughter.

"Simple. If I'm not the leader, then you'll be out a lead singer, Ben, and you'll be on your own, Spooks, to hide from the law." Amberlin paused to let her words sink in. "But most of all, because I care for you both and will do my level best to keep everyone's interest at heart. That's not to say that you all don't have important roles to play as well. Ben, you're in charge of making the initial contacts and booking gigs. Your job is also to maintain the van and musical instruments. Spooks, you're in charge of logistics: getting us from point A to B, keeping the books, our schedule, arranging our meals, etc. If either of you needs money you come to me."

There was a long pause as Ben and Spooks considered her points. Finally, Ben spoke up. "Speaking of money and maintaining the van..." Before he could complete his thought, the VW suddenly sputtered and jerked a few times before dying, slowly coming to a stop.

"What I was trying to say back there several miles ago. We need to stop for gas."

Grenwald

The trio arrived in Atlanta close to midnight. A trip that usually would take three to four hours had been extended to close to nine. Not only had it taken Ben over an hour to walk to a gas station to refuel, but shortly after they resumed their journey, the VW stopped again, this time with smoke exiting from the engine. Fortunately, a tow truck happened by and was able to tow them to another service station, but they had to pay premium rates to get a mechanic to make repairs. So, not only were they several hours later in arriving, but their scant savings had taken a big hit as well.

As Ben pulled into the parking lot across from the Peach Tree Bar where Grenwald maintained an office, everyone was hot, tired, and ornery. Amberlin had finally called for a cease-fire about an hour outside of Atlanta.

"That's it. Both of you are to shut up and not say another word until we arrive. Do you hear? Not one word." Ben and Spooks both started to object, but Amberlin stopped them. "Not a word from either of you."

"Okay, talking is now permitted," Amberlin finally said as Ben turned off the engine and collapsed on the steering wheel to rest his eyes. "But if you can't be civil when you speak to each other, then I don't want to hear it. Understand?"

Ben and Spooks both nodded, apparently too tired to argue the point. "So, this is to be our first gig, right?" Amberlin asked in as pleasant a voice as she could muster.

"Yeah, that's right," Ben replied sitting up and stretching. "It's a bit of a dive, but usually draws a pretty good crowd, especially on the weekend. It's a start."

"Good. Let's go see if Grenwald is in," Amberlin said as she opened the door and climbed out, stretching her tired limbs.

"Oh, he'll be there," Ben assured her. "I called him from that last service station and told him what had happened. "I swear I think he sleeps here most nights, at least when he's not traveling around looking for new bands."

But as they entered the bar, they discovered their troubles were far from over. The woman behind the bar sporting tattoos on both arms stared as they

71

approached. "What'll you have? We're still running a special on Long Island Ice Teas."

"No thanks," Ben replied. "We're your new group, come to entertain and keep the folks out there thirsty."

The bartender blinked a few times before replying. "There must be some mistake." She pointed to a motley crew of four other people sporting matching t-shirts huddled at the end of the bar. "They're the band this week and next. They're just on a break."

"Really?" Ben asked. "I could have sworn Grenwald said we'd be playing here starting tomorrow. Maybe I misunderstood."

"Misunderstood?" Spooks exclaimed. "Hell no, you didn't misunderstand. We're just getting the runaround here. Now you listen to me, Missy..."

Amberlin stepped between Spooks and the bartender who'd taken a step back and started reaching for something under the bar. "Is Mr. Grenwald in? I'd like to talk with him to see if we can clear up the confusion." She smiled pleasantly at the tattooed lady who nodded towards a set of stairs across the room.

"Yeah, he's up there, though I don't know what good it'll do you."

"Thank you," Amberlin replied, then motioned for Ben and Spooks to follow her.

As they climbed the stairs, she looked over to the two of them. "Ben, introduce us when we get up there, then let me do the talking. And, Spooks, I want you to stay down here and stay out of trouble until Ben and I return. Can you do that?"

"I'd prefer going up and helping..." Spooks started but then stopped as Amberlin glared at her. "Oh, all right. Whatever you say."

Harvey Grenwald was known throughout the SouthEast as the Band Booker Extraordinaire in large part because that's how Harvey had branded himself. A man in his late fifties with a bulging midsection that covered his belt, Harvey had a fondness for rings which he wore on most of his fingers, as well as one in each ear. He preferred wearing gaudy colored shirts like those you'd find on an ocean cruise to Hawaii. His shirts seldom matched his pants. A pair of black high top Keds completed the ensemble. Also notable, Grenwald tended to sweat a lot as he was on the evening Amberlin and Ben met him in his office.

"Well, hello, come right on in and make yourself at home," Grenwald belted out in his normally boisterous, booming voice as he came around from behind his desk. "So good to see you again, Ben, and this must be the little lady I heard the other evening."

"Hi Harvey," Ben replied. "Good to see you too. Sorry for the delay. Probably should sell that pile of junk and get me a good set of wheels, but ol' Nelly and I have been through so much together, just wouldn't be right."

"I understand, I do. Loyalty is a valuable virtue even if it is to a pile of junk. Now, what can I do you for?" he asked as he leaned his rotund body against the edge of his desk which creaked its objections.

Amberlin took that question as her opportunity to step up. "Mr. Grenwald..."

"Harvey, please. Mr. Grenwald is my papa, and he's worm food now."

"Well, Harvey, it appears we have a misunderstanding to clear up..."

"Yes, Mamie called up from the bar to let me know, but I'm afraid she's right. The Grubs are, well, they're like family here. They had a cancellation come up, and so they came to me, asking if I could extend their stay here. They've been one of our most loyal and popular groups. Draw a good size crowd every night. It's nothing personal, ya hear? It's just business. Like I said, loyalty is an important virtue."

"Yes, I understand," Amberlin said. "As is keeping one's word." As she said this, she reached out with one hand and touched Harvey lightly on the shoulder. She held it there as she continued to smile at him. "I'm new to the music business, and I really appreciate the opportunity you've given us. I think if you give us a chance, we'll draw a good crowd as well. New bands can draw a different set of customers. Ones that can become loyal to the Peach Tree Bar." As she talked, she used her intuitive skills looking for a chink in Grenwald's armor. It didn't take long before she found it.

"Well, I understand, Missy. I really do," Grenwald replied in a condescending voice. "I had to make a difficult decision, but that's my job. I'll be happy to call around and see if there's anyone else in the area..."

"Harvey, could I sing you a song?" Amberlin suddenly asked, and before he had a chance to answer, she started singing "My Mother's Eyes." It had been one of her grandmother Rose's favorite songs that she sang to her granddaughter on those nights when it was her turn to put Amberlin to bed. Something told Amberlin that such a tearjerker might just melt this grumpy old man's heart a bit. She was right.

"Why that's one of my favorite songs," Grenwald said, a look of pleasure mixed with confusion growing on his face. Amberlin smiled and continued to sing.

By the end of the song, Grenwald was close to sobbing as his tears mingled with sweat. He reached into his back pocket and pulled out a damp handkerchief and wiped his face. He turned to his desk and picked up the phone. After a moment, he said to the person on the other end of the line, "Tell the Grubs, I'm sorry, but I've got to keep the schedule as it was. They'll need to find another venue for next week."

As he dropped the receiver back on its cradle, he turned back to Amberlin. "That had to be the most beautiful rendition of that song I've ever heard. Thank you."

Later, as the three of them left the bar and started back to the van, Ben walked close to Amberlin and whispered, "What was that about? How did you know that was his favorite song?"

"I didn't," Amberlin whispered back. "While he referred to his deceased father as worm food, I could sense that he had a much different relationship with his mother—much more loving. So, I thought that song might sway him back to making the right decision. I was just as surprised as you how well it worked."

"You even got him to offer to take care of our lodging," Ben added. "He never does that, especially not for new groups."

"Again, I was just as shocked as you," Amberlin replied. But as they reached the van and started to climb in she thought, I learned an important lesson tonight about the power of music to change lives. It was certainly having that effect on her.

Hotel Fleabag

1

As the three of them filed through the door of their motel room, Spooks glanced around as Ben turned on the lights. "Wow, Grenwald appears to be a master of understatement," she said as she dropped her suitcase on the floor. "He said 'it's nothing fancy' which I now know to interpret as 'it's the lowliest fleabag in Georgia.'"

Ben nodded as he collapsed on one of the two beds. "Yeah, but at least we're not footing the bill."

"Hey, don't get too comfortable there." Spooks pointed to the couch across the room. "That's your bed over there."

"Who says?" Ben countered as he placed his hands behind his head in an effort to look as comfortable as possible.

"I say," Spooks replied, the edge of anger growing in her voice.

"That's enough, you two," Amberlin said as she entered the room. "It's important that we treat each other with respect. Spooks, you and I will share a bed and Ben will sleep in the other one."

"Yeah, and the next night Amberlin and I will share a bed, and you can have the other bed to yourself," Ben added with a broad smile on his face.

"That's not going to happen," Amberlin replied.

"Damn right," Spooks agreed.

"Okay, okay. I was just joking." Ben swung his legs onto the floor. "Now that we have our sleeping arrangements settled, I'll go get the rest of the stuff from the van."

"Good for you," Amberlin. "That's the spirit."

On the way to the van, Ben took a detour to the payphone he'd seen as they had checked into the room. He reached into his pocket and took a handful of coins out. Picking up the receiver, he dialed a number, paused for the prompt, and dropped several coins into the slot. He waited until the ringing stopped and a husky voice answered on the other end. Apparently, he'd awoken them.

"It's me," he said without bothering to identify himself. "We're here...no troubles to speak of. I'm keeping a close eye on both of them." He paused for a moment before adding, "Don't worry. They aren't going to give you any trouble, and you're going to leave them alone. That was the deal." He paused again for several seconds listening to the response from the other end. "Okay...okay. I got to get back. Yeah. Love you too, Mom. Tell Dad to break a leg." Another pause, then, "It's a saying for someone about to go on stage. It means good luck." He took a deep breath as he waited for his mother to stop talking. "Okay, I got it. Doing God's work isn't the same. I'll call you in the next week or two. I don't have a clue where we'll be."

He hung up the phone without waiting for a reply and resumed his trip to the van, feeling like a lowly worm of loathing. At the van, he reached under the driver's seat and pulled out a plastic bag from which he took a small pipe. Just a few tokes, he thought as he lit up. I've earned it today. Besides, no telling how long it will be until I have another chance to relax like this. By the time he started back with his arms filled with luggage, the feeling of loathing and self-hate had all but disappeared.

2

A few days after their arrival in Atlanta, Ben entered their motel room and dropped a card on the bed where Amberlin was lounging. "What's this?" Amberlin said as she picked it up to examine it.

"It's your fake I.D. just in case," Ben replied dropping into the couch that now doubled as his bed.

"In case? In case of what?"

"In case one of our places gets raided by the cops, or if we run into a persnickety manager and asks to see proof of your age. Neither is likely to happen, but it's best to be prepared."

"Oh, I see," Amberlin replied continuing to study the card. "So, I'm now twenty-one and licensed to drive in Georgia. How in the world did you manage to get this and in just a few days of our being here?"

"I didn't get it. Grenwald pulled the strings. He was covering his own ass as much as yours. Put it away somewhere safe and hope to hell you don't need it."

The next several weeks were filled with a whirlwind of activity as Grenwald booked them in an assortment of night spots in the Atlanta area before announcing that their next gig was to be in Nashville, Tennessee.

"You'll love it in Nashville," he told Amberlin and Ben as they sat in his office hearing the news for the first time. "And they'll love you too. Be sure to sing 'My Mother's Eyes.' Maybe plan on closing the first set with it so they'll be hungry for more."

"But I was hoping we'd get to stay here in Atlanta a bit longer," Amberlin started to protest, but Ben cut her off.

"That's great, Harvey. We'd love the opportunity to sing in the country music capital of the world," he said as he turned and gave Amberlin a wink.

"But we don't really sing country music," Amberlin whispered back. "I'm much more comfortable sticking with folk."

"This could be a great opportunity to expand our horizons," Ben replied. "Plus it would be best not to stay in any one town too long...you know what I mean." He nodded over his shoulder towards the office door indicating where they'd left Spooks.

"Yeah, maybe so," Amberlin replied, still unconvinced. It would be good to get out of the fleabag of a motel and Nashville wasn't that far away. Just a few hours drive. They'd taken some of the money they'd made and invested it in a general overhaul of their VW bus so it was unlikely it would give them any more problems, at least for a little while.

Unfortunately, Grenwald was wrong once again. Amberlin didn't love Nashville. In fact, she hated it, and the feeling was mutual. Except for "My Mother's Eyes," the rest of their repertoire was received with little enthusiasm, and several of the folk ballads were downright booed. The only high spot Amberlin could claim from her "Nashville experience" was hearing President Kennedy's speech to a joint session of Congress.

The three of them had decided to take in a movie to raise their mood which had dropped steadily since arriving in Nashville. They each had their own vote as to which movie they wanted to see, but Amberlin won out with "Breakfast at Tiffany's." It was in the Movietone News that preceded the main attraction where they watched history being made.

The news clip started with Kennedy speaking about the rapid changes happening in space:

"Finally, if we are to win the battle that is now going on around the world between freedom and tyranny, the dramatic achievements in space which occurred in recent weeks should have made clear to us all, as did the Sputnik in

1957, the impact of this adventure on the minds of men everywhere, who are
attempting to make a determination of which road they should take."

Amberlin sat up straighter. She enjoyed hearing the President speak with
his Boston accent and New England directness. She nudged Ben and Spooks
who were sitting on either side of her.

"Listen. I think he's about to say something really important."

Kennedy went on to point out how the Soviets were clearly ahead in the
race for space, but that didn't mean America shouldn't do whatever it could to
catch up.

"For while we cannot guarantee that we shall one day be first, we can guarantee that any failure to make this effort will make us last."

"I think I'm falling in love," Amberlin whispered as she leaned over to Ben.

"Well, if I'd known going to the movie would have that effect, I would have
invited you long ago," Ben replied.

"Not you, silly...him." Amberlin pointed to the screen.

"Oh."

Amberlin couldn't help but hear the note of disappointment in that one
word. She was still thinking about it when she heard Kennedy say, "I therefore
ask the Congress, above and beyond the increases I have earlier requested for
space activities, to provide the funds which are needed to meet the following
national goals: First, I believe that this nation should commit itself to achieving
the goal, before this decade is out, of landing a man on the moon and returning him safely to the earth. No single space project in this period will be more
impressive to mankind, or more important for the long-range exploration of
space; and none will be so difficult or expensive to accomplish."

"What did he just say?" Ben asked, sitting up straighter in his seat.

"He said we're going to the moon!"

"No way."

"Well, you just wait and see. Our President is a man of vision. I grew up
with such a man, my Papa Herb. He once told me, 'We never know what we're
able to accomplish until we try, and trying starts with a declaration.' President
Kennedy just made such a declaration."

Southern Stuggles

1

T he intrepid trio hung out in Nashville for a month. Each day Ben would take a stash of coins to the nearest payphone and spend an hour or more calling every connection he had in the music industry trying to find a new venue where they could play, preferably the folk music they all preferred.

Finally, after over a week of steady calling, Ben returned to their motel room, a broad grin on his face. As he entered, Spooks was walking out of the bathroom. He grabbed her and swung her around the room.

"What the hell are you doing?" She gasped but started laughing despite her best effort to feign anger.

"We have a new gig," Ben shouted as he let Spooks down but continued to dance around the room. "But not just any gig. I have us booked for a glorious night at the Shadow in Washington, D. C. Whoop, whoop."

"One night?" Spooks asked.

"Yeah, that sounds like a long way to travel for just one night," Amberlin agreed.

"Oh, it'll be more than that, I'm sure," Ben replied. "That's all I could get them to commit to without hearing us...well, really, hearing you, but when they do, I'm sure we'll be in tight. Plus, my God, it's the Shadow. They specialty is folk music."

Spooks and Amberlin looked at each other with perplexed looks on their faces.

"Ahh, sorry Ben, but neither of us has a clue what that means," Amber finally said.

"The Shadow is only one of the top jumping off spots for emerging talent...like you, us. This could be the start of a whole new chapter in our musical careers."

"But only one night?" Spooks reminded him.

"Yeah, only one night to start," Ben conceded, "But it'll be a night to remember plus it gives us an excuse to blow this damn town."

"That's good enough for me," Amberlin said. "Let's pack up. We're going to D. C. Maybe I can meet Johnnie Boy and get his autograph."

"Johnnie Boy?" Ben asked.

"Yeah, you know, our President of the United States, John F. Kennedy."

"Oh, I didn't know you were on a first name basis." Ben chuckled.

"We aren't," Amberlin said. "Least not yet."

2

The three of them were up early the next morning, checked out of the motel, and on the road before 7 a.m. arriving in D. C. just in time for the five o'clock traffic, but since the VW had made it without any breakdowns, everyone was still in high spirits. They drove up to a plain gray building on the corner of

35th and M street.

"You say this is one of the top showcase clubs in the country?" Spooks asked with a scornful look on her face. "It's a hole in the wall."

"Yep, that's right," Ben replied undaunted by her sarcastic tone. "It's a cozy little venue where fans get to rub elbows with up and coming music legends. and we're going to be singing here night after next."

"On a Wednesday? We don't even get a weekend slot?"

"We will if you'll keep your razor tongue to yourself and let Amberlin sing her magic," Ben replied with just a hint of edge to his voice. "Come on, let's let them know we're here."

Amberlin climbed out of the van and looked up at the marque. "Who or what is a Mugwump?"

"I'm not sure," Ben replied. "I'm guessing it's the name of a band, but I've never heard of them. But then again, they've never heard of Amberstovers."

"Who?" Amberlin and Spooks asked at the same time.

Ben's face turned red as he repeated, "Amberstovers...that's us. I know it's not the greatest name in the world, but the guy at the Shadows caught me off guard. It's the best I could come up with on the spur of the moment. Besides, it's at least as good as Mugwump."

"Well, that's true," Amberlin agreed. "Amberstovers." She tried the name out to see how it rolled off the tongue. "Amberstover. Oh, I get it. The first part of my first name and your last name. I kinda like it."

"You do?" Ben asked in amazement. "Well, good. That's who we'll be from here on out."

"Hey, wait a minute. How about me?" Spooks asked belligerently.

"You're the manager. Bands aren't named after managers," Ben replied. "Come on. Let's go see if Gerald is in."

"And he is?" Spooks asked as she opened the van door.

"He's the friend of a friend of a friend that I ended up talking to in order to get the gig."

As they entered the Shadows, Spooks muttered, "Had no idea you even had a friend." Ben either didn't hear or chose to ignore the comment.

Gerald Appleblum was as overly tall as Harvey Grenwald had been overly obese. He'd make a good Mutt to Harvey's Jeff, Amberlin thought as she shook hands with him. "So, you're the one with the angelic voice?" Gerald asked. He wore a dark blue t-shirt with "1960 Kennedy/Johnson for America" emblazoned across its front. Amberlin liked him instantly.

"I don't know about that," Amberlin replied, smiling despite herself, "but I am the lead singer, if that's what you mean."

"Wow, a self-deprecating musician. I didn't know such an animal existed. It's a pleasure to meet such a rare species," Gerald said returning the smile. "Here's the deal. I'll start you guys out on Wednesday night and see how you do. You do okay the first night, we'll give you that night for a few weeks. The Wednesday crowd isn't nearly as large as the weekend, but they're also not as rowdy. They seem to appreciate the chance to hear new talent. How's that? Fair enough?"

Amberlin and Ben nodded as Amberlin flashed a stern look at her mother to make sure she kept her two-cents out of it. They'd learned the hard way that Spook's managerial skills were best saved for renegotiating contracts when she could play the "bad cop" to Amberlin's "good cop."

"Any chance of getting a second night?" Amberlin asked. She was all too aware of their diminishing savings.

"Not immediately," Gerald replied. "But I can get you in touch with a friend of mine over in Alexandria. He's got a nice little place over there. We often trade-off talent. Just remember, I have first dibs on you if it turns out you really do have an angelic voice."

Amberlin laughed. "It's a deal."

3

On the third Wednesday night while Ben and Amberlin were in their last set for the evening, Amberlin thought she saw a face in the crowd that looked vaguely familiar, but then it flitted away before Amberlin could get a good read on who it might be. Then again as she sang "Where Have all the Flowers Gone?" that had become their closing number and signature song for the last few weeks, she saw the face once again, this time more clearly.

As the two of them took their final bows before leaving the stage, Ben leaned over to Amberlin. "Third night in a row that the crowd is larger than the previous Wednesday. We're getting known."

"Yes, we are," Amberlin agreed distractedly. "Listen, see that young girl over there with the spaghetti strap blouse and tattoos on her arms? Do you recognize her?"

Ben looked in the direction that Amberlin was nodding. "No, but I'd like to. She's cute...wait a minute. No, it couldn't be, but hold on. Those dimples when she smiles. There's only one person I've ever met with dimples like those."

"Hannah!" Amberlin shouted as she jumped off the stage and wove her way through the people, tables, and chairs. The woman was turning away towards the bar, so she shouted again. "Hannah...Hannah Barrington. Is that you?" But she was certain by this time that it was her old friend from Golden Acres despite the somewhat different hair color and the brilliantly colored tattoos on both arms. "Wait up!"

The two women pushed their way through the thinning crowd to each other, coming together in the middle of The Shadow's music hall in a powerful hug that spun them around. Amberlin found herself laughing and crying at the same time. She felt momentarily embarrassed until she realized Hannah was doing the same. Finally, out of breath and dizzy from spinning around each other, they pulled apart at arm's length, continuing to hold onto each other's arms.

"What in the world are you doing here?" Amberlin asked as she slowly guided them to the bar, suddenly conscious of her friend's limp from the weakened left leg.

"Come to see you, of course," Hannah replied. "You were wonderful...and Ben wasn't half bad."

"Where is Ben?" Amberlin started to turn back to the stage.

"Last I saw him he was being mobbed by a bunch of women, and I'd say from the smile on his face enjoying every minute of it."

Amberlin laughed. "Yep, it's been happening with increasing frequency. "Gosh, we have so much to catch up on. How long are you in town?"

Hannah shrugged. "Not sure. Taking each day as they come."

"Or are you living here now?" Amberlin asked, realizing that was possible as well.

"Yeah, you could say that...for now," Hannah replied cryptically. "But tell me, how did you and Ben get started as a group?"

"Yep, a lot of catching up to do," Amberlin repeated. "Let's get a couple of drinks and head back to the dressing room where it won't be so noisy. What will you have?"

"Do they have soft drinks here?"

"Yeah, more varieties than most bars," Amberlin replied. She leaned closer to Hannah. "I can get us something a little stronger if you like."

"Really? I had a devil of a time getting past the bouncer. I had to slip in a back way. Well, in that case, how about a beer. Anything on draft."

"Coming right up." Amberlin caught the bartender's attention. "Can we get two beers. One for me and one for...for Ben?"

"Coming right up. Ben's got himself some beautiful tattoos since last I saw him," the bartender said as he slid the beers toward her and winked.

"Thanks, Tommy. You're the best."

As the two girls walked back to the dressing room area, Amberlin asked, "Where you staying tonight?"

Hannah shrugged again. "Haven't given it much thought."

"Well, don't. You're staying with us. We have a room not far from here. Nothing fancy, but it's relatively clean, and we can put Ben on the floor for the night, or round up a cot or something. It's so good to see you again." She handed one of the beers to Hannah and opened the door to their dressing room. "Now, tell me about those tattoos, girl."

Hannah's Request

1

"So, how have you been? How's Golden Acres?" Amberlin asked as they entered the small dressing room. She waved Hannah to the one comfortable chair in the corner, and she sat in the straight back chair.

"I'm doing okay," Hannah replied as she sat down and took a long drink of her beer. "As for Golden Acres, I really couldn't say. I haven't lived there since shortly after my mom passed away."

Amberlin almost choked on her beer. "Your mom died? When, how? Oh, you poor thing. I'm so sorry."

"It's okay," Hannah replied. "It wasn't long after you and Papa Herb disappeared. She suddenly took ill and passed within the month. She tried to cover it up because we couldn't afford a doctor, but I knew something wasn't right. Before she died, she contacted her sister which is where I went to live afterward. Boy, I hated it there. She made me feel like I was such a burden on them, and well, my uncle, he's a borderline pervert. He seemed to really like me being there but for all the wrong reasons. So, I ran away. Let's see, it's been almost a year."

Amberlin slid her chair closer to her friend and reached out to grasp her hand. She could sense that her friend was telling her the truth when she said she was okay, but underneath that veneer was a layer of heartache that was far from healed. "Where did you go when you ran away?"

"The only place I knew to go," Hannah replied after she took another swallow of beer. "Asheville. I'd heard good things about Asheville, and I'd always wanted to check it out. Seemed like a good time to do it. It went okay there. I was able to get a job at a small restaurant off the main drag. I think the lady who ran the place took pity on me." She pointed to her leg. "Who says being a gimp doesn't have its advantages at times." She looked up to the heavens. "Sorry, Mom. I didn't really mean that. Betty, the owner of the restaurant, gave me room and board as partial payment for my working for her. I had to stay mostly in the back, washing dishes, cleaning up after hours. I also ran errands for her,

84

and she'd give me a tip whenever she could. It wasn't too bad. I was able to save up a little money."

"And then what?" Amberlin prompted her. "How did you get yourself to D.C.?"

"I heard about you."

"Really? You heard about my singing all the way from D. C. to Asheville?"

"No," Hannah replied, then hesitated before continuing. "Not your singing...your healing."

Amberlin didn't know what to say to that, so she merely replied. "Oh, I see."

The two of them stared at each other for several seconds before Hannah continued. "I heard about a young woman who was reported to have amazing healing abilities. I thought, wondered, prayed, it might be you. Finally, I had to go find out for myself. Betty wasn't too thrilled to see me leave but she gave me a little extra money as a going away present and packed me some food for the trip."

"But how did you travel?"

Hannah stuck out her thumb. "Hitchhiked, the only way to go...that is if you're broke and can't drive." She chuckled. "I'm pretty good at it. I think some of your intuitive skilled rubbed off on me. When I approach a car, if I don't have a good feeling about it, I don't get in. I've been chasing you around for weeks that way."

"Really?"

"Yep, first I had to track down where the 'miracle worker' lived, then I had to convince your friends, Miriam and Canyon, that I was an old friend of yours and not some nut job. That took some doing, believe me. Then, it was hitchhiking to Atlanta. Good thing you'd sent that postcard to Miriam with the Peach Tree Bar on the front. Of course, I missed you there. You'd already moved on." Hannah stuck out her thumb again. "So, on to Nashville. By then I knew I was looking for a two-person singing group. Canyon had told me about your musical ability. Where did that come from, girl? Anyway, I finally tracked down the last place you sang. Boy, what a dive. One of the bartenders told me where you guys had been staying. Evidently, he'd had his eye on you, so he'd done his own checking up."

"Really?" Amberlin said again, growing more amazed by the minute by Hannah's story. "I bet that was Derrick. He was quite the charmer."

"Yeah, that was his name and yes, he was a charmer. I was tempted to hang out in Nashville for a while, but I felt like I was getting closer to finding you, so I talked to the people at the hotel. One of the maids said they'd thrown away a map of the Washington D. C. area with the words, "The Shadow" scribbled on it. I didn't know what that meant until I arrived here today and opened up the Yellow Pages. And now I'm here," Hannah said as though it was the most natural thing in the world.

"Wow!" Amberlin replied. "You're amazing. I could never have done that for all the tea in China."

"Yeah, I know better than that," Hannah replied with a laugh. "I saw you track down your mother when you weren't even sure she was still alive, but I am pretty proud of myself. It's been quite a trip."

"I'll say."

"By the way, whatever happened with that search for your mom?"

"Oh, I found her," Amberlin tried to reply as casually as Hannah. "She's back at the room which is where we should be heading. Want another beer before we go?"

"No thanks, I'm good. I could stand a little something to eat."

"No problem. There's a great little burger place on the way. We'll stop and get everyone something to munch on. Ready to go?" Amberlin asked as she stood up.

Hannah remained sitting as she took a final swallow of her beer. "Don't you want to know why I went through all this to find you?"

"Well, sure, I guess," Amberlin replied, puzzled by the question. "I kinda thought it was because you missed your old friend."

"Yeah, that's true enough, but that's not all," Hannah said rising as well. "I want you to heal my leg."

2

AMBERLIN STOOD LOOKING at her friend stunned into silence by the request. Not knowing what to say, she decided to say nothing. Instead, she walked towards the door as though she hadn't heard Hannah's question. "Let's go get those burgers," she said over her shoulder and was relieved when she heard Hannah's footsteps behind her. But then she continued to hear the limping footsteps all the way to Burger Palace, their distinct sounds haunting her every step. The two of them sat at one of the table waiting for their takeout order to arrive.

"Well?" Hannah finally asked after a couple minutes of silence passed.

"Well, what?" Amberlin shot back though she knew exactly what Hannah was asking.

"Will you do it? Will you heal my leg?"

Still not knowing what to say, Amberlin just stared at her friend.

"Listen, I know how much you hate to use your powers," Hannah continued. "You think that nothing good ever comes from them, but I beg to differ. I wouldn't ask except, well, I'm so tired of being held back by this damn leg. No one sees me, not the real me. All they see is a little girl with a bad leg. The best I can hope to get is their pity, and I don't want their pity. Pity is for losers, and I'm not a loser. At least, that's what dear ol' Mom tried to drum into me, and it worked. But it doesn't matter that I know I'm not a loser if everyone around me thinks I am. So, will you help me? Will you at least give it a try?"

Amberlin started to reach over the table to clasp Hannah's hand, but her friend pulled it out of the way. "Stay out of my head, will you? Just answer my question."

"Hannah, you know how much I care about you, right?"

"Yeah," Hannah answered, a note of suspicion in her voice.

"But the claims you heard about my ability to heal were greatly exaggerated. They were based on an accident that happened this past winter."

"Yeah, I know. Miriam told me about how you saved her son's life. That sounds like pretty powerful stuff to me."

"But she wasn't there," Amberlin replied. "Matty had fallen through the ice. Canyon was the one who saved him, not me. I just covered him with my body and my warmth helped to wake him up."

"That's not how Canyon reported it to me," Hannah replied impatiently. "Listen, it seems like everyone around you realizes how special you are. Everyone but you. Don't you think it's about time to give up the act?"

"It's not an act!" Amberlin was about to scream, but then stopped with her mouth half open as she heard an all too familiar voice. *She's right, you know. It's time to stop trying to convince everyone that you're just like they are. You're not. It's time to step into your power,* Papa Herb urged.

"You guys just leave me alone," she shouted instead and stood up to rush out of the restaurant, but instead bumped headlong into a startled waiter holding a bag of burgers.

"I'm so sorry," Amberlin said as she grabbed the man's arm to keep him from falling. "How much do I owe you?"

"Pay at the cash register," the waiter replied, pointing to the front as he handed her the bag and backed away keeping a close eye on this lunatic patron.

"Let's go, Hannah. We'll finish this outside."

Black Horse

1

A mberlin paid for the burgers and stormed out of the restaurant and down the sidewalk towards the motel. She listened to see if Hannah was following her. I don't really care if she does or doesn't, she told herself, but even as she thought it, she knew it wasn't true. She was thrilled that Hannah had tracked her down even if it had been for the wrong reason, even if she couldn't honor her friend's request. It was good to have her back in her life. So, as she continued back to the motel, she slowed her pace to allow Hannah to catch up.

"I didn't mean to upset you," Hannah said as she pulled up beside her, obviously winded from the effort.

"I know," Amberlin replied. "It's not that I don't want to help you. I just don't know how."

They walked on for the next few blocks without saying anything. Finally, Amberlin pointed to a ramshackle building outlined with pink neon lighting with several gaps where the lighting no longer worked. "There it is, our palatial home, the Black Horse Motel."

"Black Horse with pink lights? I don't get it," Hannah said.

"Neither does anyone else," Amberlin replied with a chuckle. "We think it was named something else when it was first built, and the neon lights were installed, then someone bought it who was from the West and renamed it. No one knows for sure. I do know that our room has a distinctive horsey smell though, but it's warm and cheap. Come on in. Spooks should still be up."

"Spooks? Is that your cat?"

Amberlin laughed again. "No, silly, Spooks is my mom. We call her that because...well, it's a bit complicated. Let's just say for now, it's her nickname, and leave it at that." Amberlin pulled a key from her pants pocket, unlocked the door to the first-floor room, and waved Hannah in.

"Spooks, you awake?" Amberlin called as she entered behind Hannah. "I brought food and someone I want you to meet."

Spooks walked out of the bathroom drying her hands on a towel. "You said the magic word, 'food,'" she said as she tossed the towel on the arm of the sofa. "And who's this?"

"This is my old friend from Golden Acres I've told you about, Hannah Barrington."

"Hannah, how nice to meet you. You're the one that got locked up in my old crypt, is that right?"

"Yeah, that's me," Hannah replied. "Not my fondest memory of those days."

"I bet. Well, I appreciate all that you did to help my daughter find me. Now, where's that food?"

Amberlin held up the bag. "Burgers from Burger Palace."

"Great, my favorite," Spooks said as she took the bag from Amberlin and began to open it. "Where's Ben?"

"He's not here?" Amberlin asked.

"Nope, haven't seen him," Spooks replied as she took a large bite from one of the burgers, closed her eyes and hummed a soft melody of pleasure.

"He's probably off with his new friends then. Hope he doesn't stay out too late."

Spooks handed the bag to Hannah who took a wrapped burger out for herself. "Hey, Sugar, where did you get those gorgeous tattoos?"

"That's right," Amberlin added. "You never told me about them."

"Not much to tell, really. There was this guy..."

"Yeah, seems like our stories always involve some guy," Spooks interjected.

"Well, he worked part-time at the restaurant in Asheville where I worked, but he was really an artist. He just worked at Betty's so he could pay the rent. He used to look at my arms all dreamy like and say what beautiful canvasses they were, and how he'd love to paint upon them one day. Ol' innocent me didn't have a clue what his form of painting was...not until it was too late. Of course, Tremble, that was his name, would have stopped but by then I was into it."

"You let a tattoo artist named Tremble work on you?" Spooks said between mouthfuls of burgers.

"Yeah, kinda ironic, isn't it," Hannah replied, and then they all started laughing.

As the three of them prepared for bed, Ben walked in looking pleased with himself. He and Hannah spent a few minutes catching up before Hannah climbed into bed next to Amberlin. Shortly after the lights were turned out, Amberlin scooted over closer to her friend.

"I know I haven't really answered your question about your leg," she whispered, "but I haven't forgotten about it. Let me sleep on it, and we'll talk about it tomorrow. Okay?"

"Sure," Hannah replied. "Thanks for at least considering it. It really means a lot to me."

2

THE NEXT MORNING AMBERLIN walked around the room in a daze. As she prepared for the day, she thought about her dreams from the night before. Ben continued to snore away on the floor, and Spooks just turned over on the couch with a grumble when Amberlin tried to wake her.

"Let them sleep," Hannah suggested as she sat up in bed and stretched. "It'll be easier if all four of us aren't trying to get into the bathroom at the same time."

"That's for sure," Amberlin agreed. "There's a greasy spoon across the street that, despite appearances, puts on a decent breakfast. Want to join me?"

"Sure," Hannah replied.

The two of them proceeded to get dressed, moving around the cramped space like a couple that had been married for years, smooth, efficient, and with a minimum of small talk, at least from Amberlin. Hannah chatted away about how excited she was to be in Washington, D. C. and all the sights she wanted to see while she was there. Amberlin tried to pay attention but found her thoughts kept returning to her dream.

Finally, as the two of them sat drinking coffee and waiting for their orders to arrive, Hannah tapped one hand on the table. "Earth to Amberlin. Come in. Where are you?"

Amberlin shook herself and smiled. "Sorry, I know I haven't been very good company this morning."

"What's up? Hannah asked. "Is it about what I asked you last night?"

Amberlin took a sip from her coffee mug before answering. "Yes, well kinda. I had a dream last night..."

"And?" Hannah prompted her after several seconds of silence.

"Well, I think I may know how to help you?"

"Really?" Hannah replied excitedly. "From your dream?"

"Do you remember my grandpa?"

"Of course. He was such a nice man. I'm sorry about what happened to him. It was in all the papers."

"Well, the papers were wrong. It wasn't Spooks who shot him. It was Reverend Stover."

"Ben's father?"

Amberlin nodded. "Yeah, but here's the thing. Papa Herb still comes to me occasionally, most often in my dreams."

"Really?" Hannah repeated, and then after a moment. "Cool."

"Well, last night I received a double visit from Papa Herb and Mo."

"Who's Mo?"

"He's kind of a spiritual guide that Papa Herb interviewed in the early days of his career. They seem to like to...hang out together."

"Awesome," Hannah replied. The two of them waited in silence as the waiter brought them their food, then Hannah leaned over towards Amberlin. "So, what did they say?"

"They told me how I might be able to help you," Amberlin replied, "if you're willing to give it a try."

"Sure. Anything," Hannah said as she picked up a slice of toast and began to butter it. "Just tell me what to do."

Amberlin swallowed a mouthful of eggs before replying. "We'll do it tonight in the room. I'll send Ben and Spooks to a movie." She paused for a moment then added. "Listen, I have no idea whether this will make any difference or not."

"I understand," Hannah replied, "but how can we go wrong? My God-gifted friend is being guided by her dead granddad and his spirit guide. I'm in good hands."

School Prayer

1

That evening, after sending Ben and Spooks to a late-night movie, Amberlin opened a paper bag from her afternoon shopping and started placing votive candles around the room as Hannah watched in fascination.

"What are those for?" Hannah asked.

"I really don't know. I guess to help set the mood," Amberlin replied. "I'm just following directions."

Hannah nodded. "Where do you want me? Shall I lie on the bed?"

Amberlin shook her head. "No, on the floor over there."

"Really, why the floor?"

Amberlin shrugged. "No idea. Following instructions again."

"Okay," Hannah replied with a weak smile. "No more questions." She lay down where Amberlin had indicated. "Ready when you are."

Amberlin walked around lighting the dozens of candles before returning to Hannah's side where she knelt close to Hannah's head. "Okay, close your eyes and take several slow deep breaths, and I'll do the same." The two of them continued like this for several minutes before Amberlin reached out and placed her hands on either side of Hannah's temples where she gently massaged them before moving her hands down to her friend's chest. Hannah's breathing increased, and her eyes fluttered, but she kept them closed.

"Just following my guidance," Amberlin whispered. "Not trying to get fresh."

Hannah smiled as she resumed breathing slowly and softly. After a few minutes, Amberlin found herself slipping into a trancelike state. She decided it was time to move her focus from Hannah's heart to her leg, but as she started to do so, she heard Papa Herb and felt his presence.

Stay in the heart, dear.

Amberlin followed his direction. A minute or two went by. Amberlin couldn't be sure how long since time seemed to have little importance at the moment. She found herself drifting in time and space and then a vision appeared before her of a small girl and a large man with muscular arms and a burn scar on one side of his face. She didn't recognize either of them at first, but then the girl looked up with a frightened look on her face and Amberlin knew it had to be Hannah at a much younger age. Amberlin estimated she couldn't be more than two or three-years-old. Hannah lay in a low lying bed with the man towering over her.

"How many times have I told you not to pee in bed," the man shouted. "Now get your ass out of there and go clean yourself up!" Without waiting for a reply, the man lurched forward and grabbed Hannah by her left leg and yanked her out of bed and across the room. As he did so, Amberlin heard the crack that sounded like a tree limb breaking and Hannah let out a blood-curdling scream. The man let go of her leg, and she dropped to the floor landing on the injured leg resulting in another scream of pain.

"Shut the hell up!" the man shouted at her. "You'll wake up the damn neighbors."

Hannah lay on the floor cowering against the foot of the bed, sobs escaping from her tear-soaked face. Finally, she looked up. "Please, Daddy, don't hurt me. I'll be good. Promise."

"Then get up and do as I told you," her father replied.

Hannah tried to do as she was told but fell back against the bed as she tried to place weight on her left leg. "I can't, Daddy. My leg hurts bad."

Her father stared down at her for several seconds blinking as though attempting to focus his eyes. He weaved to one side then righted himself. He's drunk, Amberlin realized. He's about to pass out. But he caught himself and looked around the room as though waking up and finding himself in strange surroundings.

"What have I done?" He asked. "What have I done?"

As Amberlin watched the scene unfold before her, she heard Papa Herb's words. *Go within to Hannah's thoughts.*

Amberlin paused for a second, wondering how she was supposed to follow these instructions when suddenly she felt herself slip into the little girl's consciousness. *Even my daddy doesn't love me. I'm no good. I'll never be any good. I'm such a loser.* These thoughts kept playing over and over in the little girl's mind. As they did so, Amberlin could feel the accompanying anguish building within.

Amberlin felt like reaching out and hugging the little girl, but before she could do so, she felt a new presence and heard a soft, familiar voice.

Your father really did love you, my dear, more than you'll ever know. But he was a sick man after he returned from combat.

Where were these words coming from? Amberlin wondered. Her gaze returned to the little girl where she found Hannah's mother sitting next to her daughter stroking her hair. *He never meant to hurt you that night, and he never forgave himself for what he'd done. He tried to make it up to you, but neither of us really knew how, but the last thing your father would have wanted for you to go through the rest of your life thinking you were unlovable or that you're a loser.*

As Hannah's mother continued to stroke her daughter's hair and talk to her, the little girl slowly transformed to the Hannah who lay on the motel floor in D. C. *It's time...well past time for you to release those false beliefs and to accept the truth. We love you, my dear. Your father had his own demons to fight from the terrible things he witnessed overseas. He made a terrible mistake on that night...one he would never get over, but it's totally false that you are unlovable. He loved you more than life itself.*

Amberlin watched Hannah's face slowly relax from her mother's words as two tears escaped between the closed lids. She suddenly realized that it was unnecessary for her to try to heal Hannah's physical body for where the true damage lay was within her heart and mind. As she sat there next to her best friend with her hands still over the area of her heart, the vision slowly faded, and she was once more in the motel room.

2

IT HAD BEEN A LITTLE over a week since the healing episode, and even though Hannah continued to limp noticeably on her left leg, she made no comment about it, including never mentioning whether she felt the attempt had failed or not. Hannah also seemed to have a much more positive outlook on life and never said anything about being a loser or less than others around her. All in all, Amberlin deemed the healing to be a grand success.

Amberlin, Ben, and Hannah were sitting around the table enjoying a second cup of coffee at the greasy spoon when Spooks stormed in, looked around, spied where they were sitting, and walked briskly over to them, slapping the morning newspaper on the table in front of them.

"Good morning," Amberlin said, momentarily startled by the interruption. Ben had been telling one of his many stories about being on the road and had the two girls in stitches until the dark cloud known as Spooks altered the mood around the table like a cloud covering the sun.

"Hardly a good morning," Spooks replied jutting a finger down to the front page of the paper where she'd circled one of the articles. "Can you believe it? Those assholes have grown so popular that they're even being quoted on the front page of the *Washington Post*."

"Who...what are you talking about?" Amberlin asked as she glanced to where her mother was pointing.

"The Stovers, who else?" Spooks replied.

"My folks are in the paper? What have they done now?" Ben asked as he slid the paper towards him. He read the headline: "Supreme Court Bans Prayer in Schools," then groaned. "That's not good. My folks will go apeshit over this."

"Read on," Spooks directed. "They already have."

Ben scanned down the article until his eyes recognized his last name. "'Most of the American people want Bible readings and Prayer in the schools...Why should the majority be so severely penalized by the protests of a handful?' said Reverend Ben Stover when he heard the Supreme Court ruling." Ben looked up from what he'd read. "Okay, what's the big deal? They're entitled to their opinion. It's a free country."

"You just don't get it, do you?" Spooks shouted, pulling the paper back towards her and pounding on it with her fist. "The *Washington Post* has no business giving such phonies as your parents so much national attention."

"Wait just a minute," Ben replied partially rising from where he was sitting. "My folks may be many things...crooked, obsessive, maybe even weird zealots, but they're not phonies. They happen to believe very strongly in what they're doing."

Hannah reached over and placed a hand on Ben's shoulder, gently pushing him back down in his seat. "Calm down you two. We don't want to get kicked out of here. Where else would we go for overcooked eggs and bacon swimming in grease?"

"Okay, okay," Ben said as he slid back down. "I'm just growing tired of Spooks' holier than thou attitude, especially when it comes to my folks."

Spooks pointed back down at the newspaper. "They're being quoted by one of the largest newspapers in the country. I read just the other day that your father, the 'weird zealot,' is drawing thousands to his revivals every night. And their believing so strongly in what they're doing makes them just that much more dangerous." With that, she scooped up the newspaper and stormed out in the direction she'd come.

Archer

1

The next few weeks flew by. As the popularity of the *Amberstovers* grew, so did their size. The expansion happened one night when Amberlin noticed Hannah standing in the back of the room swaying to the music and following the beat with a tambourine. After the break, as they started back on stage, Amberlin grabbed her friend's hand. "Come with me and bring that thing with you."

"What? No, I was just..." Hannah started to protest.

"We need a percussion section," Amberlin asserted, "and you're it."

As the three of them climbed onto the stage, Ben looked first to Hannah and then Amberlin, a surprised look on his face.

"It's okay," Amberlin said. "She's our new percussion section...and maybe our second backup singer." She turned to Hannah. "If you know the words, watch Ben. When he sings, you sing or at least mouth the words. We'll work out the details later."

"Are you sure?" Hannah asked. She turned to Ben who shrugged.

"Her name comes first in the band's name for a reason," he said. "Welcome to the *Amberstovers*."

The night went so well that Gerald booked them for a second night each week. He also promised them top billing on a weekend if they continued to draw well, but fate had other plans for them. Ben entered their motel room one evening with a broad grin on his face.

"I've got our next gig!" he shouted dancing around the room. "It's going to be great." He glanced around. "Where's Spooks?"

"She went for a walk," Amberlin replied. "Something about the spaghetti she had not agreeing with her. I didn't realize we were looking for a new gig. Things seem to be going well here. Did Gerald tell you something I don't know about?"

"No, no, nothing like that," Ben replied as he sat down on the edge of the bed. "This one just fell into our lap, and it's simply too good to pass up."

"How's that?" Hannah asked from the couch. She was sitting leafing through the latest issue of the *Spectator*, a local paper highlighting the entertainment of the area. "It says right here that *The Shadow* is the top spot for folk music in the area."

"Yes, in D.C." Ben replied, "but we're heading to the Big Apple."

"New York?" Amberlin asked, suddenly growing excited as well.

"Yep, and not just any part of New York. We're heading to *Cafe Wha* in Greenwich Village."

"*Cafe Wha*?" Hannah asked. "Never heard of it."

"It's only the hottest place in the world," Ben replied.

Amberlin looked at Hannah before replying. "But we like it here. Can't we play this out first and then move on to New York?"

Ben shook his head. "No. I really think it would be in our best interest to move on. Remember, it's hard to hit a moving target."

Amberlin remembered what that catchphrase meant. "What else is going on, Ben?"

Ben hesitated then took a deep breath. "My folks are coming to town. They're supposed to meet with some uppity Senator...a Senator Barry Gold something or other. I don't remember his name, but he's a big wig conservative. They're going to meet about this school prayer controversy. If Spooks finds out about it...well, I just think it would be best if we could avoid such a confrontation."

"I'll say," Amberlin agreed. "But how did you learn about this?"

Ben's gaze flickered from Amberlin to Hannah and back again. After a moment, he stuttered, "I...I...I read about it in the paper. It was a follow-up story. It was buried pretty deep, so hopefully, Spooks won't see it."

Amberlin studied his face before finally replying. "Okay, so when do we head out?"

"As soon as possible. I'll talk to Gerald in the morning. I'll tell him we have a chance to play at *Cafe Wha*. He'll understand."

Amberlin nodded. "Okay, it's off to the Big Apple we go."

2

"IT WAS A STANDING ROOM only crowd!" shouted Ben as he entered their dressing room without knocking.

Spooks and Amberlin glanced up with matching startled looks on their faces. "Well, I don't know if that's quite accurate," Amberlin said with a broad smile on her face. "Besides, how could you see anyone in the back of the room, as dark as this place is?"

"Don't you ever knock?" Spooks asked, but despite her attempt to be critical, she smiled as well.

"Well, I used my x-ray vision and saw several glowing figures in the back, so I say it was standing room only," Ben asserted as he dropped onto the over-stuffed chair next to the makeup table where Amberlin sat.

"It was a good crowd tonight," Amberlin agreed. "Even better than last night. We seem to be a hit in Greenwich Village."

"I'll say. Spooks, I think you should talk to the manager about keeping us over another week. What do you say? I mean, we're a hit at *Cafe Wha*. Let's play it for all it's worth."

"Already done that, Mr. Smarty Pants," Spooks replied. "He was in total agreement. I was even able to negotiate a little raise. Like I've said countless number of times, let me handle the business dealings. You just keep the van working and keep plucking on that guitar of yours."

"All right. Whatever you say," Ben replied. "It's too great a night to bicker. Where's Hannah?" But before anyone could answer, a loud knock on the door interrupted them.

Spooks rose to open it. "Probably someone from Ed Sullivan," she said jokingly as she opened the door.

It wasn't.

Instead, a tall, handsome, well-dressed man stood with his hand up prepared to knock again. He wore a suit and tie, though the tie was loosened around his neck. His look brimmed with signs of wealth from the tailored jacket and pants to the diamond-encrusted pinkie ring.

Maybe he is with the Sullivan show, Spooks thought staring up and down at him in fascination, but as her gaze moved up to his face, another face from the past flashed before her eyes. But no, it couldn't be...could it?

"Archer?" Spooks asked. "Archer Bowlins?"

"It is you," the man proclaimed excitedly. His strong tenor voice resonating around the room. "I knew it."

"Is it really you?" Spooks asked, continuing to stare at him in disbelief.

"Yes, it's me. It's so good to see you again after all these years. May I come in?"

Still flabbergasted, Spooks stepped aside to let him in before she realized what she was doing. By the time she did, it was already too late.

"Hello, there," Ben said sitting up a little straighter in his chair. "Come by for an autograph or two, did ya?"

"Well, no, not really," Archer replied with a jovial smile. "But I'm sure it won't be long before you have folks flocking to the backstage door for just that. No, I came to see Evelyn, if that's okay?"

Amberlin stood up and took a step toward him, her hand outstretched. "How do you know my mother?" she asked.

Spooks closed the door and circled around to step between the two of them. "I guess introductions are in order," she began and was dismayed to hear the shaking in her voice. She tried again. "Amberlin, meet Archer Bowlins. He's your father."

"I am?" Archer said, now as shocked as Spooks had been a moment before. His face transitioned through various looks, from being startled by Spooks revelation to confusion, finally settling on recognition. "So that's why you disappeared on me?"

"Yeah, that's pretty much what happened," Spooks replied. "Look, everyone, sit down. It's time for me to come clean about a few things."

"I'll say," Ben blurted out from where he remained seated. "I thought Reverend Stover was Amberlin's father."

"That's not right," Amberlin interjected. "That was just a rumor. My father's name was Harry—Harry the Handyman. That's what Rose told me."

Evelyn held up her hands. "Hush, everyone. Please, let me explain." She pointed to a straight back chair in the corner of the room. "Pull up a chair, Archer my dear. I have a story to tell."

Coach House

1

Spooks looked at the three of them seated before her: Ben slouched in the overstuffed chair, Amberlin, who had returned to the chair in front of the makeup table, and her old sweetheart, Archer, sitting in the straight back chair with a stunned look on his pale face. He's apparently still shaken by the bomb I just dropped, Spooks thought, then realized Amberlin and Ben wore similar expressions. I really know how to blow shit up, don't I?

Spooks looked around for another chair, but not seeing one, decided to stand. She began to pace as she tried to figure out how to begin. Begin at the beginning, her mother, Rose, often said. For once, she decided to take her mother's advice.

"It was many years ago," she started. "I wasn't much older than you are now, Amberlin, but I was different growing up. I was...well; I was on the wild side. I hated where I lived. Golden Acres felt like a straightjacket on my life. It wasn't until later I realized just how confining a straight jacket could be. Anyway, I started rebelling against Golden Acres' rules, but I did it the southern-nice way. I began sneaking out on nights and weekends. I'd hitchhike into town where I discovered *Dottie's Cafe*. That's where I met him. She pointed to Archer.

"Yeah, I still remember how radiant you looked that first night," Archer said. "Like there was a sun rising behind you or some Hollywood spotlight shining down on you."

"That radiance was probably the glow of sweat from my trekking into town during those sweltering summer days. Anyway, it turned out *Dottie's* was a favorite hangout of the Morrison High School crowd which is where Archer, here, went to school and as I soon learned was Mr. Big Shot."

"Well, I wouldn't say that," Archer denied.

"Everyone else did, and that humility of yours helped to win me over. All conference track star, football team quarterback, straight A's in school, lead singer in the glee club...and on top of all that, you were nice."

"Yeah, and you were Miss Mystery. No one knew who you were or where you lived. You'd just show up at Dottie's and order a milkshake."

Spooks laughed. "I don't think I ever paid for a single one of those."

"Paying for your shakes was the only way I knew to get your attention." Archer chuckled. "Besides, Chuck Smitters had his eyes on you as well."

"Chuck never had a chance," Spooks replied, "but I wasn't ready to let you know that at the time. A little competition never hurt anyone." Spooks stopped pacing for a moment before continuing. "Anyway, it didn't take long before I'd fallen for you, and yes, I realized you'd fallen for me as well. Then, there was that one special night..." Spooks let her voice drift off as she remembered back to that evening.

Everyone was quiet for several seconds until Spooks finally shook herself and started pacing again. "Anyway, it wasn't long before I realized the consequences of that evening. Truth be told, I think I knew the moment it happened...the moment we were together that it was going to result in my becoming pregnant, so I cut it off."

A moment of stunned silence stretched out until finally, Ben spoke up. "But you told my dad that he was the father."

"Yeah," Spooks replied. "I was mad as hell at him. He'd been trying to get into my pants for weeks. Wouldn't take no for an answer, so one night I took a bottle of booze over to his office and got him drunk. It was easy. The next morning I told him that we'd slept together, but we never did. His guilty conscience made it an easy sale a few weeks later when I told him I was pregnant with his child."

"But why?" Ben asked.

Spooks shrugged. "I don't know. Like I said, I was mad at him, plus I figured if everyone thought our holier than thou preacher was to blame, they'd keep it quiet. My main concern was to make sure no one ever learned about what really happened."

"So Amberlin and I aren't half brother and sister?" Ben asked, a note of relief in his voice.

Before Spooks could answer, Amberlin turned to look in Ben's direction with a stunned look on her face, then said, "Brother and sister? Is that what you thought all this time? Wait a minute. My grandparents told me that my father was Harry, the Handyman."

"Yeah, that was a rumor Missy started, and I let it slide," Spooks replied. "Of course, I didn't have a clue what lengths Missy would go to keep me quiet. Then it was too late. The baby, you," she nodded to Amberlin, "was suddenly on her way and next thing I know Missy, my trusty midwife, had chloroformed me. I woke up in the worst hellhole ever, where I learned what a real straight jacket feels like."

Everyone remained silent for a minute, each deep within their own thoughts when the door to the dressing room opened and in strolled Hannah. "Hey, everyone, let's go get a bite to eat. I'm hungry enough to eat a...oh, hello, who are you?" She directed the question to Archer.

There was a long pause before everyone burst out laughing. "That's not an easy question to answer," Spooks finally replied. "Let's go get something to eat, and I'll bring you up to date."

As they started filing out the door, Spooks leaned over to Ben and whispered, "Keep your filthy hands off my daughter and your dirty mind on other things, you hear?"

"Whatever do you mean?" Ben asked with a look of pure innocence, but Spooks wasn't buying it.

2

"I KNOW A REALLY NICE bistro just down the street," Archer said as the group left Cafe Wha.

"Do you mean the Coach House?" Spooks asked. "That's a little upscale for our wallets."

"Oh, please, it's on me," Archer replied.

Spooks smiled, then noticing the rest of the group nodding vigorously, said, "Okay, sure thing. The Coach House it is."

"I don't make it down to the Village all that often these days, but whenever I do, I make it a point to visit the Coach House. Leon Lianides may be Greek, but he cooks some of the best American food anywhere," Archer added. "Be sure to try the corn sticks. He refers to them as Celestial cornbread. It melts in your mouth. They go well with the black bean soup. Leon once told me his secret to the soup is a hint of Madeira."

By the time they arrived at the restaurant, Archer had Amberlin and everyone else salivating. It was clear from how the hostess treated him that Archer was a regular at the restaurant.

"So, do you live in New York now?" Amberlin asked after they were seated and drinks were ordered.

"Just outside New York," Archer replied. "My wife and..." He paused a moment, his face suddenly red as he glanced in Amberlin's and Spooks' direction. "I'm married now with two beautiful children. Archer, Jr. is ten, and Miranda is eight."

"Of course you are,"Spooks said to hide her disappointment. "You're too good a catch to go all these years without someone hooking you. I just hope you're happy."

"That I am," Archer replied. "I never did anything with sports after high school, but being active in the glee club eventually led me to my career today."

"Oh, and what's that?" Amberlin asked, then waited for the waitress to distribute the drinks around the table to hear the reply.

"I'm also in the music business," Archer replied as he raised his glass of white wine. "I'm an opera singer."

"So, you must be where Amberlin gets her celestial tones," Ben said, then took a long swallow of his beer.

"Maybe," Archer replied. "My folks both love to sing as well, even though they never pursued it professionally."

Everyone was silent for a couple of minutes as the breadsticks were delivered and everyone filled their mouths with the delectable food. Finally, Hannah spoke up. "I met the nicest person this evening at Cafe Wha. Her name is Mary-something-or-other. I forget her last name, Travis or something like that. She's waitressing there temporarily, but she's part of a new group. She told me that they recently signed a record deal that their agent put together. His name is Albert Grossman."

"You met someone who knows Grossman?" Ben asked. "I've heard of him. He's a big deal in the record world, though I hear he can be a pain to work with."

"Oh, Al's not so bad," Archer interjected, "if you know how to work with him."

"You know him too?" Spooks asked.

"Yeah, not too well, but the music industry is fairly small; a close-net community. Before opera, I tried my hand at some different types of music, but my tenor voice kept people thinking opera even if I was trying to sing something else. I met him back in those early days, and my agent knows him pretty well. Al is passionate about the music business and especially for those he represents."

"Well, Mary said he'd gotten her group a gig at the Bitter End. She thought we might want to talk to him at some point."

"I'll say!" Ben replied. "That would be great."

"I can probably make that happen," Archer said. "Just say the word."

"Whoa, wait a minute," Spooks said. "I'm the manager. I don't think we need anyone else..."

"Well, you'd still be the manager," Archer replied, "but Grossman could be a valuable connection if you want to cut a record...which, by the way, is where the money is these days."

"If Spooks doesn't feel it's a good idea to contact Mr. Grossman, then we'll wait," Amberlin said. "Like she said, she's our manager."

Ben groaned and opened his mouth as if to say something, but Hannah placed a hand on his and shook her head. Amberlin noticed the move and wondered what it was all about, then shrugged it off. It was not so easy to shrug off that her father, her real, true-to-life father, was sitting across the table from her. Her gaze kept drifting back to him despite her best effort to not stare. He really is quite handsome, she thought. I wonder what his wife and children are like?

It appeared she wasn't the only one caught off guard by her mother's confession. She noticed Archer glancing her way from time to time. Finally, their gazes locked on each other and they both laughed embarrassed at being caught.

"What did you say your wife's name was?"

"I didn't," Archer replied, "but it's Marva."

"That's a beautiful name. I look forward to meeting her," Amberlin replied, then knew she'd said something wrong by the look of alarm on Archer's face.

He glanced over to the rest of the people at the table who were busy ordering food. He leaned over towards Amberlin. "You know, this has all been quite a shock tonight. In a million years, I never thought I'd ever see Evelyn again, then to have her suddenly show up like this and, on top of it all, find out I have another daughter..." Archer paused, perspiration beading his brow.

"Yes, it was quite a shock to me as well," Amberlin replied. "Did I say something wrong?"

"Well, it's just that my wife comes from a very conservative upbringing. I'm not sure how she'd take to learning that I have a child out of wedlock, not to mention what that could do to my career."

"Oh, I see," Amberlin replied. "I hadn't thought of that. I certainly wouldn't want to cause you any trouble. I just thought..." What had she been thinking? Of course, he couldn't just up and take her home to introduce her to his family. She was illegitimate, a byproduct of one night of passion—two young lovers who had gone too far.

Archer reached across the table and grasped her hand. "I'm so sorry. You're a lovely girl and if there was any way..."

"Yes, Amberlin is a lovely young lady," Spooks broke in correcting him. "But neither of us are looking to cause you any grief with your perfect little family or your perfect career. Let's just chalk this up as one more pleasant evening and let it go at that."

Archer frowned but nodded. "Yes, perhaps that would be best, but if there's ever anything I can do..."

"...Introduce us to that Grossman fella," Spooks cut in again. "I've changed my mind. If he can help Amberstovers move ahead, who am I to stand in their way?"

"Yes, sure, I'll be only too happy to do that," Archer replied with a sigh of relief. He took a handkerchief from his jacket pocket and wiped his brow. "I wish...I wish it could be different."

"Yeah, me too," Spooks said as she patted Archer's hand then gently lifted it from Amberlin's. "But life isn't made up of what we wish it could be. I learned that lesson years ago back at Golden Acres, and it was driven home many times at the asylum."

Club 47

1

A few days after the gathering at the Coach House, Amberlin had a message from Archer to give him a call. Had he had a change of heart, Amberlin wondered? The thought stirred her heart which only served to confuse her more about how she felt about her real father. As she walked to the pay phone a couple blocks from the basement room where they were staying, she pondered the recent meeting. Archer might be my biological father, she thought, but her real father had been Papa Herb. He and Rose had been who had raised her, provided for her, loved her. While she could be thankful to Archer for giving her life, she really had no reason to expect anything else from him, and she certainly didn't want to disrupt his life any more than she had already done. He'd also made that perfectly clear as well. So, what could he want now?

"I've been in touch with Grossman as I said I would, and he'd like to meet you and hear you sing," Archer said after they exchanged awkward salutations.

"Really?" Amberlin asked, excited by the news, despite herself. "When, where?"

"Well, that's the thing," Archer replied. "He's up in Massachusetts right now checking out some groups. He said if you can make it up there, he'll arrange to have you play a set at Club 47. If he likes what he hears, he'll arrange to meet with you afterward."

"Okay, I guess that'll work," Amberlin replied, though something didn't feel quite right about it. "When?"

"He said there's no hurry. He'll be up there at least a couple weeks, maybe longer, but I'd suggest you get up there as soon as possible. Strike while the iron is hot, you know."

Or at least while the iron is lukewarm, Amberlin thought. "Okay, I'll let everyone know...and thanks. I appreciate this."

"It's the least I can do," Archer replied then after an uncomfortable pause. "You take care of yourself, you hear?"

"Sure thing and you do the same."

"CLUB 47! WE HAVE A gig waiting for us at Club 47? That is a big deal. I've heard good things about that place," Ben shouted as he did his happy dance around the room. "And we get to meet with Al Grossman? This is great news!"

"Well, we get a set, probably two or three songs, and maybe we'll get to talk with him," Amberlin corrected him. "Seems a long way to go just for an audition."

"Are you kidding?" Ben replied. "I'd go to California for such an opportunity. This could be a big break. Grossman represents some of the up and coming names in folk music."

"Okay, if you say so. What do the rest of you think?"

"Sounds good to me," Hannah replied, "though I'm pretty much just along for the ride. I know my vote doesn't really count."

"Sure it does," Ben spoke up before Amberlin could. "You're our percussion section."

Hannah giggled, but there was a sultry sound to it that caught Amberlin off guard. What was going on with those two?

"How about you?" Amberlin asked turning to her mom.

"Doesn't much matter to me," Spooks replied. "My vote probably means less than Hannah's."

"Why do you say that? You're still our manager."

"Yeah, for now," Spooks replied, then smiled. "Sure, let's do it. I told Archer to arrange the meeting, and he did. Wouldn't be right for us not to follow through."

"Okay! We're off to Harvard Square!" Ben exclaimed in an imitation Boston accent.

2

FOR THE NEXT SEVERAL weeks, the standing room only crowds continued even with an additional wing being added to the tent. The stack of bills disappeared and was replaced with a stack of newspaper clippings and letters inviting Rev. Stover to various events. Suddenly, the reverend was in high demand for speaking events and other social occasions, most of which Missy had to decline, but there was one she knew better than to refuse. It came in a plain white envelope with no return address postmarked from Los Angeles. At first, Missy almost ignored it, but then something prompted her to open it. Inside she found a handwritten letter. Her eyes fell to the signature at the bottom of the note: *Randolph Hearst.*

Holding her breath, Missy struggled to read the scrawling handwriting. The gist of the letter was direct and straightforward. Hearst was inviting them to a small soriée at the end of the month at his luxurious castle on his 168,000-acre estate in San Simeon, California. The invitation both excited her and mystified her. Why extend such an invitation in such a manner? Didn't most such social events come in the form of an engraved message, especially from one of the wealthiest and most powerful men in the world?

And most curious of all was the P.S. *Destroy this letter upon receipt.*

Before doing so, Missy showed the letter to Rev. Stover.

"Don't you find it strange?" she asked as she watched him read the letter.

"Strange?" Rev. Stover replied, and he flipped the letter over. "Well, yes, perhaps, but Hearst is known for his strange ways. Perhaps this is just one more example. That date is on a Monday, I believe. Seems odd he'd schedule such an event on a Monday as well. What do you think? Should we try to go?"

"Are you kidding?" Missy answered, taking the letter and folding it back up. "Of course we're going. This is the man who, with one short telegram, turned our crusade from a bankrupting failure to a huge success. You don't refuse invitations from such powerful and influential men. Besides, it'll be an opportunity for us to get away for a day or two. We could both use a little downtime."

Rev. Stover nodded. "Fine by me. You'll make all the arrangements?"

"Of course," Missy replied. "That will include a shopping trip for some appropriate attire as well...for both of us."

Rev. Stover groaned. "Really? Do we have..." then noticing his wife's facial expression, nodded. "...Whatever you say, dear."

3

IT TOOK THEM A LITTLE over a week to tie up matters in New York. With Hannah's help, Spooks was able to negotiate Mary and her trio to take over Amberstovers' gigs. In the process, Mary told Hannah to be sure to introduce herself to Paula Kelly. "She started Club 47 with Joyce. I forget Joyce's last name, but Paula is much nicer anyway. Tell Paula how much I miss her. She's a sweetheart and will treat you right." Mary turned to leave then stopped. "And keep an eye out for another singer, Joan. Last I heard she was thinking of dropping out of Boston College so she could devote more time to her singing. She's often around Club 47, and she's another Mensch."

"Pardon?" Hannah asked, confused by the term.

Mary chuckled. "It means she's really nice too. I'm sure you'll get along well with her. Good luck up there with your audition, and thanks for the gigs here."

Ben called ahead to make sure someone at Club 47 knew that they'd soon be arriving, and they were off once more in the van arriving at dusk.

"I booked us a room at a local motel," Spooks told them as they neared Boston, "but we'll need to find somewhere cheaper as soon as possible."

"That shouldn't be a problem," Hannah replied. "Mary gave me a few names of people in this area. Besides, Ben has a knack for making friends, most of the female persuasion, so we shouldn't have any trouble finding other accommodations."

"What's that? Did I hear my name being used in vain," Ben said from the front of the van. He looked at Hannah in the rearview mirror. "You know you have my heart and allegiance."

"Yeah, right," Hannah replied with a snort of laughter. "Until the next pretty face shows up," but it was obvious from the smile on her face and the twinkle in her eyes that Ben's comment had hit home.

Once again, Amberlin wondered what was going on with her two friends. Were they becoming an item, and if they did, how would that affect the dynamics of the group? Already she'd seen plenty of other singing groups breakup when members became involved with each other and jealousy set in. It was understandable. Most of the groups were made up of young men and women, many still in their teens and a few more in their mid to late twenties, who spent much of their time singing about love.

What could you expect? If she was honest with herself, she'd even considered what it would be like to move her friendship with Ben to some next level, especially now that she knew for sure that they weren't half-siblings. But life was already complicated enough, so she'd resisted the urge. But could she really expect Ben and Hannah to do the same? Probably not, especially when you consider how closely packed their lives were right now. Finances required that they all room together which usually meant rotating two women sleeping in one bed while the other got the luxury of sleeping alone. That left Ben to sleep on the couch or a cot if one could be found.

Life on the road was far from glamorous, but everyone had seemed to adjust pretty well so far. Would that continue to be the case if Ben and Hannah became more than just friends? *I might just have to speak to Mom about this,* Amberlin thought. In the meantime, she'd just keep an eye on them and try to do her part to keep anything from escalating further, at least until she was sure what was going on.

When Spooks called to speak to someone at Club 47 the next day, she was informed that Amberstovers were slated to sing two songs the day after tomorrow. "Really?" Spooks said. "What are we supposed to do in the meantime?"

"I don't know and don't really care," came back the reply. "Tour historical Boston for all I care."

"That was probably Joyce, one of the owners," Hannah replied when Spooks told the rest of them the news. "I've heard that the farther north you go, the more abrupt people are."

"Well, let's stay the hell out of Canada then," Spooks replied.

"At the same time," Amberlin interjected. "Why not do what she said. I don't think any of us have ever spent any time in Boston. I, for one, would enjoy playing tourist for a day or two. Who's game?"

"Sure," Ben and Hannah replied.

"Yeah, I guess," Spooks answered far less enthusiastically.

"Great! Ben, how about going to the lobby? I think I saw some free information about the area. Everyone else, get your most comfortable shoes on. We're going walking."

"Yeah, like I have more than one pair of shoes," Spooks replied, but with less of an edge.

For the next two days, the four of them explored both Harvard Square and the many other sections of Boston proper. In the process, they also discovered the MTA.

"Oh, oh, we've got to go on that!" Ben said pointing to one of the signs.

"What is it?" Amberlin asked.

"It's the M.T.A.," Ben replied, then added when the perplexed look remained on Amberlin's face. "It's the Metro Transit Authority—a subway. It can take us all over this city for next to nothing."

"Really? Cool," Amberlin replied.

"How come you know about it?" Hannah asked.

"From one of my favorite songs by the Kingston Trio," Ben replied. "It tells the fanciful story of a man named Charlie who takes a ride on the M.T.A. only to never be heard from again. He sang the first verse.

"It goes on, but you get the idea," Ben finished.

"That's a really fun song," Amberlin said, and both Spooks and Hannah nodded. "Maybe we could learn it in time to sing it as part of our spot in a couple days. It'll give us something to do as we walk around Boston and take rides on the M.T.A.."

"Sure, why not?" Ben said. "I already know the words and chords. Shouldn't be hard at all."

"Isn't it a little too light-hearted for such an important audition?" Spooks asked.

"Maybe," Amberlin replied, "but if Mr. Grossman can't enjoy a light-hearted, fun song along with our more serious ones, I don't want to work with him."

The other three nodded agreement.

Touring Boston

1

F or the next two days, Amberlin acted as their tour guide even though she knew as little about the area as the rest of them. With a stack of brochures in hand, she guided them through the streets and boroughs of Boston. She even dipped into their meager savings so they could enjoy some of the local cuisines. During their two days, they sampled Boston cream pie, Sam Adams beer, and even some Boston baked beans. They visited Paul Revere's House, the Old North Church, and Faneuil Hall Marketplace then hung out for hours at Boston's fifty-acre urban park known by the locals as the Boston Common where British troops were reportedly hosted during the American Revolution.

As the days passed, Amberlin continued to notice Ben and Hannah spent a lot of time together, often flirting and joking with each other. She was appalled by how much her jealousy continued to grow, but what could she say? Even Spooks didn't seem to mind their playful antics. She was happy when their big night finally arrived, and she could focus on the music and try to make a good impression on Al Grossman.

They were only allowed enough time to sing two songs. Everyone agreed that one of them needed to be Kingston Trio's song about the MTA, but the second song was up for debate; a debate that quickly turned into an argument between Ben and Hannah.

"The MTA song is a good one to start with because the local crowd will get into it. But we need to keep the second song upbeat as well," Hannah insisted.

"No, we need to show Grossman our range," Ben countered. "I say we follow up with a tear-jerker, something like Your Mama's Eyes."

"That'll have everyone crying in their beer."

"So, what's wrong with that? It'll show how we can move a crowd from laughter to tears."

"But if we keep the mood light and fun loving, it'll prove we can keep them coming back for more."

"Well, sorry, but you're just the percussion section. I'm going to have to overrule you on this one," Ben replied and started to walk away.

"Oh, so that's how it is?" Hannah all but screamed as she reached out and grabbed him by the arm and swung him around.

"Hey, hands off the merchandise." Ben pulled his arm away angrily.

"Enough, you two," Amberlin finally said. "You both have valid points. We could go in either direction, and we'd be fine. So, here's what we're going to do. We'll start with the MTA song and then follow up with 'Turn, Turn Turn.'"

"What?" Ben and Hannah asked at the same time. "Why that song?" Ben continued.

"Because I like it," Amberlin replied and walked off, leaving her two friends staring at each other.

Finally, Ben shrugged and nodded to Hannah. "What she says goes. Let's go wow some people."

2

AND WOW THEM THEY DID. The crowd of mostly Bostonians loved the MTA song and sang along with the chorus, then drew respectfully quiet as Amberlin sang Turn, Turn, Turn accompanied by Ben's acoustic guitar and Hannah's tambourine. Amberlin's clear, melodic voice cut through the silence with the last line: "A time for peace, I swear it's not too late."

A hush continued for several seconds as Ben, Hannah and Amberlin looked at each other. Had they blown it after all? Then the crowd burst out in applause, as many in the audience leaped to the feet with whistles and cat calls. The three musicians broke out in smiles and sighs of relief before exiting the stage despite several calls for an encore.

"Wow, I'm sure glad that's over," Amberlin said as she turned to the others. "I don't think I've ever been so nervous."

"It sure didn't show," Ben replied.

"Not at all," Hannah agreed. "You were marvelous. I don't think I've ever heard you sing better."

Spooks rushed up to the three of them and hugged them all. "You were wonderful. You had the crowd eating out of your hands. If that Grossman fellow doesn't sign you, he's tone deaf and an idiot."

"Hush, mom," Amberlin warned, though she was laughing at the same time. "We don't know where he's sitting. He could be any one of these people around us."

"Not likely," Spooks replied. "Bigwigs like him sit at some large table in the back with his entourage around him."

"How would you know?" Ben asked, chuckling as well.

"I've seen it in movies," Spooks replied with a smile.

"Excuse me, Miss," one of the barmaids said as she tapped Amberlin on the arm. "I have a message from Mr. Grossman. He'd like for you to join him at his table over there." She pointed to the back of the room.

"See, I told you," Spooks said with a smirk.

The four of them started to follow the young girl who then stopped to look at them with an embarrassed look on her face. "I'm sorry. Mr. Grossman was very explicit with his directions. "The invitation was extended only to you," she said as she pointed to Amberlin. "The rest of you can wait over there at the bar if you like."

3

A WEEK AFTER CALLING the number in the letter and leaving a message that they happily accepted Hearst's invitation, Missy received a call back informing them that a limousine would pick them up the following week on the day of the event, and they'd be driven the six hours to the San Simeon estate.

"Lunch will be served during your travels," Hearst's English sounding assistant informed her. Do you have any particular dietary needs that I should know about?"

Dietary needs? Missy thought, perplexed by the question. "Well, Rev. Stover enjoys a good steak from time to time."

"Filet, sirloin, or ribeye?" the man replied without hesitation.

"Oh, well, huh, ribeye, I guess," she replied. I think I'm going to enjoy this mini-vacation, she thought.

"How would Rev. Stover like it cooked?"

"Medium rare," Missy replied, though it had been so long since they'd had steak, she wasn't sure that was her husband's preference.

"And for you, Madame?"

"Oh, I'll have the same...a little more well done I suppose." That way, if medium rare proved not to her husband's satisfaction, she could share her steak with him.

"Very well, and would a baked potato and Caesar salad be to your liking?"

"Oh yes, very nice," Missy answered.

"And do you and your husband partake of wine on occasions? We have some fine Bordeaux that would go well with the menu."

"Yes, yes. I'll leave that to your discretion."

"Very well," the man replied. "Your car will arrive no later than ten o'clock. You have the number if you need to reach me for any reason."

Winter

1

The waitress escorted Amberlin to a large circular booth around which seven or eight people sat, but it was apparent to Amberlin who she'd come to see. Everyone had their attention on a short, chubby man with graying long hair and sunglasses even though the room was already dark. As he held up his hand, the group's chattering instantly stopped.

"Everyone, run on for a bit," Al said as he waved his hand dismissively. "I need to chat with this young lady for a few minutes."

Without another word, the assortment of men and women rose from their seats and disappeared into the night leaving Amberlin standing alone with him. "Have a seat," Al said. "Would you like a drink?"

"No, no thanks," Amberlin replied as she slid into a seat at the table.

Al waved the waitress away. "You have quite a voice, young lady. Unique and melodic."

"Thank you," Amberlin replied, suddenly aware how nervous she was.

"I think you could go far in this business," Al continued. "The folk music craze is just beginning to pick up speed. It will revolutionize music as we know it. You could make quite a mark for yourself, not to mention the money that's available for someone with your talent."

"Thank you," Amberlin repeated, not knowing what else to say.

"Just one thing. You need to dump the rest of your group. I can find you another guitarist to accompany you with far more talent than your guy, and you don't really need someone to rattle a tambourine. You can learn to do that yourself. No, you're the star...or at least you could be if you give yourself over to me."

Amberlin's high spirits suddenly dashed down to the sub-basement level. Give up playing with Ben and Hannah? No way. Sure, they got on her nerves from time to time, and who knew where their playful flirting might lead, but there was no way she would turn her back on them. Besides which, she didn't like the idea of giving herself over to this Al Grossman or anyone else for that matter.

Trust your instincts, she heard the familiar sound of her Papa Herb. How many times had he told her that? It has always served her well. No point in changing that strategy now.

"I appreciate all that you say, Mr. Grossman..."

"Just call me Al. All my clients do."

"As I was saying, Mr. Grossman. While I appreciate your comments and compliments, I'm afraid the Amberstovers is a package deal. You want me? Ben and Hannah come along, as does our manager. These people are my friends as well as co-workers. It was Ben's idea to start a group in the first place."

Al stared at her, apparently surprised that she'd not responded more positively. Finally, he said, "Let me paint you a picture of what's possible. Imagine, standing on a stage with a microphone in your hand and a full accompaniment of musicians around you. You gaze out to the crowd of admiring fans, thousands of them. They've all come to hear you sing. Why? Because they've already bought your records and now they want to see the real thing—the woman who's transformed the music industry and brought folk music into the mainstream. That could be you, and I can make it happen."

Was this her purpose knocking at the door, and was she refusing to answer it? What a difference she could make from a platform like that? She could sing the songs she wanted to sing, songs of peace, of prosperity, of possibilities for all of humankind. And all she had to do was to turn her back on her friends and mother. No way.

"I thank you for your time," Amberlin replied. "It's a beautiful picture you paint, but unfortunately, you'll have to find someone else to fulfill it. I won't turn on my friends. We're a package deal." With that, Amberlin slid out of the booth and walked away.

As she returned to the bar, Ben, Hannah and Spooks encircled her. "What did he say? Will he help us get a record deal?" Ben asked.

"He said..." Amberlin paused, unsure how to continue. Finally, she took a deep breath and continued. "He said we weren't quite what he was looking for. He told us to keep singing together, and maybe something would come available in the future. He was very nice and positive, but no record deal tonight."

"Damn," Ben said. "Really? I had such a strong vibe that this was our big break."

"Yeah, me too," Hannah added.

"Maybe I should go talk to him," Spooks said. "After all, I'm Amberstovers' manager. I should be the one to negotiate the deals."

Amberlin reached out to put a hand on her mother's arm. "Thanks, but no. That won't be necessary. While I'm as disappointed as you all are, I feel certain it's for the best. We just aren't a good match. But buck up. I'm sure something else will come our way."

No sooner had she said those words than a middle-aged lady walked over to them. "Wow, our crowd loved you guys! I've never seen them so captivated with just two songs." She stuck out her hand to Amberlin. "I'm Paula Kelly, one of the owners of Club 47. I'm wondering if you could hang around for a while. I think we can find some other dates you could play. What do you say?"

Amberlin glanced around at her fellow band members and smiled. "I think that would be great."

2

ALTHOUGH NO ONE EXACTLY planned for it to work out this way, Club 47 became their fall and winter home and sanctuary. Paula Kelly turned out to be the much nicer and more helpful owner as Mary Travers had said. She referred the band members to other jobs in the area. Ben started working part-time teaching guitar at the same music school where Amberlin taught singing. Hannah was content waiting tables at Club 47. Paula also gave Amberstovers two regular slots at Club 47, including one every Saturday night.

During this winter period, Amberlin continued to follow the news, especially anything that had to do with the new President who was often covered in the newspaper and on TV.

On September 25th, President Kennedy addressed the United Nations General Assembly, saying that the United States intention was to "challenge the Soviet Union, not to an arms race, but to a peace race," and Amberlin fell more deeply in love with him.

Less than a month later on October 6, Kennedy warned of a possible nuclear attack. The newspaper article read: "President Kennedy advises citizens to be ready for nuclear attack, and build family bomb shelters." By the end of the month, the USSR had tested its first hydrogen bomb. At fifty-megaton, it was the biggest explosion in history. Amberlin watched and wondered what was happening to the world. Had everyone gone crazy?

New Year's Eve finally rolled around, an opportunity for a fresh start, Amberlin thought. Spooks was nursing a cold but insisted the others go out and celebrate, so they did, starting at Club 47. Their original plan was to tour the other hot spots in the area, but the atmosphere felt too comfortable to them to want to change. There'd been more than the normal amount of disagreement among them over the past several weeks, but on this night they all agreed to do their best to put their strained feelings to the side for the night.

As the midnight hour approached, Ben pulled out a plastic bag with several small mints. "Take one," he offered as he pulled one out for himself and held the bag out to the two girls.

"What are they?" Amberlin asked, as she took one and stared at it.

"Just a little sweet for two of the sweetest girls in the world," Ben replied. Both girls groaned. "Happy New Year. Who wants to dance?"

Hannah's hand shot up, and the two of them headed to the dance floor. Not long after Amberlin swallowed the confection, she began to feel odd. Within minutes, Amberlin began to notice the colors of her fellow celebrators' outfits were more vivid and seemed to be vibrating in time with the music—the clearest music Amberlin had ever heard. It sounded like celestial angels singing to her, so beautiful that she was moved to tears. At the same time, she knew something wasn't right. She looked around for Ben and Hannah, but they were nowhere to be found on the dance floor. She wandered around the room for several minutes searching for them. The next thing she knew, she was outside but couldn't remember how she got there. Looking around, nothing seemed familiar, in part because everything was both vivid and distorted.

She began to cross the street, intent on trying to find her way home, or at least back to Club 47 when suddenly she heard a deafening blare and a flash of blinding light. She jumped back as a speeding automobile whizzed by, missing her by inches.

She turned slowly around, now afraid for her life. On the third rotation, she felt the firm grip of hands on her shoulder. She turned to find a diminutive old woman smiling at her with a worried look on her face. Amberlin shook her head to clear it. The woman was the spitting image of her grandmother, Rose, but that couldn't be. Rose was dead. She'd read about the devastating fire that had burned down the Gentry's home with her inside.

"Come with me child," the woman said, sounding precisely like Rose even though Amberlin's hearing was distorted. The woman patted her shoulder reassuringly and slowly guided her away. The two of them walked for blocks with the old woman continuing to talk soothingly to her, assuring her that everything would be okay. But how does she know? Amberlin thought. I may be dying, or maybe I'm already dead, and this is hell. It sure wasn't heaven, not any heaven she wanted anything to do with.

The two of them finally arrived at a small basement apartment that reminded Amberlin of where they'd stayed in D. C. Were they back in Washington now? That didn't seem possible, but then again, nothing she'd experienced since taking the mint from Ben had appeared real either. The old woman Rose lookalike unlocked the door and guided Amberlin inside to an ancient couch. She helped Amberlin lie down.

"You just shut your eyes and get some sleep," she said. "I'll fix us some tea. You still like cream in your tea, don't you?"

As Amberlin closed her eyes, she wondered how in the world this stranger could know how she liked her tea...unless, she really was who she appeared to be? It was the last thought she had before drifting off to sleep, stepping from one world of unreality into another. She found herself floating in a sky of multi-colored and fragranced clouds. As she drifted through a pale blue one, she caught the whiff of blueberries, like the ones she often picked with Papa Herb in the woods behind their home. Drifting to a second cloud, this one pink in color, the fragrance changed first to apples and then strawberries. All of the smells reminded her of her childhood, and her heart ached from the memories. As she drifted from cloud to cloud, each one reminded her of other parts of her early years.

She began to hear someone singing, but she didn't recognize the words.It started with a question asking if anybody had seen an old friend by the name of Abraham. Abraham who? Amberlin wondered? The song continued to describe him as someone who had freed a lot of people. She recalled reading about Abraham in the Bible but couldn't remember if he'd been involved with freeing people or not.

The verses continued, but each time the names changed, first to John then to Martin. Who were these men? Were they real people or just figments of the songwriter's imagination, but that didn't make sense. Surely, they must be famous people. Why else would someone want to immortalize them in a song? She recalled that one of Jesus' disciples had been John, but Martin? Who the hell was that? Then she heard the last verse, different from the others and with a new name—Bobby. That sure didn't sound like a Biblical name. There had been a Bobby in her Sunday school back at Golden Acres, but no way would he have become worthy of being captured in a song. Whoever these four men were, they seemed to all have turned up missing which was the only common element Amberlin could make.

As the song ended, she woke up. *What a strange song*, Amberlin thought as she turned over and sat up. Just as strange was how moved she found herself by the lyrics. Who were these men and why had she dreamt about them?

She glanced around at the small cubbyhole of a room. Where was she and what the hell had happened? She closed her eyes for a moment and shook her head to clear it. When she opened her eyes again, she spied the slip of paper on the orange crate that served as a table next to the bed. She picked it up:

I have your back. Watch out for Ben.

R

R? Could that be Rose? Could her grandmother still be alive? Had she, somehow, managed to escape the fire that devastated her home? A wave of emotions threatened to overcome her. She closed her eyes again and took a couple deep breaths. Her relationship with her grandmother had always been a complicated one. While Papa Herb consistently showed her unconditional love, the same could not be said for Rose. Still, despite their many disagreements, she loved her grandmother and had been heartbroken when she'd learned of her death, but had she really died? It seemed too much to hope for, not to mention it seemed impossible that she could now be here, so many miles away from their home in North Carolina.

Amberlin sat on the edge of the bed waiting for the mystery lady to return, but after an hour, hunger and a need to pee took over. She decided to head back to her own place and return later to thank whoever it was that had looked after her last night.

Upon returning to their small apartment, she found only Spooks home.

"Where's Ben and Hannah?" she asked.

"No idea," Spooks replied as she sniffled then blew her nose. "I've been sleeping most of the time. They might have come and gone for all I know. This cold has knocked me for a loop."

"Let me fix you some more of that chicken soup," Amberlin offered.

Spooks nodded. "That would be nice, dear. It's the only thing that I can even taste at this point."

Amberlin went about warming enough soup for both of them. It was widely accepted in the Gentry family that chicken soup was not only good treatment for a cold but could also work as a preventative. The last thing she needed right now was to come down with what her mother had.

It wasn't until later in the afternoon when Ben and Hannah finally showed up. Both looked haggard and in need of a good bath, but otherwise no worse for wear. No one seemed ready to talk about the previous evening. Amberlin finally decided to ask Spooks, Ben and Hannah about the song to see if they were familiar with it? They weren't.

The next day she started asking the other musicians that hung out at Club 47 as well, but no one knew what she was talking about. It was from one of them that she learned what had happened on New Year's Eve.

"Sounds like you had quite a trip," the musician said. He had some of the loveliest tattoos Amberlin had ever seen. Everyone knew him simply as Tat Man.

"Trip? No, we stayed right here in the neighborhood," Amberlin replied.

"Not that kinda trip. An acid trip," Tat Man replied.

"What's that?"

"Listen, did anyone give you something during the evening? Maybe in the form of a sugar cube or..."

"Wait a minute," Amberlin said. "Ben had some mints..."

"Yeah, they were probably laced with LSD," Tat Man replied. "He didn't tell you ahead of time what was in them?"

Amberlin shook her head.

"Not cool, man, not cool at all, but it doesn't sound like you're any worse for the experience. As for those lyrics, never heard them. Probably just a product of an overly active brain. I wouldn't worry about it."

It seemed like good advice to Amberlin. Unfortunately, her mind wouldn't let it go. She found herself repeating the lyrics over and over at the strangest times.

A day or two later, Amberlin returned to the basement room to thank the woman who'd been her guardian angel but was disappointed to learn from one of the neighbors that the woman had checked out the previous day leaving no forwarding address.

Hearst Castle

1

T rue to his word, a royal blue Rolls Royce pulled up to their trailer at 9:55 on the morning of Hearst's soireé. The chauffeur quickly loaded their bags into its trunk, and they were off to San Simeon. As they left the congested traffic of Los Angeles, the window separating the driver from the rear compartment slid open.

"There are mimosas in the fridge there to your right, if you care for any," he said, glancing back at them in the rearview mirror.

"Mimosas?" Missy asked, then silently kicked herself for asking the question. The last thing she wanted to do was come across as some country hick or southern red neck, though in truth she was a little of both.

"Yes, madame," the chauffeur replied, nonplussed by the question. "It's a delightful mix of California champagne with our very own California grown orange juice, freshly squeezed, of course."

"Sounds divine," Missy replied. "Thank you." She turned to Rev. Stover who sat beside her grinning broadly. "Would you care for a mimo...what are you grinning at?"

"You, my dear," he said as he reached over and patted her knee. "You're very cute this morning, and yes, I'd love a mimosa."

Missy found herself blushing as she opened the small fridge and pulled out the pitcher of OJ. This trip was exactly what the doctor had ordered...well, in truth, what God had decreed. She just knew it. She'd even dreamt about it the night before. Their lives were about to take a significant leap forward, and maybe, she shouldn't worry about being viewed as a hick or redneck. Her 'southern nice' charm had a way of winning people over. It had already worked once with Hearst. Why not continue it with all his highfalutin friends?

As the Rolls Royce floated across the California highways north to San Simeon, Missy found herself nodding off. She glanced over at her husband who was already snoring quietly beside her. Good for him, she thought. He really needed the rest. For that matter, so did she. She closed her eyes and was asleep in moments.

She was awoken by the sound of the separating glass once more opening.

"I'm so sorry to disturb you," the chauffeur said in a soft voice little more than a whisper, "but we'll be arriving at the rest area where Mr. Hearst has arranged for your lunch to be served. If you like, I can call ahead and make other arrangements."

"Oh, no. That won't be necessary," Missy replied as she wiped away the drool from her cheek. "I'll wake my husband, and we'll be ready in just a moment."

"Very well, Madame," the chauffeur said, and he closed the window.

The 'rest stop' was located at a pull off that provided a spacious view of the Pacific Ocean. A large open-aired tent had been erected sheltering the table laid out for two from the hot, early afternoon sun. To one side, a hibachi sat where a chef complete with a towering chef hat stood putting the final touches on their meal. A lone butler stood nearby to serve the food and to take their drink order.

"You don't happen to have iced tea, do you?" Missy asked as she sat down and stared at the fine china before her.

"Yes, ma'am, I do. Would you prefer sweet or unsweetened?"

"Oh, sugar, sweetened, of course, with lemon if you have it. I'm from the South where sweet tea was invented."

The meal was prepared and served to perfection. Before she knew it, they were back on the road again, and it wasn't long before Rev. Stover was once more asleep beside her, but Missy wasn't sleepy this time. She passed the time gazing out the window to the California landscape as it passed by, mesmerizing her into quiet contemplation.

What was this trip really about? Why would a man of Hearst's power and importance include a small town, southern preacher for one of his social events and on a Monday, no less? After receiving the invitation, she'd asked around town about the newspaper mogul, but no one seemed to know all that much about him except that he was insanely rich, more than a little eccentric, and private to the public eye.

"He prefers reporting the gossip of the underbelly of society than being a part of the gossip," one man who'd lived in California his entire life had said.

One thing for sure, she'd have to stay on her toes and not be overwhelmed by the opulence of the man's lifestyle. Not an easy task for an ol' southern belle who was raised in the backwoods of the North Carolina mountains.

2

Hearst Castle sat in the middle of nowhere, where the rolling hills of the countryside met with the desolate landscape of the Pacific Ocean, empty of almost all growth, except hill after hill of dry grass occasionally broken up by small groves of dwarfed trees with no signs of civilization anywhere.

Missy had dozed off and on for the last two hours, until the Rolls Royce came over one last hill and there, off in the distance, were the twin towers of Hearst Castle, like one she'd imagined in the fairy tales her grandmother had told her as a child.

She reached over and tapped on the glass, then waited for the chauffeur to lower it. "Is that our destination?" she asked.

"Yes, Madame," he replied. "That's the castle of Mr. Hearst, his pride, and joy. When we arrive, there will be someone to show you to your rooms. I'll bring your bags up straight away. May you have a pleasant stay. It's been a pleasure to serve you." And with that, he once again raised the window.

While the countryside around the Hearst Estate might be dry and brown, the grounds around the castle were a paradise of gardens, pools, and sculptured shrubs unlike anything either of the Stovers had witnessed before. As the Rolls pulled into the circular driveway, a butler in formal attire opened their door and escorted them to their rooms. On the way, the two of them gawked at room after room filled with priceless antiques.

"The newspaper business must be doing pretty well," Rev. Stover whispered as they strolled behind the butler.

"I'll say," Missy replied.

As they arrived at their room, the butler opened the door and waved them inside. Magically, their luggage had managed to arrive ahead of them and was sitting on the floor next to the most massive bed Missy had ever seen.

"It's like the Pacific Ocean of beds," she said as she walked over to it and, giggling like a schoolgirl, bounced on it several times.

Rev. Stover frowned at her antics but didn't say anything. He started to give the butler a tip, but the butler held up his hand.

"That's not necessary. Mr. Hearst takes excellent care of all his staff."

"And how many is that?" Missy asked.

"Oh, I really don't know," the butler replied. "Somewhere south of a hundred fifty I should think. Dinner will be served promptly at six. Someone will come to show you to the dining room. "

"Oh, that won't be necessary. I'm sure we can find it," Missy replied.

"With over a hundred and sixty rooms, it's quite easy to get lost," the butler replied. "Besides, Mr. Hearst prefers his guests not wander the halls. He's already lost too many of them that way."

"Really?" Missy asked, amazed by the thought of such a fate.

"No, Madame. My apologies. That last statement was my attempt at a little levity."

"Oh, I see." So, let's see just how gullible the country bumpkin is, Missy thought, suddenly embarrassed.

After the butler left, Missy strolled around the room, touching the ornate furniture, and checking out the masterpieces hanging on each wall. She then wandered into the walk-in closet that then led to the bath.

Walking back into the bedroom, she said, "The closet is larger than our trailer, and the bathroom is twice the size of the closet."

"Nice digs, huh?" her husband replied.

"I'll say. I think I could get used to living like this."

"Well, don't. Such opulence always comes with a hefty price tag."

"What is that supposed to mean?" Missy asked as she joined her husband who was lying on the bed.

"Just that for one to accumulate such wealth, one must have sold their soul to the devil, probably more than once."

"Oh," Missy replied, then added with a smile. "Well, all I can say is Mr. Hearst got a really good deal on his soul in that case."

New Snow

1

P romptly at 5:50 PM, Rev. Stover heard a light tapping on their door. Upon opening it, he discovered a lovely lady dressed in a maid's outfit smiling at him. "I'm to escort you and your wife to the dining room," she said. "It's a little way away, and Mr. Hearst grows irate if his meal isn't served promptly at six. Are you ready?"

"Yes," Rev. Stover replied. "Missy, let's go. Dinner is ready."

Missy came out of the bathroom drying her hands on a plush towel which she dropped on the bed. "And who is this young little thing?" she asked as they stepped into the hallway.

"I'm Lucinda, Madame," the young woman replied. "I'm to make sure your stay is as enjoyable as possible."

"I just bet you..." Missy started, but Rev. Stover reached over and pinched her arm to silence here.

Missy threw him an angry stare but refrained from saying anything else. They arrived at their destination as a large grandfather clock in the entryway to the dining room struck six times.

Like most of the rooms in Hearst Castle, the dining room was larger than life and could comfortably accommodate at least fifty guests, but on this night, the monolith of a table was only set for three.

Rev. Stover glanced at Missy and then to Lucinda. "Where are the other guests going to sit?"

"There are no other guests," Lucinda replied as she pulled out a chair for him then did the same for Missy.

As the clock struck its final chime, Hearst walked through the door and took his seat at the head of the table. He nodded to Lucinda who waved to someone at the far end of the room, and the feast began.

As the food was brought in, Hearst turned to his two guests. "Welcome to my humble abode. I do hope your journey wasn't too terrible."

"Not at all," Stover replied. "We found it quite enjoyable. I thank you for providing such a pleasant mode of travel. I'm a bit surprised to find we're the only guests this evening."

"Well, yes, my message to you may have been a bit misleading for which I apologize," Hearst replied as the wine steward approached the table and started pouring the wine. "What I wanted to talk to you about, well, let's just say it's of a sensitive nature. I do hope you'll forgive me. I'm someone who values his privacy, particularly when it comes to matters of politics."

"Politics?" Rev. Stover asked as he picked up his wine glass and took a sip. "But I'm just a man of God. Matters of politics are not my forte."

"Really?" Hearst replied. "Well, let's see if that's true. What are your views on Communism?"

"Why, Communism is the plague of the devil and maybe the world's greatest threat in our time," Stover replied without hesitation.

"And what do you think of our current President? This John F. Kennedy fella?"

Rev. Stover paused in cutting up the steak that had been placed before him. He stuck a piece in his mouth to give himself a little more time. This second question wasn't nearly as easy to answer. He didn't know what Hearst's political leanings were. He glanced over at his wife. She probably knew. Missy was always good about doing her research in advance, but Hearst hadn't asked her the question and the newspaper baron was now staring straight at him, not his wife. He took another moment to swallow the steak, then took a long sip of his wine. He picked up his napkin and dabbed his lips before replying. His pappy had taught him a lesson many years ago. "When you don't know what to say, the truth is always your best bet," he'd often said.

"Well, I, along with many other clergymen, are not at all comfortable about having a Papist in the White House."

"Exactly!" Hearst shouted as he banged one hand sharply on the table, spilling his wine. The wine steward was immediately at his side with a towel to clean up the mess which Hearst ignored.

"When the chips are down, to whom will he answer? The American people or the Pope in Rome? And especially when it comes to those pinko Commies?" Hearst shouted, then took a deep breath before continuing in a calmer voice. "That's what I wanted to talk to you about." He reached over and patted the reverend's hand. "You see, I'm a member of a small conclave of other patriotic citizens who have some real concerns about the direction our country is taking, especially with such a peace-loving dove in the White House. Did you hear his speech a few months ago? Something about challenging the Soviets to a peace race instead of an arms race? Ridiculous."

As the long pause lingered, Rev. Stover grew more nervous. He so wanted to glance over at his wife, to get even a small amount of reassurance from her, but Hearst continued to keep him locked in with a hard stare. Finally, when he couldn't stand it any longer, Stover cleared his throat. "Like I said, I'm only a man of..."

"Yes, yes, I realize that," Hearst interrupted, waving his hand dismissively. "But even men of God need to step up and stand for what they know to be right. Isn't that correct?"

"Yes," Stover agreed, "but what does any of this have to do with me?"

"Glad you asked. I've been watching you closely these past few weeks, and you are rapidly becoming a voice of reason within the Christian faith, with a little help from me, I might add."

Stover nodded. "Yes, you've been most gracious in helping to spread the word of God."

Hearst waved his words away again. "Of course such free publicity is rarely free in the long run if you get my meaning."

"No, I don't believe I do," Stover answered, a frown growing on his face.

Hearst glanced over to Missy. "Is he always this dense?"

Missy nodded. "Yes, but usually only about matters of politics." Seeing her opening, she continued. "Why don't you just tell me what it is we can do to level the scales as it were."

Hearst laughed. "I can see I haven't been giving you enough credit. So, as I was saying, my colleagues and I are concerned about the direction this country is heading, and we need someone who can carry the banner for democracy among the Christian community. I believe your husband...well, your husband along with your guidance and assistance...can be that voice of Godly reason."

Missy went to pick up her glass of wine before noticing it was empty. Hearst waved to the wine steward to refill it. She took a moment to sip it before replying. "I'm sure we're at your service, Mr. Hearst. As my husband said, Communism is a plague from the devil, and we're all about fighting Satan wherever, and however, he raises his head."

"Very well," Hearst replied. He raised his glass of wine. "Then a toast to our newest members. To God, democracy and the fall of evil."

The three of them drank from their glasses, then Hearst suddenly tossed his against the closest wall. Missy followed a second later, and then with a shrug, Rev. Stover tossed his as well.

Hearst leaned over close to the two of them. "Matters are developing in the coming months that will serve, in effect, to cut the head off the particular devil corrupting our country. We'll need you ready to lead the many millions of dedicated Christians to use this opportunity to take back our country from those who would sell it out to the dark forces of Communism. Can you do that?"

As he asked the question, he glanced first to Missy, then to the reverend, and back to Missy again. "I believe it's why we were placed on his green Earth," Missy answered for both of them.

2

Six inches of new snow fell on Harvard Square on February 22nd, the same day that John Glenn became the first American in space. Amberlin couldn't remember seeing so much snow any other time in her life, and she was well past ready for spring. Unfortunately, long time residents of New England assured her that they'd likely have at least six more weeks of cold weather.

"YOU MIGHT WANT TO TAKE in the Flower Show," one of her neighbors advised. "I go to it each year, and for several hours I can forget that winter is outside. It truly is a breath of fresh spring weather."

The idea sounded good to Amberlin, so she shared it with the rest of the troupe.

"I'm in," Hannah said immediately.

"Me too," Spooks replied. "Can we go today?"

"Unfortunately, it doesn't start until mid-March," Amberlin replied. "How about you Ben? Want to go smell the roses?"

"Dunno," Ben replied. "I'll see."

Ben had been in one of his moods for the past several days. Amberlin almost asked him what was troubling him but then decided at the last minute to hold off. *He just needs a little space to work things out,* she thought.

Later that evening when everyone was ready to go out for dinner, Ben was nowhere to be found.

"Should we wait?" Amberlin asked.

"No way," Spooks replied. "I'm hungry as a bear just waking up from its winter hibernation. He'll know where to find us."

Hannah nodded her agreement, so the three of them left, leaving Ben a note just in case he showed up.

He couldn't figure out how his parents had managed to track him down once again. They'd done everything they could to keep a low profile, but they had been at Club 47 for several months—probably too long. Paula had handed him the letter. Ben had immediately recognized the handwriting as his mother's and his gut twisted. What the hell did she want now?

The letter was short and not so sweet:

Call me when you get this letter. It's urgent!

Mom

Despite the urgent part of the letter, Ben had waited two days before deciding to do what his mom asked. He found a pay phone several blocks away from the apartment in a dive of a bar that he knew no one that knew him would frequent. He pulled a fistful of coins from his pocket and arranged them on the shelf next to the phone. He pulled the door shut and felt and heard the whirl of a fan turn on. He called the long distance operator and gave her the number, then waited for her to tell him how much money to deposit, then stopped. Why was he spending his hard earned money on a call that he didn't even want to make? He decided to reverse the charges and told the operator as much.

He waited for the connection to be made and listened while the operator informed the other party that they had a collect call. "Will you accept the charges?"

"Yes, of course," Missy Stover replied. "He's my son."

"Hello darling," Missy said when the connection was completed. "It's so good to hear from you. I was beginning to think my letter might not have gotten to you."

"Yeah, it came today," Ben lied. "What do you need? Is everything all right? Is father okay?"

"Yes, yes, we're both fine," Missy replied. "I've just been missing my baby, that's all."

Ben groaned. He didn't believe that for a moment. "I'm fine. Just been busy, that's all."

"And how's your sister?" Missy asked. She couldn't help but get to the real purpose of the letter and the call.

"She's not my sister," Ben replied before he had a chance to think about it.

"Well, your half-sister then. How is she?"

That's right. Neither of his parents knew the truth about who Amberlin's father really was. Shouldn't he tell them? Wouldn't that relieve their minds? Isn't that what any good son would do?

"Hello, Ben. Are you there? Did we lose the connection?"

"Yeah, I'm here," Ben replied, his brain swirling from the realization. "Amberlin is fine," he finally continued. So much for the notion of being a good son. It was too late for that. "Listen, everything is fine here, and everything is apparently okay where you are, so what's the purpose of this call?" He didn't even try to disguise his irritation.

"Leave the boy alone for." He could hear his father shout in the background.

"Your father sends his love," Missy said.

Like hell he does. "I really have to go," Ben replied. "I'll check in more often in the future, but otherwise, just leave me alone, okay?" He hung up without waiting for a reply.

He sat in the phone booth for several minutes playing with the stack of coins in front of him. Why did he allow her to get to him so easily? Why had he even bothered to call her? Because if I hadn't, she would probably have ended up on my doorstep, came the reply.

When he finally felt calm enough to walk home, he opened the door. As he did so, he noticed an old lady slipping out the door in front of him. Her movement seems strangely familiar, but he couldn't figure out why. He finally shrugged. Probably just a little residual effect from those New Year's Eve drugs. Yep, I'm sticking with good ol' pot in the future. He pulled up the collar of his coat as he prepared to walk home. As he opened the door, he noticed it had started snowing again. He really missed the south.

Part Three

Whistle Blow

1

Amberlin sat in the booth in the diner near her apartment sipping on her second cup of coffee in an attempt to wake up even though it was close to eleven in the morning. They'd had a late gig the night before, and she'd been the only one awake when her hunger forced her out of bed and to the diner, leaving everyone else still asleep.

"Don't turn around," a voice behind her whispered so softly at first Amberlin thought she might have imagined it. Before the meaning of the words had registered, she'd already started turning.

"I said, *don't* turn around," the voice said again much more loudly and this time recognizable. It was the mystery lady from the other night. Ignoring the command, Amberlin turned in her seat and gazed into the steel gray eyes of her grandmother Rose—her supposedly deceased grandmother who sat in the booth next to hers apparently alive and kicking.

"You never were very good at following orders," Rose said, but with a smile that cushioned the comment.

"How in the world...? What are you..." Amberlin started and stopped, flabbergasted by Rose's appearance. She slid out of her booth and slid in across from Rose.

"The reports of my death have been greatly exaggerated," Rose replied with a chuckle, "but also necessary and intentional," she added.

"But how?" Amberlin asked as she reached over and clasped Rose's hands and squeezed them tightly. Rose briefly explained how Ben had saved her life by helping her to escape the fire by hiding in the root cellar.

"That's why this is so hard to have to say," she added at the end of the story.

"What's that?"

"Ben is treating you wrong," Rose replied.

"Well, I know we have our arguments from time to time..." Amberlin started.
ed.

"That's not what I mean," Rose interrupted. "He's been in touch with his folks and letting them know what's going on with you."

"No way," Amberlin said, shocked by the news. "How? Why?"

"I've caught him making calls to them. I can only imagine why. I'm afraid he's up to no good."

Amberlin sat there feeling her anger grow at the thought that one of her best friends could betray her this way.

"The Stovers are very good at getting over on people," Rose added. "Believe me, I know. Missy Stover had me convinced for years that she was my best friend and only had my best interest at heart. Meanwhile, she used and manipulated me, which is part of the reason I decided it best to fake my own death."

"I see," Amberlin said. "But it was Ben's idea to go out on the road like this."

"Well, I think Ben is a troubled boy. Conflicted might be a better word to describe him. I think he really likes you, but at the same time, he feels compelled to do what his mother expects of him. Missy has a particularly strong though misguided power to persuade and manipulate, and she's not afraid to use it on her friends or family members."

As the two of them sat there holding hands, Amberlin could feel the tears welling up in her eyes, and her heart ached. They had all been through so much together these past several months while on the road.

At that moment, Ben walked through the front door. Seeing Amberlin, he waved and started towards her, but then stopped as he noticed who she was sitting with. His smile wavered for a moment then broke out into a wide grin.

"If it isn't Mrs. Gentry as I live and breathe," he said as he resumed approaching the table then stopped once more, his face contorting into a mixture of confusion and doubt. "Wait a minute. Were you in the bar the other night? Hey, have you been following me?"

Rose and Amberlin both stared at him without either saying a word. A long pregnant pause later, Ben finally shook his head. "Now, if you'll give me a minute I can explain everything."

"I bet you can," Amberlin fairly screamed at him. "You Stovers have a knack of explaining everything no matter how bad it looks. Unfortunately, those explanations are always packed with lies and deceit. But you've run out of rope this time, Mr. Ben Stover. I'm through with you."

Ben started to take a step forward to slide into the booth, but Amberlin threw up a hand in a gesture of a traffic cop. "Stop right there. Turn yourself around, go to the apartment, get your stuff packed and get the hell out of my life. I'll give you an hour. If you or your stuff is still there when I get back, I'll call the police. Is that understood?"

"Well, I'm not sure that's such a good idea," Ben replied with just a moment of hesitation. "The police might be more interested in Spooks than me, especially when I explain who she is."

Amberlin felt something letting go within her. It felt like all her control was leaking out from a myriad of cracks in her makeup—cracks that had been forming for months as she realized that Ben had been deceiving her for close to a year. She felt Rose squeeze her other hand more tightly. She paused and took a deep breath, then slowly let it out.

"You're right," she finally replied. "We'll keep the police out of this. I'll let Tattoo and a few of his friends take care of you. He's offered to do so more than once. Of course, I doubt he'll be nearly as gentle as the boys in blue."

Amberlin watched as the blood drained from Ben's face. He'd already had a few close calls with Tattoo and his other band members. Ben slowly nodded, then shrugged. "Okay, if that's how you want it." He turned to walk away but stopped before reaching the door. "You know I'll have to take the van, and that will leave you without any transportation."

"Fine," Amberlin answered. "Just make sure all of my stuff, as well as Hannah's and Spook's, is out of it."

"What if Hannah decides to come with me?" Ben asked.

"She's on her own now and can make her own decisions," Amberlin replied. Though the thought did trouble her, there was nothing she could do about it now.

Ben nodded again. "Okay, see you around."

"Not if I see you first," Amberlin replied.

2

AFTER BEN HAD LEFT the diner, Amberlin sat in the booth across from Rose and stared down at her hands. She felt the first tears escape from the lids of her eyes and trickle down her face. She felt her grandmother's hands squeeze her own.

"I've really done it now," Amberlin finally said with a sniffle and cough. "No guitarist for the group, no van, and maybe no backup singer. What am I going to do now?" She looked up at Rose who smiled back at her.

"You'll do what the Gentry women have done for generations when life gets hard. You'll go on. You'll persevere, and in the process, you'll grow stronger."

"But I'm almost out of money, and I've effectively broken up the group, so I'm probably out of a job as well."

"Maybe, but you don't know that for sure," Rose replied. "Listen, I'm here for you, and I don't really think you want me to buy into your limitations. Papa Herb, may he rest in peace, never did, and I'm not about to do it this time. So, who do you need to check with to see if you still have a job or not?"

"That would be Paula at Club 47. I know my teaching job is still okay, but it doesn't pay all the bills."

"Well, as far as the bills go, I can help you out there," Rose replied, patting Amberlin's hand. When Amberlin opened her mouth to protest, she added, "Consider it a loan or an investment in your future. It's what grandparents do. Besides, I have some making up to do with you. Let this be a start."

Amberlin finally managed a smile. "Okay. Thanks, Grandma. I really appreciate it, but you know that's not the biggest thing. I've come to really love singing. I'm going to miss it."

"And why would you say that?" Rose replied. "Just because you may have to reorganize your group is no reason to quit now. I've heard you sing." Amberlin looked up at her. "Yeah, yeah. I've hidden in the back of the room a few times," Rose continued. "You're good...no, you're better than good. You're fantastic. Like I said, I'm investing in your future—your future as a folk singer."

The two of them paused as the waitress approached their table, and Rose ordered a coffee as the waitress refilled Amberlin's cup. After she left, Rose continued. "What was it that Papa Herb told you so often? Something about you having a divine destiny, wasn't it?"

Amberlin nodded. "Yes, that's right."

"Well, I think your music ability plays a significant role in that, so you can't let this bump in the road stop you. I simply won't allow it."

Amberlin smiled at that last statement. "Oh, you won't, will you?"

Rose chuckled. "No, I won't. There's an old saying. 'It's always darkest before the dawn.' Well, I have a feeling your dawn isn't that far off. So, let's have one last cup of coffee, then you head back to the apartment and see how many folks are still there. If Hannah is gone, I'll start practicing the tambourine."

The two Gentry women looked at each other for several seconds then burst out laughing.

Mouthpiece

1

In the months following the meeting with Hearst, Rev. Stover became more outspoken against the evils of Communism, especially attacking the role the Soviet Union played in trying to take over the world by crushing democracy. He even started questioning the role Cuba might play in the Soviet's plans.

Without referring directly to JFK, his message often included questioning America's leadership both in Congress and the White House. Missy couldn't remember a time when she'd seen her husband so involved in politics, and she was equally surprised how good he was. Of course, she did her part to guide him in this new direction, encouraging him in every way she could to keep swinging for the fence.

Hearst continued to do his part as well by being sure that their tent revivals continued to receive front-page coverage whenever possible. It was his idea to take their message to a broader audience.

"You've had a good run here in L.A.," he told them during one of his infrequent personal visits. "But there's so many more dens of iniquity across the country, as I'm sure you're aware. I want you on the road for God. After all, you're a revival, right? Got the tent and everything. And don't worry about small crowds. I've laid out a map that will take you to areas where my newspapers will give plenty of free publicity even before you arrive. By the time you've set up your tent, there will be long lines waiting to get in. How does that sound?"

"Sounds fantastic!" Missy shouted before Rev. Stover had a chance to comment. "It's exactly what God would want us to do, spread his message to the masses just like Jesus."

Hearst smiled, then looked at the reverend. "You in?"

"Of course, he's in..." Missy started but then stopped when Hearst shot her a nasty look.

143

"Thanks, I can speak for myself," he said to Missy, then turned his attention to the newspaper baron. "Yes, I'm in. It sounds like a good plan, though pulling up stakes and moving from town to town can be quite expensive."

Hearst waved his comments away. "Hell, don't worry about that. I'll cover whatever extra expenses you incur." He stopped for a moment, chewing on his lower lip. "There's just one thing I'd like you to do a bit differently. I've noticed you never mention Kennedy by name. You just refer to the evils of Washington as coming from Congress and the White House. I want you to be more direct. It's time to name the serpent. Do that, and all those extra expenses will be taken care of."

Stover glanced over at his wife who was nodding vigorously but keeping her mouth shut. Those extra expenses could easily mount into thousands of dollars over the next few months, but all he had to do was drop Kennedy's name a few times. Point out the dangers of having a Papist dove as their Commander-in-chief. He nodded.

"Yeah, I can do that. No problem." The two men shook hands.

2

As Amberlin and Rose entered the apartment, Spooks leaped off the bed where she'd been lying reading a magazine.

"Is Ben gone?" Amberlin asked without any preamble.

"Yes," Spooks answered. "What the hell happened? I couldn't get a word out of..."

She stopped in mid-sentence and stared at Amberlin's companion.

"Mom? Is that you? What in the world?" Spooks stammered.

"Hello Evelyn," Rose replied. "It's so good to see you again." The two rushed over to each other and hugged. "It's a long story. I'll fill you in later. For now, just know that I had to fake my death to get some nasty people to leave me alone."

"Missy and Reverend Stover?" Spooks asked.

"Yes, that's right, and now we're dealing with their son."

"Well, not anymore," Spooks replied as she pushed her mother out to arms length and stared at her, still not sure if she believed her eyes. "He stormed in here a little while ago, packed up his stuff and stormed out. I couldn't get a word out of him."

"Did Hannah go with him?" Amberlin asked.

"No, I did not," Hannah said as she entered from the bathroom. "He did talk to me. I ran into him as he was getting in the van. He told me his side of the story and asked me to go with him, but I declined. Truth be told, I didn't believe him, especially the part about Mrs. Gentry being alive. I can see that at least that part was true."

"What was his side of the story?" Amberlin asked.

"He said that you had accused him of being dishonest and wouldn't give him an opportunity to explain. He felt like you were just looking for an excuse to break up the group. That just didn't sound like you at all, so I decided to stay and hear your side."

Amberlin explained what she'd learned at the diner.

"So, the part where I accused him of being dishonest is true," Amberlin finished.

"Wow! He's been spying on us all this time for his folks? Creepy," Hannah said with a shudder.

Hannah, Amberlin, and Spooks had migrated to the bed, leaving the overstuffed chair to Rose.

The four of them looked at each other for several seconds before Spooks finally said, "Okay, so what do we do now? The group is effectively broken up, we've no transportation, we're hundreds of miles from home, and oh yeah, our little stash of money is just about to zero."

"And we have our health, each other, and believe it or not, God is still on our side," Rose added in an attempt to balance her daughter's negativity.

"Grandmother is right," Amberlin joined in. "I don't agree that the group is necessarily broken up. We're just in a period of flux, that's all. I've seen this happen with some other groups and some of them have bounced back even stronger than before."

"I'm with Amberlin," Hannah said. "I'm going to miss Ben. I think we all will...yes, even you Spooks," she said before Spooks could interrupt. "But what's done is done, and we must move forward. Besides, Amberlin is who everyone wants to hear. We can get another backup singer and guitarist. Right?"

"Maybe," Amberlin replied, "but that may not be necessary. I have another idea that might just work."

"What's that, dear?" Rose asked.

"Well, first I have a confession to make. I haven't been completely honest with everyone either?"

"Oh, boy, here goes," Spooks said. "What deep, dark secret have you been keeping from us."

"Remember when I met with Al Grossman a while ago?"

"Sure, he wasn't interested in working with us," Hannah said.

"Well, that wasn't exactly true," Amberlin replied. She went on to share what Grossman had really said.

"So, you turned him down?" Spooks asked when Amberlin finished.

"Yeah, sorta. I just wasn't interested in his conditions."

"But now..." Hannah started.

"Well, I could go back to him and see if he'd be willing to reconsider," Amberlin finished for her. She glanced around at the other women.

No one spoke for close to a minute. Finally, Rose said, "I think it's a good idea. Of course, I'm the newest member of this troupe, but I'm also the senior member, and I've been with Amberlin the longest." She reached out and clasped her granddaughter's hands. "You are special. I mean, we're all special in our own ways, but your Papa Herb was right. You have a divine destiny, and as I told you earlier, I'm convinced that your singing will play a major role in your fulfilling your purpose. I vote yes. Go talk to this Al Grossman. Maybe he's finally woken up and realizes what a mistake he made the first time."

Spooks nodded. "I agree. Even dense men come to their senses every now and then."

Hannah nodded as well. "Yes, go talk to him. None of us have to be part of the group. We could just be your entourage, where you go for support and nurturing when the pressure of fame and fortune become too much."

Amberlin looked into each of their faces, tears welling up in her eyes for the second time that morning. Finally, she said, "You are already that place of support and nurturing. Now, let's go see if we can find a bit of that fame and fortune."

They all cheered and danced around the room. Finally, Spooks asked, "How are you going to get in touch with Grossman? Didn't he leave several weeks ago?"

"Yes," Amberlin agreed, "but I bet Paula will know how to reach him. In the meantime, I'll go to her, hat in hand and beg her not to give our spots to anyone else. Maybe I can get Tattoo or one of his band members to take Ben's place for a few gigs."

"Sounds like a good plan to me," Hannah said. "Paula really likes you and Joyce, her partner, really likes the crowds you draw. We'll make it through this. I just know it."

"Okay," Amberlin said as she rose from the bed. "How about a group hug before I go plead my case to Joyce?"

The four of them came together in the center of the room. As they embraced each other, Rose added, "Could I also say a little prayer for us?"

"Please do," Amberlin replied.

Rose paused for a moment before saying, "Dearest Heavenly Father, we come with grateful attitude for all you have already provided to us through the years, and we ask for your continual blessing and protection. Please look over my dear Amberlin, as she takes this next leg of her journey to fulfill your will. In your Son's holy name we pray. Amen."

"It's been a long time since I was part of a prayer circle," Spooks said as they separated.

"Never hurts to acknowledge the Source of all our bounty," Rose said. "And as my Herb often said, now it's time to move our feet as we pray."

Bay Of Pigs

1

The meeting with Paula went better than Amberlin expected. Paula assured her that the two spots a week were still hers and that between the two of them they'd find a temporary replacement for Ben. The best news of all was that Al Grossman was planning a trip back to Club 47 the following week.

"He's still looking for that special group or solo singer," Paula said. "I'll be happy to put in a good word for you when I talk with him later in the week. I'm sure he'll be interested in talking with you again, especially since he's not found that perfect act yet."

The rest of the week flew by, with Tattoo offering to sit in for Ben. His style of playing was a bit different, but he knew most of Amberlin's regular songs and was a quick study in picking up the songs he wasn't familiar with.

Before she knew it, Grossman had arrived and had scheduled a time to talk with her.

"Don't bother bringing any music or an accompanist. I know how you sing. We'll just need to see if we can sort out the details," he told her over the phone. "How about meeting me at the diner down the street from Club 47 around seven? It'll be quieter there, and I can get a bite to eat before going to the club."

Amberlin stood outside the diner a few minutes before seven, too nervous to go in. So much was riding on this meeting, not just for her, but for her mom, grandmother, and best friend as well. What if she blew it? What if Grossman wasn't really interested in working with her, but just wanted one more opportunity to rub it in how much of a mistake she'd made before? Only one way to find out, she thought as she pushed the door opened and walked inside.

As she expected, Grossman had taken a seat at the far end of the diner away from everyone else. He wore a houndstooth jacket and looked more like a college professor than someone who could make or break aspiring folk-rock singers. All except the hair that, while gray like a college professor's was likely to be, it was also much longer than most college campuses would tolerate from a member of their faculty.

Seeing her across the diner, he waved and at the same time motioned for a waitress.

"Good to see you again, Amberlin. It is okay if I call you that, right?" Grossman said as he partially stood up and motioned her to sit across from him.

"Certainly, Mr. Grossman," Amberlin replied.

"Al is fine," he answered. "I'm on a first name basis with all my singers."

"I see," Amberlin replied, "but I'm not one of your singers just yet."

"And that's the reason we're talking again, aren't we?" Grossman said with a chuckle. "I like someone who gets right to the point. Have you come to your senses?" He smiled to take the edge off the question.

"Let's just say that my situation has changed somewhat, so I thought it would be worthwhile for us to explore the possibility of working together again."

"Yeah, I heard you dumped your guitar player," Grossman said. He paused as the waitress approached their table. "What would you like? Their beef stew is more than a little credible but stay away from their beans and franks. Gas city."

"Oh, nothing for me, thanks. I just came for the conversation."

"Nonsense. You've got to eat." He turned to the waitress who stood there with a bored look on her face, snapping her gum, pad in hand. "How about rustling us up a couple bowls of that stew of yours and a platter of rolls. Can you do that, sugar?"

The waitress shrugged, wrote down the order and disappeared without saying a word. "The service here is some of the worst in the area, but the food ain't half bad. Now, onto business. So, you dumped your guitar player, right? Smart move. Even a smarter move to want to talk to me. Like I said in our first meeting, you have talent and a unique sound that I think could be big...with the right guidance, of course."

"And you're the one to provide that guidance?" Amberlin asked.

"Listen, babes, in this business it's as much about who you know as what you can do. It really takes both. You've got the chops, and I have the contacts. It's a match made in heaven."

"And all I have to do is dump my friends and my manager, who happens to be my mother, by the way, and give myself over to you," Amberlin said. "Oh, and by the way, my grandmother has recently been added to the mix."

"Your grandmother? Really?" Grossman asked.

Amberlin nodded. "Yep, she's quite a pistol. I think you'd like her, though she's probably a little old for you."

"I may have been a little hasty before," Grossman replied. "I know friends are important, and well, you did dump one of them. Perhaps we can find some common ground here." He paused a moment. "Really? Your grandmother is in the picture now?"

Amberlin smiled. "That's right, but I don't expect her to be on stage with us. In fact, I don't care if any of them are on the stage or not, and they're fine with that as well."

"Okay, good," Grossman said with a sigh of relief.

"But," Amberlin continued, "You're right, friends and family are important. I need them to be included in some way. Consider them my support staff. Would that be a problem?"

Grossman paused a moment as the mute waitress brought two steaming bowls of stew to their table and a basket of freshly baked rolls. As she set the dishes in front of them, Amberlin suddenly realized just how hungry she was. She took a moment to bow her head and give thanks before picking up her spoon and digging in.

The two of them sat silently enjoying the meal. Within minutes, the rolls were gone, and Grossman waved for some more. Finally, he looked up from his almost empty bowl and asked, "So, do we have a deal? Will you allow me to make you rich and famous?"

Amberlin placed her spoon down and wiped her lips with the paper napkin. "Yes, at least in spirit if not in the details. I'll have Spooks get in touch with you to work those out. After all, she is my office manager, and given that she's also my mother, I know *she'll* have my best interest at heart." The emphasis of that one word made it clear she wasn't yet convinced that she could say the same thing about Grossman. She extended her hand across the table to shake his hand.

As their hands parted, she smiled at her new agent. "Just one more small detail. I want to make it clear that I'm not your sugar or your babes, or any of the other demeaning titles you may refer to your other singers by. Neither are any of my gals. We all have names. Mine is Amberlin, then there is Hannah and Spooks or if you prefer, her real name is Evelyn. You may refer to my grandmother as Mrs. Gentry, at least until she says otherwise. Do we understand each other?"

Grossman swallowed his last bit of stew. "Sure, ba...I mean, Amberlin. I don't mean anything by those words. It's just my style."

"Well, I imagine we will both need to make a few adjustments in our *styles* if this relationship is going to work." She rose to leave. "You have a pleasant evening, Mr. Grossman. I'll tell Spooks that you'll be in touch in the morning."

2

HEARST HAD ONE LAST condition for picking up the bill for the travel expenses. They had to rename the revival to "Saving Our World from Communism Revival." Stover wasn't thrilled with the name, but it only took looking at Missy's projections of what it was going to cost to go on the road for him to consent to the change.

Hearst also began to send him telegrams filled with bullet points to make against Communism and more specifically against President Kennedy, so Rev. Stover started inserting most of them into his sermon each night. As promised, at every town they reached, there was a crowd waiting to stream into the revival tent. The crowds were unusually large and boisterous in the midwest where tent revivals were not uncommon, and there wasn't a lot else to do for entertainment.

Before their first night in Wichita, Kansas, Rev. Stover received another of Hearst's telegrams:

POUND JFK ON BAY OF PIGS DEBACLE

"Bay of Pigs?" Rev. Stover read out loud.

Missy glanced up from the magazine she'd been reading as she lay on the couch of their 4-star hotel, one of the added perks of being funded by the largest newspaper tycoon in the world. "What was that, dear?"

"Hearst's most recent telegram," Stover said, waving the yellow slip of paper in his hand, "says, 'pound JFK on Bay of Pigs.' What the hell is a Bay of Pigs? I mean I know we're in pig country but..."

"Not that kind of pig," Missy said, trying unsuccessfully to stifle a giggle. "Back in April of last year, just a few months after Kennedy took office, a report came out about the CIA trying unsuccessfully to overthrow Fidel Castro in Cuba. Surely, you must have read about it. It was quite embarrassing for Kennedy."

"Oh," Stover replied. "Maybe I did read something about it, but in April most of my time was taken up preparing for our trip to L. A."

Missy stood up, dropping the magazine on the coffee table. "Look, you go ahead and prepare the rest of your sermon. I'll put together some notes for you on the incident and how that's just one example of how the President is letting down God-fearing citizens and allowing Communism to take over the world. I read just the other day that Cuba is just over a hundred miles from Florida. Imagine, Communism is right in our backyard, and our newly elected President botches our best chance to throw ol' Castro out of the country."

"Maybe I should let you give that part of the sermon," Stover said. "You certainly have the fire for it."

"No, no, that podium is your second home. I'll get you the relevant notes, so all you'll need to do is add the fire and brimstone."

Stover nodded, feeling more confident he could pull off Hearst's latest request. After a few minutes, he looked up from updating his latest sermon. "Remember when we first met Hearst at his castle?"

Missy nodded but didn't look up from the magazine she'd picked back up. "He made some comment about something happening in the coming month, something about cutting the head off of a particular devil or something like that. What do you think he meant by that?"

Missy thought about it a moment before replying, "I don't really know, but the way I look at it, beheading any device is a good thing and aligned with our work for God, right?"

"Yeah, I guess so," Stover replied though he wasn't entirely convinced it was true.

Swan Song

The last several weeks had been a whirl of activity, so much so that Amberlin had missed the Boston Flower Show that she'd been looking forward to attending. But Grossman, true to his word, was taking major steps to make his newest singer rich and famous and, in the process, himself a good bit wealthier as well. The whole deal had almost been nixed in the bud when he'd insisted on a twenty percent cut of the profits from record deals as well as concerts and public appearance. Spooks had countered with ten percent which sent Grossman into a tirade. It took Amberlin to step in to make peace between the two of them, though she knew it was a fragile peace that could break out into warfare again at any moment.

Grossman had sent Amberlin to a studio in the area to record a demo tape. He started circulating the tape around to the area radio stations as well as sharing it with some additional night spots that were beginning to showcase folk singers. Finally, as winter moved on and gave way to spring, Amberlin declared she needed a break, so Grossman reluctantly postponed a couple of her appointments with radio DJs.

Upon Rose's advice, Amberlin agreed to meet her grandmother at Boston's Public Gardens to help make up for missing the flower show. The Public Gardens was a favorite spot for the locals, especially in the spring when the flowers were in full bloom and the swan boats mingled with real swans on the lake.

When Rose had mysteriously reappeared in her life, Amberlin had assumed her grandmother would stay in the apartment with the rest of them, but Rose declined the invitation, insisting it was important for her to stay on her own. "Don't worry, dear, I'll be around and stay in touch. I just don't think it's a good idea for three generations of Gentrys to be under the same roof all the time."

Amberlin arrived early to the gardens so she'd have a little time to herself before her grandmother's arrival. As she walked along the paths beside the lake, she let her mind wander over the last few hectic weeks. There was no question her star was rising. Grossman had seen to that, but she wondered if she was truly on target with the divine destiny her Papa Herb had insisted she'd been born to fulfill. She'd seen other people get so caught up in the frenetic pace of life that they ended up burning out or straying from what truly made them happy and fulfilled.

It was good to step off the merry-go-round even for a couple hours to check in with her own guidance. As she had the thought, a lone swan changed its direction and started swimming towards her. It reminded her of the other animals who had served as guides along her journey. Did this one have a message for her? She'd no more asked the question then the answer came to her.

Hello, Dear heart, I feel your anxiousness and want to let you know all is well, the swan's voice resonated in her mind.

Well, that's good to know, she replied. Would she ever grow used to animals communicating with her in this way? She wondered. Probably not. In fact, she didn't want the wonder of such a miracle to pass.

Many new things will unfold for you in the coming days, the swan continued.

Yes, they've already started, Amberlin agreed.

I'm here to encourage you to get your feet wet in these new endeavors, but avoid jumping in blindly.

Amberlin smiled at the play on words. *Those are wise words coming from a smart bird.*

Patience and balance are your watchwords, the swan continued. *The doors to manifesting your dreams and exploring new realms are before you. You are ready, even if you're not sure that you are.* As the swan made this last comment, she turned to swim in the direction she had come, but then stopped, turning her head back towards Amberlin. *Oh, one last thing. Don't become a swan too soon. Let the beauty of your life unfold in its own time.* And with that, the swan resumed its journey.

Amberlin watched her go, a sudden sense of peace rising within her. She remembered one of Papa Herb's favorite sayings, "All is in Divine Order even when, and especially when, it doesn't look or feel that way." She closed her eyes and took a couple deep breaths, enjoying the fragrance of new growth that surrounded her.

Hearing a sound behind her, she opened her eyes and turned to see her grandmother approaching.

"There you are, child. I thought we agreed to meet at the swan boats," Rose said, but without any edge to her words.

"I was heading in that direction when a real swan stopped to talk with me," Amberlin replied, then realized how that might sound to her grandmother.

"Don't tell me the animals talk to you as well?" Rose replied. "They would never leave your grandfather alone," she recalled. "I guess that's a trait you inherited from him. What did your swan friend have to say?"

"My watchwords are patience and balance," Amberlin summarized.

"Ahh, I see. Never had much of the first and the latter has become a little hard to come by of late." The two of them started walking along the path in the direction of the world-famous swan boats that had been a hallmark of the Public Gardens since the 1800s.

Neither of them talked for several minutes, enjoying the fresh air of spring and each other's company. Finally, Rose spoke up. "Do you know what yesterday was?"

Amberlin stopped to consider the question. "Let's see, today is May twentieth so that would make yesterday the nineteenth. Right?"

"Right, as far as it goes, but do you know what happened yesterday? Think national news," Rose responded.

Amberlin twisted her face in an exaggerated expression of thinking hard but finally shrugged. "I have to admit, I've been so busy lately I've not kept up with any news, much less national happenings."

"There was a big celebration for our President's forty-fifth birthday," Rose replied.

Amberlin thought about it for a moment, then replied, "Wait a minute. I thought his birthday was at the end of the month." She'd even thought about sending him a birthday card but hadn't gotten around to picking one out yet.

"True," Rose said with a chuckle. "I think his actual birthday is the twenty-ninth, but they jumped the gun. Maybe Marilyn Monroe had another engagement on that date."

Amberlin looked at her grandmother, perplexed by her last statement.

"Marilyn sang Happy Birthday to him," Rose added. "It was on the news last night. That poor girl," she added. "She looked exhausted like she'd been up all night. I don't know what's going to come of her."

"What do you mean?" Amberlin asked as they resumed walking.

"I don't know. Just that every time I see her or read about her in the paper, seems like some man is taken advantage of her. I don't think she's a very happy person."

"Marilyn Monroe not happy? How can that be? She has everything, doesn't she? She's beautiful and famous. I'm sure she'd not hurting for money. How can she not be happy?"

Rose stopped again and turned to her granddaughter. "That's my point and why I brought up that little bit of trivia."

Amberlin thought about it for a moment, a smile slowly forming on her face. "Are you another swan trying to deliver a message to me, too?"

"Could be," Rose replied. "In my day, I had a pretty long neck." She reached out to grasp one of Amberlin's hands. "Just be sure that you're not mesmerized by the glitter and gold of celebrityhood. Remember your purpose."

"But I don't even know what that purpose is yet!" Amberlin replied, suddenly frustrated by Rose's comment.

"Well, I think you do," Rose argued. "Let me ask you, what's a common theme you've seen developing in your life?"

"Common theme?" Amberlin asked. "What do you mean?"

Now it was Rose's turn to pause. "Darn, I wish your Papa Herb was here. He was always much better at this sort of thing. Anyway, think of it this way. Imagine there's been a common thread unfolding in your life, probably something that's so natural for you that you've taken it for granted, but it's a special part of your nature."

Amberlin scrunched up her face again, but then decided it might be better to relax and just let the answer come to her. When she did, she suddenly knew the answer. "Peace," she answered. "I've always wanted people to get along, whether it's just two people or the entire world. I mean, we have so much more in common than we have differences, but seems like nowadays everyone is only focused on the differences."

"Yes!" Rose exclaimed. "That's true, and I hear that same theme in many of the songs you sing. 'A time for peace, I swear it's not too late.'"

"You're right," Amberlin agreed, but then frowned. "But how can one lone folk singer have any hope of bringing peace to the world?"

Rose patted Amberlin's hand. "Well, for starters, you're not the only one singing about world peace. You've got a lot of partners in fulfilling this purpose.

Truth be told, it may not be fulfilled in your lifetime or ever for that matter, but do it anyway. Having such a grand purpose to your life will assure you that you'll never get bored or run out of ways to express your deepest self."

Amberlin slowly smiled. "You know, grandma, you're not half bad at this purpose stuff. Living with Papa Herb for all those years, it must have worn off on you." They reached out and embraced each other.

"Let's go take a ride on one of those swan boats," Rose said as they finally stopped hugging each other. "My treat."

Cuba

Amberlin looked up from her copy of the *Boston Globe*. She'd developed the habit since arriving in Boston of picking an issue up each morning and bringing it to breakfast to stay up on what was going on around her. Truthfully, it was as much to stay up to date on what President Kennedy was doing as anything else. She still hoped to someday have the opportunity to meet him and shake his hand. Actually, in her daydreaming, she never bothered shaking his hand but instead gave him a big hug, though she doubted his Secret Service agents would ever allow such shows of affection. This morning she had to pause in her reading to take a few deep breaths in an attempt to settle herself.

"What's up?" Spooks asked, noticing the look of concern on her daughter's face.

"It's this issue with Cuba," Amberlin replied. "Do you know that the Soviet Union plans to put nuclear weapons there?"

"Really? That doesn't sound good," Hannah said between mouthfuls of eggs. "How far away is Cuba, anyway?"

"I don't know exactly," Amberlin answered, "but it's not that far away from the coast of Florida, and it's a whole lot closer than Russia."

"What's the paper saying we're going to do about it?" Spooks asked, a look of concern growing on her face as well.

"It says President Kennedy is warning the Russians that he won't allow them to bring in more nuclear weapons," Amberlin replied. "It's also saying that we may be on the brink of nuclear war?"

"Holy Mother," Spooks replied. "That would be awful."

"Yeah, it would sure put a crimp on record sales," Hannah quipped, then seeing the looks of astonishment on her two friends' faces, added, "Sorry. Just trying to soften what's happening with a little humor."

Amberlin nodded, then reached out and clasped her mother's and Hannah's hands. "I know war is the last thing Kennedy wants, but at the same time, he can't let the Russians just walk all over us. Can we take a minute...?" She paused as her gaze wandered back to the front page of the paper and to the article besides the one she'd been reading. The headline read:

Reverend Stover Blasts JFK for Mismanaging Global Crisis

"Oh, no," Amberlin said with a groan.

"What now, dearheart?" Spooks asked, as she also glanced down at the paper. She picked it up and read the headline, her face growing red as she did so. "You've got to be kidding? This can't be our Reverend Stover, can it? Not the small town, small-minded preacher from the North Carolina mountains that we've all grown to hate?"

"I'm afraid so," Amberlin replied. "It says here that Kennedy told one of his close friends, that he wanted on his epitaph, 'He kept the peace,' and that he'd told another friend, 'I am almost a peace at any price president.'"

"What's wrong with that?" Hannah asked. "Isn't that what we want—someone who won't go off half-cocked looking to blow up the world?"

"Not according to Rev. Stover," Amberlin replied. "He says it's time for our President to quit pussy-footing around with Khrushchev and show him who's boss."

Now it was Hannah and Spooks who groaned.

"As I was saying," Amberlin continued. "Let's take a minute to pray for our President, and while we're at it, let's say a prayer for Rev. Stover and his wife. Somehow, they've managed to find their way to the front page of the *Boston Globe*. I suppose on the positive side, they'll be too busy with their warmongering to give us any more trouble."

"We can pray for that small miracle," Spooks replied, "but I wouldn't count on it. You're growing in popularity as well, and your message of peace and love is diametrically opposed to theirs of war and fear. I don't see them losing interest in us anytime soon."

"I'm afraid you may be right," Amberlin replied giving her mother's hand an extra squeeze, "but we can pray for it anyway. After all, God works in mysterious ways, right?"

"Yeah, I'll say," Spooks replied. "Stranger and more mysterious every day."

The three of them bowed their heads in prayer. After a couple of minutes of silence where each of them delivered their own silent prayers, Amberlin finished with an "Amen," then glanced at her watch. "Whoa, I need to get going. I'm supposed to meet Mr. Grossman in a few minutes."

"Do you want me to come with you as your business manager, of course?" Spooks asked.

"Sure, if you'd like," Amberlin replied. While she didn't really think it would be necessary, she also didn't want her mother to feel like she was being replaced in her role as business manager. "He wants to go over what we need to do over the next few months. Wants me to cut another demo tape, audition some back-up singers, and he has a guitarist he thinks would be a good match for my style of singing. Stuff like that."

"Yeah, I better be there too," Spooks replied. "I still don't trust this dude."

"His name isn't dude," Amberlin said. "It's Mr. Grossman. Please remember that. I won't let him call any of us babes or sweetie, so I can't very well let you get away with calling him, dude."

"And to think I'd gone out of my way to clean up what I wanted to call him," Spooks answered back, but she was smiling, so Amberlin let the snide comment go.

Joan and Bob

1

T he next several months flew by. Besides the gigs at Club 47 with Tattoo and Hannah as accompaniment, Amberlin also had to maintain her voice teaching schedule, plus find time for the long list of to-dos that Grossman kept expanding. These tasks included several recording sessions for a demo tape, meeting with potential backup singers, and finding the perfect guitar player who Grossman felt would be a good match for Amberlin. One of the first changes Grossman insisted upon and to which she agreed was getting rid of the name, Amberstovers.

"You have a beautiful name as well as an angelic voice," he assured her. "So, that's how you'll be known. Just one name—Amberlin."

She continued to read about the increasingly inflammatory comments Stover aimed at the White House and President Kennedy. It appeared that the more vocal he became, the larger the crowds grew at his revivals which then prompted him to be even more outrageous with his slanderous accusations. Somehow Rev. Stover had become the spokesperson for conservative Christianity.

Meanwhile, Amberlin began to read about another southern preacher by the name of Martin Luther King who had a completely different message that resonated much more strongly with her vision and purpose. His message was one of nonviolence in the face of many egregious acts against the black community. Somewhere along the way, Amberlin realized that her mission for peace on Earth had to include justice and equality for all people no matter their skin color, where they were born, or who they chose to love.

"Someday I'd like to meet this Mr. King and shake his hand," she told Hannah and Spooks one morning over breakfast. "Maybe even sing one of the ballads he's reported to love so much."

"Who's that, baby?" Spooks said, peering over the rim of her coffee mug.

"Martin Luther King," Amberlin replied. "If there is such a thing as a balancing force in this world, Mr. King is on the other end of the scale from Rev. Stover."

"Is that a fact? Well, more power to him then," Spooks replied. "By the way, have you heard from your grandmother lately?

"No, not for a couple of days," Amberlin replied. "Why?"

"Oh, no reason. I just get concerned when she disappears like this. She's not getting any younger, you know."

"Well, I wouldn't worry too much about her. She's survived her home burning down around her, and taking care of herself since then, including trailing around behind us for the past several months. I'm sure she'll turn up soon." Amberlin glanced at the clock at the far end of the diner. "I need to get going. I have another meeting with Mr. Grossman in a few minutes."

"Why didn't you tell me," Spooks mumbled as she stuffed the last of her scrambled eggs in her mouth.

"Well, primarily because I don't need you to come with me this time. He just wants to introduce me to a couple of other folk singers he's working with."

"Oh, who are they?" Hannah asked.

Amberlin took a slip of paper from her jeans pocket and unfolded it. "Let's see." She read from the paper. "Someone by the name of Bob Dylan and Joan Baez."

"Never heard of them," Hannah replied.

"Me either," Spooks said. "Can't be all that good."

"Whoa, wait just a minute," Amberlin said, holding up her hand. "No one has heard of me yet either. Does that mean I'm not any good?"

"Of course not, dear," Spooks replied. "You're not just good, you're great. After all, you're my daughter."

Amberlin leaned over and gave her mother a kiss on the forehead. "Love you too, Mom."

2

AMBERLIN RUSHED INTO the practice room in the basement of Club 47 where she'd agreed to meet Grossman and his two folk singers with just a minute to spare. She could hear them talking and laughing as she came through the door. Well, they sound friendly enough, she thought, relaxing a bit. She'd been nervous about meeting two other singers who she felt must undoubtedly be farther along in their careers than she was and no doubt more talented as well.

She straightened her shoulders and berated herself for having such thoughts. As Papa Herb had told her many times, "You're as good as you allow yourself to be. Never look down on another human being, especially not yourself."

"Sorry for being late," she said as she plastered a smile on her face that she didn't feel.

"You're not late at all," Grossman replied, glancing at his watch. "You're right on time. It's us that are ahead of time." He turned to his two companions. "I want you to meet the next great talent of the folk singing world, Amberlin Gentry. This is Bob Dylan, a great poet who insists on singing his poetry, and Joan Baez, who'll be right up there in the starry lights with you."

"Yeah, that is if we're to believe this man's blarney," the young woman with long, black hair said, stepping forward to offer Amberlin, her hand. "Of course, I guess we all did believe at least part of it, or we wouldn't be here, would we? I'm Joan. Pleasure to meet you."

"And I'm the poet," the young man with the curly disheveled hair that looked like he'd just crawled out of bed said. "I actually caught a part of your act the other night. For once, Al's right. You have a beautiful voice. You should go far."

"I wanted the three of you to meet," Grossman continued. "I just got Joan and Bob an invitation to sing at the upcoming March on Washington. It'll be covered by all the major TV channels. Hopefully, at least some of the stations will include the entertainment that's slated for earlier in the day, but whether they do or not, it'll be a good opportunity to be seen and heard by a lot of folks."

"Not to mention it's a worthy cause," Joan added. "Why don't you come with us? The paper says there's likely to be thousands of people marching for civil rights there. I'm sure Al can get you a backstage pass so you won't have to fight the crowd."

"It sounds interesting," Amberlin replied. "When is it again?"

"This coming Wednesday," Bob replied. "We'll be driving down the day before. We've plenty of room in the van. How about it?"

Amberlin looked at the three of them and smiled. "Okay, I'm in."

The four of them continued talking for a few minutes before Grossman needed to leave for another meeting. After he'd left, Amberlin felt comfortable enough with her new friends to ask a question she'd been asking others about for weeks.

"Listen, have you all ever heard a song that referred to four people—Abraham, someone named Bobby, another one was John, and another one named Martin?"

The two of them looked at her and slowly shook their heads. "Doesn't ring a bell," Joan replied.

"Me either," Bob said. "Certainly not one of my songs."

"Okay," Amberlin said. She'd grown accustomed to such a response. She was preparing to leave when Joan stopped her.

"Sorry, we can't help you with your mystery song. The only thing that came to mind when you asked was that one of the people scheduled to speak at the march is a southern preacher by the name of Martin Luther King."

"Really?" replied Amberlin. "I've been reading about him in the paper. He's really going to be there?"

"Yep, he's one of the main speakers," Joan replied.

Amberlin thought about the possible connection. She'd been talking to Spooks and Hannah just that morning about wanting to meet Reverend King someday, and now, less than an hour later, she'd been invited to attend an event where he'd be speaking. Interesting? Could he be the Martin in her mystery song? After all, she'd figured that the Abraham referred to in the lyrics must be Abraham from the Bible so it would figure that at least some of the other names might be preachers or somehow connected to the Bible as well. There was John the Baptist and also wasn't one of the disciples named John as well? But who was Bobby? She was pretty sure there wasn't any Bobby in either the New or Old Testaments. It was a modern sounding name, so maybe he was another preacher. She looked at her two new friends. Whoa! Wait a minute. Bob was just short for Bobby. Could this Dylan fella be part of the mystery sound?

"Are you okay?" Joan asked, studying her carefully.

"Oh, yes, sorry," Amberlin replied, realizing she'd been so deep in thought that several seconds had elapsed without a word being spoken. "I'm just trying to put the pieces of a puzzle together in my mind."

"I know how that can be," Dylan replied. "Sometimes I get a song I'm working on stuck in my head, and I can hardly function until I get it down on paper."

"Maybe that's what I need to do," Amberlin said. "Write down all the different pieces to see how they fit together. Thanks for the suggestion."

"Well, why don't we plan to meet here on Tuesday afternoon," Joan said. "Try to pack light. Bob keeps his van on the edge of being condemned with all his paraphernalia."

DC March

1

"You're going where, with whom, for what?" Spooks asked with a motherly edge to her voice that often put Amberlin on the defensive, but she vowed not to go there this time. Instead, she took a couple of deep, calming breaths before answering the questions.

"I'm going to Washington D. C. to take part in the March on Washington which is about all people having equal rights under the law. I'll be with my two new friends, Bob Dylan and Joan Baez. Grossman has booked them to sing earlier in the day before the speakers. I'm going because it's a great opportunity to meet new people, maybe even Reverend King who'll be one of the speakers. Also, I feel strongly that it's part of my divine destiny that Papa Herb spoke about so many times."

"Oh," Spooks replied, apparently caught off guard by Amberlin's calm and deliberate response. "I see." She thought about it for a minute longer before adding. "Okay, as long as you know this is right for you."

"Unequivocally," Amberlin replied. "So, if you'll excuse me, we're heading out fairly early tomorrow. I want to get a good night's sleep. Can we please turn out the lights?" She leaned over and gave her mom a peck on the cheek before walking over to the bed and turning back the covers. Hannah was already snoring away on the pull out bed, so she waited for her mother to climb in bed beside her before cutting off the light. She was still thinking about the trip to D. C. tomorrow as she drifted off to sleep, so it wasn't all that surprising that she dreamt of being on the road with her two new friends. What did surprise her was that the three of them were singing the mystery song as they traveled down the road. It seemed completely normal that all three of them knew the lyrics by heart. As they approached the end of the song, one phrase stood out to Amberlin:

"Didn't you love the things that they stood for?"

Suddenly, she was awake and sitting up in bed, that phrase still reverberating in her head. Funny, she hadn't noticed it before, but now it seemed to carry some special meaning, some clue she couldn't quite decipher. It was "what they stood for" rather than "what they stand for." So, did that mean whoever these four men were, they were part of history and not of the present? That would make sense for Abraham had lived thousands of years ago as did John the Baptist and Jesus' disciple named John. But what about Martin and Bobby? She couldn't recall anyone in history by either of those names. Of course, she was far from an expert on history. It had been one of the subjects Papa Herb had insisted including in her homeschool curriculum, and somehow he had managed to make it enjoyable by focusing more on the people and their lives than just dates and special events.

She lay back down in bed, but sleep didn't come immediately. She continued to ponder what her dream was trying to tell her, but it wouldn't be until the next evening when she and her friends arrived in D.C. when it started to become clear how far off the mark she might have been.

2

It was evening on the twenty-seventh when the three folk singers pulled into Washington D. C. The city was always a hub of activity, but especially so on the night before the March on Washington that many people projected could be one of the most massive peaceful demonstrations in the nation's history.

"Do you mind if we check out the venue for tomorrow," Dylan, who'd insisted on driving the whole way, asked. "I know Grossman has promised that all the sound equipment and everything would be all set, but I still would like to see where we'll be participating in history being made."

"That's fine with me," Joan said, and Amberlin agreed. After all, she was just along for the ride, besides which she was curious to see the location as well. They ended up having to park several blocks away due to security that was already in place for the next day. Fortunately, they all had stage passes that served to get them through security as long as they didn't mind walking.

The three of them were busy talking about the next day and taking in the sights of the nation's capital, so the trip passed quickly. They approached their final destination just as the day moved into evening. Suddenly, Dylan, who had taken on the role as tour guide, stopped and pointed ahead. "There it is, the Lincoln Memorial."

Just as he spoke, the lights of the Memorial flashed on highlighting the sixteenth President of the United States sitting there is all his glory.

"Wow!" Joan exclaimed. "What great timing."

"At your service," Bob said as he bowed deeply.

Amberlin just stood there, frozen in place by the colossal statue in front of her, but more than the icon was what it had sparked inside her. Suddenly she knew she'd been wrong this whole time about the mystery song. "Not Abraham of the Bible," she whispered, "But this Abraham...Abraham Lincoln!"

"He freed a lot of people, but it seems the good die young,"

Of course, Abraham Lincoln had freed the slaves. That's why the focal point for the March on Washington was to be at his Memorial. The pieces of the puzzle were beginning to fall in place. And who would be speaking at the Memorial tomorrow? Martin Luther King. He had to be the Martin of the song, didn't he? But wait, he was still alive, so maybe the song wasn't just about people in history but also about people in the process of making history.

"Hello, Earth to Amberlin...come in." Joan's words finally came through to Amberlin.

"Girl, you can zone out better than anyone I've ever met," Joan said as Amberlin shook her head to clear it.

"Sorry," Amberlin replied, smiling self consciously. "I didn't sleep all that well last night. Must be kinda tired. Plus this is all so overwhelming. I never realized the Lincoln in the Memorial was so large."

"Yeah, pictures just don't do it justice, does it?" Joan said.

"I'll say," Amberlin agreed, "Plus I think I understand a bit more about my strange dream and the lyrics that keep buzzing in my head."

"Oh, yeah?" Joan asked.

Amberlin pointed to the giant statue in front of her. "This is the Abraham in the song, not the one from the Bible."

"Are you sure?"

"Yes. I don't know how, but I am. Plus, it makes sense for the rest of the verse."

"Then, I guess you just need to find out what the common denominator that all of the people mentioned in the song share," Dylan replied.

"That and who the other people are," Amberlin agreed. "I mean, Martin could only be Martin Luther King, right? After all, he's going to be speaking here tomorrow about freedom and justice, but who's John and Bobby?"

"Well, there are a lot of Johns and Bobbies around," Dylan said.

"But none more famous than our current President," Joan added.

"Yeah, who also happens to have a brother that goes by Bobby," Amberlin finished the thought. "I have to admit I've had a strong affinity for this President that goes all the way back to his inauguration address."

"Yeah, me too," Joan agreed. "Not to mention that he's not all that bad to look at."

"Well, there is that, too." Amberlin laughed.

"So, what's the common denominator?" Dylan asked as the three of them walked up the steps of the monument to get a closer look at Lincoln.

Amberlin pondered the question for several seconds before replying. "I haven't the foggiest idea." But something tells me that it's tied in with my own divine destiny, she thought.

Lincoln Memorial

1

The three musicians returned to downtown D. C. early the next morning to an entirely different atmosphere. Already, throngs of people mingled around trying to find the ideal place to locate themselves to hear the speeches. Thousands more arrived as the morning unfolded.

The full name of the event was the March on Washington for Jobs and Justice and was to take place on the National Mall which many people were calling "America's Front Yard." The march started with a rally at the Washington Monument, attended by several celebrities and musicians including Joan and Bob. Participants then marched the mile-long National Mall to the Lincoln Memorial where some prominent leaders of the black community spoke.

The highlight of the day was the speech by Reverend Martin Luther King. Though Amberlin didn't have the opportunity to shake the Reverend's hand, she and her two companions had ideal seats close to where all the speeches were taking place. The most significant moment for Amberlin was about midway into King's speech. Joan had taken the opportunity earlier in the day to introduce Amberlin to Mahalia Jackson, another of the musicians scheduled to sing that day.

"I've been told that Mahalia is one of Reverend King's favorite singers," Joan said during the introduction.

"I don't know about that," the black gospel singer replied, blushing, "but I do know I'm looking forward to hearing him speak."

The four singers ended up sitting next to each other, only a few yards from the speakers of the day, including Reverend King. As his speech progressed, Amberlin noticed Mahalia appeared to grow more agitated, and she started to squirm in her seat. Amberlin could hear her mutter a few times but couldn't quite make out the words.

Finally, Mahalia closed her eyes for a few seconds, mumbled a few words as though praying, then opened her eyes and spoke out loud and clear, "Tell them about the dream, Martin. Tell them about the dream."

Reverend King paused for a moment from his prepared speech and glanced over to Mahalia and smiled before continuing, "And so even though we face the difficulties of today and tomorrow, I still have a dream. It is a dream deeply rooted in the American dream. I have a dream that one day this nation will rise up and live out the true meaning of its creed: "We hold these truths to be self-evident, that all men are created equal."

What had she just witnessed? The young black singer of gospel had spoken two short lines that had suddenly altered the direction of this national leader's speech. Amberlin continued listening, growing more moved by each sentence, as was the teeming crowd around her.

Finally, as King finished speaking to a roar of applause and cheers, Amberlin leaned over to Joan. "Did you see what just happened?" she asked unsure if she could trust her own eyes and ears. Joan nodded. "Yes, I did. That was really something, wasn't it?"

"Oh, my word!" Amberlin exclaimed. "I've never seen anything like it. Mahalia just asked Reverend King to share his dream, and..." She wasn't sure how to finish the sentence.

Joan smiled. "Sometimes it's just a matter of being in the right place at the right time and taking the right action. When that happens, spirit takes over, and life is altered."

"Yeah," Amberlin replied. "That's exactly what just happened." She sat there half listening to the rest of the speeches. I wonder if I'll know when the time is right? Will I have the courage to make the right move?

2

The phone rang in the hotel room. Who would be calling this late, Missy wondered, as she leaned over in bed to pick it up. Her husband was still in the bathroom preparing to join her in bed.

"Yes?" Missy said as she answered the call.

"Oh, good evening, Mrs. Stover. This is Randolph. Please forgive me for calling so late."

"That's okay, Mr. Hearst. We're both still awake. If you hold a minute, I'll get my husband."

"That won't be necessary. I was really hoping to speak to you if that's okay."

"Me? Sure. What can I do for you?" Missy replied, flattered that such a remarkable man would want to talk to her.

"You may recall in our first meeting, I mentioned that something was being planned that I wasn't at liberty to talk about at that time."

"Yes, I remember," Missy replied.

"Well, I'm afraid that I'm still not at liberty to share the details, but I want to give you a heads up about it so you can prepare your husband. We have it on good authority that the Kennedy brothers are planning to pull our troops out of Vietnam, which is ridiculous. It would be admitting defeat for the first time. We just can't have that."

Missy wondered who the 'we' were that Hearst was referring to but decided she really didn't want to know. "What do you want my husband to do?" she asked instead.

There was a long pause on the other end of the line. Finally, Hearst said, "First, make sure he doesn't go off the deep end when it happens so he can help stabilize the rest of the country."

Another non-specific pronoun, Missy thought, but once again she was certain she didn't want to know any specifics. She knew she could fulfill her part of the assignment. There had been some times in their long marriage where she'd had to keep him from going off the deep end. Why should whatever was about to happen be any different? "I can do that," she replied. "Can you give me any idea when this 'event' will be occurring?"

Another long pause before, "Most likely sometime in November," Hearst replied, then added, "In Dallas."

That soon, huh? Missy nodded and squared her shoulders as she sat up in bed a little straighter. "You can count on me, Mr. Hearst."

"I knew I could. You and the reverend have a pleasant evening. I'll be in touch." And with that, there was a click on the other end of the line just as Rev. Stover walked out of the bathroom and over to his side of the bed.

"Who was that calling this late at night?"

"No one, really. Someone trying to sell me a set of World Books. I told him I was already married to one of the smartest men in the world and didn't have any use for them."

"I bet he's never heard that reason for not buying."

"Yeah, he didn't seem to know what to say after that. Good night, dear," Missy said as she leaned over and gave him a peck on the cheek.

3

This time, as the mystery song played somewhere off in the distance, Amberlin saw Papa Herb walking toward her out of the mist that surrounded her. As he approached, she realized that he was humming along to the tune.

"Do you know that song?" she asked as he came nearer.

"No, not really," he replied. "Not yet, anyway."

"What do you mean, not yet?"

"I'll know it when Donovan gets around to singing it," came the cryptic reply.

"What is that supposed to mean?" Amberlin asked.

"Well, you know dreams aren't always tied to time," Papa Herb replied. "Time is a lot more fluid in the spirit world than over there in the physical realm."

"So, this song that keeps bugging me hasn't been written yet? Then how is it possible for me to know the words?"

Papa Herb shrugged. "I'm not sure. It's a mystery. But if I had to guess, it might have something to do with you fulfilling on your divine destiny, but that's just a guess. I'm pretty new to this spirit realm myself."

Amberlin thought for a moment before asking, "Is that it? Can't you give me anything else to work with?"

Papa Herb smiled. "Yes, dear. Pay attention and trust your heart."

Road Trip

1

As October turned into November, and it looked like they'd be wintering over in Boston for the second year, Al Grossman threw Amberlin a curve by suggesting that she make her way South.

"Baez and Dylan are down in Austin, and it's a really happening place right now for folk music. I'd like you to join them down there if you don't mind?"

"Austin, Texas?" Spooks asked. "That's a long drive. Are you going to cover the gas?"

"Ever the business manager, aren't you?" Grossman replied, then smiled. "Yeah, I'll cover the gas, and I'll make sure you have some decent venues to play as well as several radio stations to visit. Besides, it'll be a lot nicer down there in the winter than up here. What do you say?"

Amberlin nodded, then pointed to the newspaper she'd been scanning. "Sounds good to me. How close is Austin to Dallas?"

"Not that far," Grossman replied. "Maybe, four or five hours driving. Why?"

"President Kennedy is scheduled to be in that area in the next week or two. I'd love to try to be there at the same time. How about you schedule a time I can sing for him like Marilyn Monroe did awhile back?"

"Sure," Grossman replied. "Just as soon as you've hit it big in Hollywood like she has. So, can I start booking some venues in Austin?"

Amberlin looked to Spooks and Hannah who both nodded. "Yep, sounds like a plan."

After Grossman left, Spooks turned to Amberlin. "Seems like a long way to drive to see the President, that is if he even keeps on that schedule."

"I think he will," Amberlin replied. "It says here that he's going on that trip in preparation for running for President for a second term, so it's likely he'll be making himself available to the fine people of Texas. Who knows, maybe I'll get to shake his hand." She decided not to tell her mother about the sudden sensation she'd felt within herself as she'd read the article in the paper. Papa Herb

174

had encouraged her to trust her heart, so this was one step in that direction. Besides, like Grossman had said, it would be a lot warmer in Texas than in Boston. She still remembered the cold, frigid months of last winter. She was ready for some warmer weather.

"Can you let Paula know that we'll be heading south soon so she can be sure to book someone else in our place?"

"Will do," Spooks replied. "You know there's one other little detail that needs handling."

"What's that?" Amberlin asked.

"We no longer have a van."

"Oh, right. I forgot about that," Amberlin replied.

"I heard Tattoo, and his group is thinking of selling theirs," Hannah said. "Want me to check with him and see if it's true?"

"Do you think it can make the trip to Texas?" Spooks asked.

Hannah shrugged. "It's at least in as good a shape as Ben's vehicle was, and it got us here."

"Okay," Amberlin replied. "We've got a little extra in the kitty I was squirreling away for something like this. See what you can find out. Sounds like it's time for a road trip."

"Road trip, road trip..." Hannah started chanting.

"I'm getting too old for this kinda life," Spooks replied with a groan.

"Hey, that reminds me. Has anyone seen or heard from Rose in the last few days?" Amberlin asked.

"Yes, she came back a couple of days ago and left this note," Spooks replied. "Sorry, I forgot to give it to you," she continued as she handed a yellow slip of paper to Amberlin. "She said if anyone needed her that she was staying at that address."

"Okay, good," Amberlin replied, glancing at the paper before sticking it in her pocket. "I'll drop by and let her know of our plans. She may want to join us on the trip."

"Or just fly down on her broomstick," Spooks said.

"What is that supposed to mean?" Amberlin asked.

"Only that our dear, sweet, Rose seems to be embracing her special powers of witchhood."

Amberlin opened her mouth to admonish her mother for the comment but then thought better of it. As she turned to leave, she muttered. "Maybe it's time all the Gentry women embraced our witchhood."

2

Over the next week, Amberlin and her troupe made plans to relocate from the wintery weather of the Boston area to the much warmer climate of Texas. They were able to acquire a van of their own from Tattoo, who even included having the van detailed and serviced to be sure it would be in tiptop shape for the long trip.

Despite several attempts, Amberlin was unable to persuade her grandmother to accompany them to Texas. "I have a few other matters to take care of here," Rose said when Amberlin tried to talk her into joining them. "I have a life outside of taking care of my daughter and granddaughter, you know."

Actually, Amberlin hadn't stopped to realize that until that moment, but when she tried to find out a few details about the other parts, Rose had clammed up and sent her on her way. "When you get down there and find a place, let me know where it is. I'll be happy to join you eventually, just not yet. Oh, and if you have a chance to meet the President, be sure to give him a hug for me."

Since there was no rush to get to Austin, the three women decided to take their time and see some of the sights along their almost two thousand mile journey. They invested in a tent and some other camping equipment so they could keep their expenses down. It turned out that Hannah and her mother had often gone on camping vacations, so she was a wealth of practical knowledge on the subject.

They even managed to find a few nightspots along the way where Amberlin sang in exchange for their food and lodging, which also included the three of them taking much-appreciated showers. While on the road, Grossman was busy checking out venues in the Austin area where Amberlin, Baez, and Dylan could all perform. He also located a small apartment that wouldn't break the bank. All in all, the transition went smoothly, and by the middle of November, they were all settled in the Lone Star state.

"He's coming, he's really coming!" Amberlin exclaimed as she waved the morning newspaper in her hand.

"Who's coming where?" Spooks asked from the stove, where she was putting the final touches on the bacon and eggs.

"Let me guess," said Hannah from the kitchen table where she sat sipping on her cup of coffee. "It has to be our illustrious President Kennedy, right?"

"That's right!" Amberlin replied, then paused. "How did you know?"

"He's the only person you'd get so excited about," Hannah replied. "Simple process of deduction. Just call me Sherlock Hannah."

"When is he due to arrive?" Spooks asked as she carried the platter of scrambled eggs and bacon to the table.

"He's in San Antonio today, and will be flying to Fort Worth tonight."

"Really, that soon?"

"Yep," Amberlin replied as she joined her mom and Hanna at the table. "We've got to go see him. We've just got to."

"Well, count me out," Spooks replied. "Grossman and I have a very important meeting scheduled for tomorrow. A meeting that will have far more influence on your future than some silly trip to see the President of the United States."

"I'll go," Hannah replied. She reached across the table to scoop some eggs on her plate and take a couple slices of bacon. "It'll be fun. We can take our camping gear just in case we don't want to sleep in the van."

"Really?" Spooks asked. "Two young girls in a van in a strange city all by themselves. My mommy genes aren't too sure they like that scenario."

"Ahh, we'll be fine," Amberlin replied. "This is the whole reason we traveled this far."

Spooks shook her head. "I thought the reason we took this trip was to advance your career as a folk singer."

"Well, yeah, that too," Amberlin replied. "Right after breakfast, we'll pack up the van and head north. Are you sure you don't want to go with us?"

Spooks shook her head again. "Nope, I'll stay here and make sure Grossman doesn't try to pull anything that would jeopardize that career of yours. Go have fun, see the President, but please be safe."

"We will," Amberlin replied. "I'll trust my inner guidance all the way."

"And your common sense," Spooks replied.

"Road trip, road trip," Hannah started chanting. "We're going on another road trip."

3

"WHERE DO YOU THINK the best place to see President Kennedy will be?" Hannah asked from the passenger seat of the van where she was serving as Amberlin's navigator.

"I've been giving that some thought," Amberlin replied. "I don't want to just see him. I also want to shake his hand."

"Wow, why not also see if Jackie will mind the two of you going out on a date?" Hannah said, chuckling at her own joke. "You do know that there will be thousands of other people wanting to do the same thing, right?"

"Yeah, so that's why I think we need to increase our odds by planning to be at more than one place."

"You can do that? I mean, I know you've got some incredible powers that us lowly humans don't, but I didn't know you could be at more than one place at the same time."

"Not at the same time, silly. The President is spending the night at Hotel Texas in Fort Worth, so I think that's one place we should be. He'll have to come out in the morning to get to the parade route that's in Dallas. While he's having breakfast and giving speeches, it'll give us time to make our way to the parade route which will be our second chance to see him."

"You've really planned this out, haven't you?" Hannah asked with a note of envy in her voice.

"I sure have. The only thing I can't plan is what to do if they make a change, in which case we'll need to be ready to adjust our plans as well."

"And so, where are we going to spend the night while the President and First Lady luxuriate in Hotel Texas?"

"Oh, that's simple," Amberlin replied. She glanced over to Hannah to see how the news landed. "We'll be secure in our little van here...in the parking lot of Hotel Texas."

"You're kidding, right?" Hannah asked, obviously aghast at the idea. "You're not kidding. Spooks would kill us if she ever found out."

"That's why we're never going to tell her," Amberlin replied. "Look, what better place to spend the night? There will be plenty of people around, including the President's Secret Service. We'll be right there in the morning so we won't need to worry about getting lost or stuck in traffic."

"I guess," Hannah finally replied. "But I doubt I'll sleep a wink the entire night."

"No worry. You can nap as I drive us over to Dallas."

Hannah was quiet for a few minutes as she tried to get comfortable with the idea of spending the night in a hotel's parking lot. Finally, she looked up from the map sitting in her lap she'd been pretending to study. "Do you know where along the parade route we should try to be?"

"Not for sure," Amberlin replied. "I suspect it'll be crowded along most of the route, but as I was thinking about it last night, I kept getting a 'hit' that we might try to get to a place along the route called Dealey Plaza."

"And why there?" As she asked the question, Hannah folded up the map of Texas and pulled out a second map, this one of Dallas. She started looking for Dealey Plaza on the map.

"I'm not sure. For one thing, it's towards the end of the route so it'll give us more time in case we get stuck in traffic, plus it's close to the final destination, so it's unlikely that part of the route will be changed. But mostly it's because I promised Papa Herb that I'd trust my guidance, and that's where it directed me to go."

The two of them traveled in silence for several minutes. Finally, Hannah checked her wristwatch. "We've been on the road almost an hour. Don't you think that's enough time to dig into that bag of goodies Spooks packed for us?"

Amberlin laughed. "Sure, let's see what we've got."

Hotel Texas

As it turned out, they weren't allowed to park the van in the hotel's parking lot but had to resort to parking on the street a few blocks away. Fortunately, the long trip along with their tour of the area had exhausted them so by nine o'clock they were both snuggled up in the rear of the van fast asleep.

Come morning, Amberlin awoke first, followed shortly after that with Hannah rolling over to gaze out the van's rear window. "Is it raining?" she asked after a minute.

"Yeah, just a little," Amberlin replied. "It's supposed to clear later this morning."

Hannah groaned. "Maybe I'll just sleep in this morning."

"No, you won't!" Amberlin replied with more of an edge than she'd intended. "We've got to get moving so we can be sure to get a good place before everyone else gets here."

"In the rain?" Hannah asked, obviously not pleased by the prospect of standing out in the rain for hours.

"It's just a light mist," Amberlin replied. She tossed a small object at her friend.

"What's this?" Hannah asked as she picked it up to study the small plastic package.

"It's a rain bonnet to help keep your hair from frizzing up so much."

"Too late for that," Hannah replied as she sat up, then leaned over to stick the package in her pocket.

"During the night, they set up a stage in front of the hotel."

"How do you know that?" Hannah asked.

"Oh, I've already been scoping everything out, and I know just where to stand so we're almost guaranteed to have a chance to shake his hand."

Hannah studied her friend for several seconds. "You're really obsessed with this, aren't you?"

Amberlin shrugged, an embarrassed look on her face. "No, not really." She grinned sheepishly. "Well, maybe, just a little."

"Why is it so important that you shake his hand...wait a minute. I remember now. Years ago back at Golden Acres, when you shook Ben's hand, you were able to find out all sorts of things about him. Are you planning to do the same with President Kennedy."

Amberlin shrugged again. "I don't know, maybe. I just know that my guidance is shouting at me to do whatever I can to get close to him. It...well, it feels like somehow it's all tied in with why I'm here, not just here in Texas, but here on planet Earth."

"You mean, your destiny?"

Amberlin didn't shrug this time but answered with a definite, "Yes, with my destiny."

Hannah stared at her before finally saying, "Cool. Let's get going."

Amberlin had to admit that Hotel Texas didn't look fancy enough for the President of the United States to stay in, even if it was only for one night. The front of it reminded her of a movie theater with a large marquee with the word, TEXAS, on top and underneath the message:

Welcome to Fort Worth

Where the West Begins

Amberlin had hoped the inclement weather might keep some people away, but it appeared to take more than a little rain to suppress Texans' enthusiasm for the 35th President of the United States. Of course, it probably didn't hurt that Kennedy had chosen one of their own in Lyndon B. Johnson to be his running mate. The misting rain also didn't appear to squelch the festive mood of the gathering crowd who were all excited to catch a glimpse of Kennedy.

By 9:45 when the President strolled out of the front of Hotel Texas, a throng of several thousand people crowded around the stage. President Kennedy wore a dark blue suit and matching tie without bothering with a raincoat even though several of those in his entourage wore them. He climbed the stairs of the stage confidently where he then stood patiently as several other dignitaries spoke, fortunately, only briefly. Then Vice President Johnson stepped in front of the microphones to loud applause and introduced the President.

The crowd surged forward to get a better look at the youngest man to ever be elected to the most powerful office in the world. Kennedy smiled graciously as he waited for the applause and cheering to die down. He then let the crowd know where First Lady Jacqueline was.

"Jackie is busy organizing herself," he quipped. "Of course, she looks better than we do when she does it." The crowds cheered once again. After a few more comments, he thanked the crowd and started towards the stairs.

"This is our chance," Amberlin said as she pulled on Hannah's hand. "Here he comes."

Sure enough, a smiling Kennedy walked off the stage and straight to where the crowd stood behind the wooden barrier. The two of them stood with their bellies pressed against the wooden board by the crowd behind them. Everyone shouted greetings to him as they waved their hand in an attempt to shake his, if only for a second or two. Amberlin held out her hand as well but with one difference. Between her fingertips was a small yellow flower she had picked earlier that morning from in front of the hotel.

As President Kennedy approached, she held the flower out to him while also sending him a mental message. "I'm for peace too," she kept repeating to herself while radiating a feeling of love to him. It worked. As he returned her smile and momentarily gazed into her eyes, he took the flower from her then shook her hand.

As contact was made, Amberlin felt a rush of energy course through her body followed almost immediately with a second wave, this one of deep shock and grief. This second wave knocked Amberlin back against Hannah, breaking the connection with Kennedy's hand, but the grief and foreboding continued for several seconds, knocking the wind from her.

"Are you okay?" Hannah shouted as Amberlin continued to lean on her for support. Amberlin tried to speak, but nothing would come out. Her throat and chest felt so constricted, she felt like she might never breathe again, much less utter a word. She managed to shake her head as she open and closed her mouth like a fish suddenly thrown out of the water and onto land.

This doesn't make sense, she thought. How could he be smiling so broadly and yet have such a sense of anguish inside him? But something about that didn't feel right either. Had those feelings truly come from him or had they come from the crowd at large and merely used him as a conduit?

Hannah continued to hold her up while also trying to elbow their way to the rear where the crowd wasn't quite so densely packed. Spying a bench not far from the stage, she guided Amberlin in that direction.

"It'll be okay, everything will be okay," Hannah kept repeating as she weaved them through the crowd, finally arriving at a bench where Amberlin collapsed, her face as pale as the petals of a lily of the valley.

"Put your head between your knees," Hannah instructed her. Amberlin did and slowly began to feel better, though when she tried to pick her head back up to look around, the dizziness and nausea returned. She dropped her head again and took several long, slow breaths.

She wasn't sure how much time passed as she sat there with her head between her knees, but when she finally was able to look up, the crowd had noticeably thinned, and there was no sign of Kennedy or his entourage.

"Is he gone?" Amberlin asked, shocked to hear her voice come out as a raspy whisper.

"Yes," Hannah replied. "Feeling better?"

Amberlin nodded. "I'm so thankful you were here with me. If I'd been alone, there's no telling what would have happened. I might have been trampled by everyone around me."

"Well, what did happen?"

Amberlin shrugged. "I'm not sure. I felt this wave of positive energy coursing through his hand into mine, but then suddenly there was this wave that washed over me. I've never felt such a massive sensation of...of anguish, shock, sadness. That's as close as I can come, but the words all seem inadequate to describe it. I couldn't tell where it was coming from either. It didn't feel like it was coming from the President, but I can't be sure."

"I think we better get you to a hospital so someone can check you out," Hannah said as she reached out to take one of Amberlin's hands.

Amberlin shook her head. "Thanks, but I don't think that'll be necessary. I'm feeling much better now. If you can drive the van to Dallas, I'm sure I'll be fine."

"Drive to Dallas? Are you kidding?" Hannah replied. She placed one hand under her friend's chin and lifted Amberlin's face to gaze into her eyes. "You're not still planning to go through with this craziness are you?"

"Of course I am," Amberlin replied. "I think it's more important than ever to see this through, though I don't think I'll be so quick to try to shake our President's hand anytime soon."

"But why?"

Amberlin paused, considering the question. "I'm not sure how to answer that. I don't suppose you'll accept, 'because,' will you?"

"No."

"Okay, let me try to explain as best as I can. I certainly don't have all the pieces of the puzzle together, not yet, but here's what I know. President Kennedy and I are connected in ways that I don't yet understand. I believe we share a common purpose though. He's for peace throughout the world, and so am I. Also, remember that strange song I've been bugging everyone about?"

Hannah nodded.

"Well, I believe he's the John mentioned in the lyrics along with President Abraham Lincoln. These two men shared some important elements. They were both for peace and freedom, and they both became the President of the United States."

"But how about the other two names? What were they?" Hannah asked.

"Martin and Bobby."

"History and civics were never my strong suits," Hannah said, "but I don't recall a President by either one of those names."

"Well, there was Martin Van Buren" Amberlin replied. "I think he was the seventh or eighth President, but somehow I don't think he's the Martin the song is about. If I had to guess at this point, I'd say it's referring to Reverend King. He's certainly for peace and justice, but I don't think he has any plans to run for President. It's all so befuddling which is why I think it's important for us to continue following President Kennedy. Truth is, I don't know what else to do at this point."

Hannah squeezed Amberlin's hand. "Okay. That's what we'll do. Do you think you can make it back to the van?"

"Yeah," Amberlin replied, then as she started to stand, she wobbled a bit. Hannah caught her. Amberlin smiled. "That is, with a little help."

When they reached the van, Hannah helped Amberlin into the passenger seat then walked around to climb behind the wheel. "Okay, you'll have to give me directions, and I must warn you. The largest city I've ever driven in is Asheville. This is going to be a whole new experience for me."

As they drove down the road, Amberlin turned on the radio to see if she could catch any updates about the President's trip. The Dallas/Fort Worth station was interspersing news updates between their songs. The President had just finished speaking at a breakfast gathering that got started late, according to the announcer, because everyone had to wait for the First Lady to arrive.

"Good," Amberlin said. "That'll give us a little more time, which it looks like we'll need, given the amount of traffic on the road. Which is probably why they'll be flying the President to Dallas even though it's a short flight. But he'll then get in a motorcade that'll take him downtown. Those motorcades move pretty slow so everyone along the way can get a good look at the President and First Lady. Did you bring your transistor radio?"

"Of course," Hannah replied. "Why?"

"Once we park the car, we can use it to stay posted on the progress of the motorcade."

"Good idea. By the way, how are you feeling?" Hannah asked after they'd been driving for about twenty minutes.

"Much better," Amberlin replied. "A bit of a headache, but other than that, I'm fine."

"And where are we heading again?" Hannah asked. "What part of Dallas?"

"We want to get as close to Dealey Plaza as we can. We'll probably need to park several blocks away and walk the rest of the distance. It's toward the end of the route the motorcade will be taking so it'll give us a little more time just in case we need it."

"Well, it looks like the weather is going to cooperate. The rain has just about stopped."

"Yeah, that's good," Amberlin replied. "That way they won't have to put them under a bubble."

"A bubble?"

"Yeah, I've seen a couple of motorcades on TV before. If the weather is bad, they use this large clear bubble in an effort to keep the First Family dry and still making it easier for people to see them."

"Yea, no bubble. I prefer not seeing my First Family under glass." The two girls laughed.

Dealey

1

The traffic into downtown Dallas was heavier than Amberlin had expected, and it became more congested the closer they got to Dealey Plaza. Finally, Amberlin, growing more frantic by the moment, made a decision. "We can walk faster than this. Look for a place we can stash the van for a few hours. I don't care if it's illegal parking. We're running out of time."

"Okay, I'll see what I can find," Hannah replied, "but calm down. We've already seen him once. I'm sure we can catch his speech on the news tonight."

"It's not that," Amberlin replied. "I have a horrible feeling that something isn't right here. That shockwave I felt back at the hotel may have been some premonition. I think I was supposed to warn President Kennedy, but I failed to do so. I've got to rectify that somehow."

Hannah stared over at her friend. "Are you sure? Maybe it was just...I don't know, maybe you misread it. How are you going to warn him? He'll be surrounded by the Secret Service. They're likely to arrest you as some kind of a nut."

"I know, I know, but I can't help it. The closer we get to the motorcade, the stronger the feeling. Look, there. Pull in there," Amberlin said, pointing to a loading zone.

"It says, 'No Parking,'" Hannah pointed out.

"I don't care, just do it," Amberlin shouted. As she did so, she grabbed the wheel and started turning them in the direction of the empty spot.

"Whoa, hands off the wheel," Hannah said as she pushed Amberlin's hands away. "I'll do it."

As she pulled the van into the spot, Amberlin opened her door and started to climb out. "Where's your radio?"

"In the back," Hannah replied. She turned off the engine. "I'll get it. You go on ahead. I can catch up."

Amberlin nodded and started in the direction the growing crowd of people were headed but then stopped. If they were separated, it might take them hours to find each other again. It took Hannah less than a minute to find the radio, and the two of them were off towards Dealey Plaza. As Amberlin led the way, Hannah switched on the radio and turned the dial to the station they'd been listening to in the van.

"The President's car is now turning onto Elm Street," the radio announcer said.

"That's it," Amberlin said. "I recognize the voice. Turn it up just a little."

"It'll be only a matter of minutes before he arrives at the Trade Mart..." the announcer continued.

"How far away are we from Elm Street?" Hannah asked, breathing heavily.

"Not far at all," Amberlin replied. They're still a little north of us."

"I was on the freeway earlier and even it was jam-packed with spectators waiting for their chance to see the President," the announcer said.

"Up there," Amberlin shouted as she pushed her way through the crowd. "I think I can see the motorcade just up ahead." She pointed to a grassy knoll about a block away. "This way."

The two of them weaved in and out among the other onlookers. They heard a crack, crack and then a third crack, and a moment later the tone of the radio announcer's voice changed.

"It...it...it appears something has happened in the motorcade route. I repeat, something has happened on the motorcade route."

Amberlin stopped so quickly that Hannah bumped into her. Tears streamed down her face. Now I know, she thought, what the anguish was for. She prayed she was wrong, but she feared she was right. Someone had just shot the President of the United States.

"Several police officers are rushing up the hill at this time." The frantic voice of the announcer continued to blare from the transistor radio.

"What is it?" Hannah asked as she noticed the tears and tormented look on Amberlin's face.

"I'm too late," Amberlin whispered. "I should have known, but I missed the connection."

"What connection? What are you talking about?"

Amberlin sat down on the side of the curb and placed her head in her hands.

"Stand by, just a moment please." There was a moment of dead air space then the announcer returned. "Parkland Hospital has been advised to stand by for a severe gunshot wound."

"Oh my God," Hannah said, looking first at the radio in her hand and then to her friend.

"The President's limousine is now going by me at a high rate of speed. Secret Service men are standing up in the limousine. They are armed with submachine guns. It appears that someone in the limousine might have been hit by the gunfire."

Hannah sat down next to Amberlin and put an arm around her.

"I should have known. I should have..." Amberlin choked and sobbed. "If I'd only been here sooner."

"Is it Kennedy?" Hannah asked. Amberlin nodded, then slowly looked up. "They've killed my President."

2

Rev. Stover leaned back in the leather office chair that his congregation had given to him shortly before he and Missy had decided to take their message on the road. How long ago had that been? And in that length of time, he'd probably sat in the chair no more than a few hours all total. Funny how things like that turn out, but it sure felt good to be back home. It was only going to be for a few days before they'd head back out on the road and the next set of revivals.

Being home had given him some much needed time to rest and to think about many things. Just this morning he'd made what felt like an important decision to not continue to berate President Kennedy in any of his sermons until he'd had the opportunity to meet the man in person and determine for himself this man's character. It felt good to have made this decision. It felt righteous. He'd become a mouthpiece for Hearst and his cronies, but not anymore, at least not until he could arrange for such a meeting with the President. That shouldn't be too hard. Hell, he'd been doing all this work for Hearst. It was time the newspaper mogul helped him a bit. Surely, he could arrange such a meeting.

He was just reaching for the phone to give Hearst a call when there was a tapping on the office door. Missy walked in without waiting for a reply, which always irked Stover just a bit. What's the point of knocking if you're not going to wait to be invited in? But fine. Now that she was here, he'd let her know his decision. He expected there'd be some blowback on it. There usually was. He'd grown to expect it, but this time he'd stay strong and see the decision through.

"Good morning, dear. It's good to see you," he lied. "I've been thinking about something, and I want to include you in it."

"Good, I'm glad I caught you in and seated," Missy replied, a troubled look on her face.

"Yes, sitting in a most comfortable chair, I might add. I wish we could take it on the road..."

"Ben, I need you to focus for a minute and let me talk," Missy interrupted him. Rev. Stover felt a knot begin to form in the pit of his stomach. Something in the tone of her voice mixed with the distraught look on her face. Whatever it was she had to say wasn't going to be good news.

"What? What happened? Is Ben Jr. okay?"

"Yes, as far as I know, Ben is fine," Missy replied, and Stover let out a sigh. "It's the President. He was shot a short time ago in Dallas."

"Shot? Really?" he replied, stunned by the news but thankful at the same time it didn't involve his son. "Is he okay? Funny, I was just thinking about him and how..."

"He's not okay." Missy interrupted again. "He's dead."

"What! Really?"

"Yes," Missy assured him. "Governor Connally was also shot, but reports say he'll be all right."

Rev. Stover sat there for several seconds as his mind tried to take it all in. Damn. Here I go finally figuring out I need to talk to the man and this happens. Wait a minute. "Is this what Hearst was talking about a few weeks ago—the big deal that was coming down?"

Missy stared at him, her eyes not meeting his.

"Missy, tell me the truth. Is it?"

She let out a deep sigh of her own before answering. "Yes, it is."

"And you knew about it before now, didn't you?" Rev. Stover said in an accusatory voice.

"No, well, not exactly," Missy stammered. "Hearst gave me a heads up that something major was about to happen, but I didn't know the specifics."

"Damn...damn...damn!" Rev. Stover shouted as he leaped from his chair and started pacing the room. "This is bad. This is very bad."

"What do you mean?" Missy asked. "You've been preaching against this man for weeks. His remaining in office could have ruined this country."

"Preaching against someone is a far cry from murdering him," Rev. Stover said. "This has gone too far. We're in way over our heads. What the hell am I going to do?" He continued to pace around his office as he ran his fingers through his hair.

"You're going to sit down and calm down," Missy said in her sternest voice. "Now...please."

He stared at her, momentarily shocked by the edge in her voice. The two glared at each other for several seconds. Finally, Rev. Stover sighed heavily, and still shaking his head, returned to the chair behind his desk where he sat, continuing to glower at his wife.

"Now, listen to me," Missy said in a calmer voice. "This is a good thing. Oh, I know it's a shock to the system, to the whole country...hell, to the world, but we'll get through this, and when we do, we'll be stronger for it. The country will be stronger and so will you and I and our mission. You've got to trust me on this.

"Now, Johnson has already been sworn in as the President, and they have apprehended the man who shot Kennedy."

"Really? Already? Who was it?"

"Some nobody by the name of Oswald, I believe."

"Oh, shit, that's not good. What if he blabs about who's behind this? It'll just be a matter of time before we have the Secret Service, or FBI, or CIA..."

"Enough!" Missy shouted, the edge of 'don't mess with me' back in her voice. "He won't talk, and no one is coming to our door. I'll be talking with Hearst later today. He wants you on the call to go over what you're to say about this tragic event. If you and I follow instructions, everything will be fine. If you go flying off the handle with Hearst or with the press...well, you won't, that's all. Do you understand?"

He nodded slowly. "I need a drink," he finally said.

"Fine. I'll get it for you, but only one, at least until after the call." Missy stood up and walked over to him. She placed a hand on his cheek and rubbed it softly. "It's going to be all right. Trust me."

He tried unsuccessfully to smile back at her. "Just get me that drink, will you?"

The Day After

The headline of the *Fort Worth Star Telegram* that set on the table between the two girls read:

KENNEDY SLAIN

CONNALLY ALSO HIT

BUT NEITHER HANNAH or Amberlin even glanced at it. They knew what it said. They'd been there. After the shooting, they made their way back to the van and slowly drove out of town. Hannah didn't know where to go so she just drove around aimlessly as Amberlin sat next to her, occasionally sobbing then abruptly stopping, taking several deep breaths before the next rain of tears began.

When Hannah saw a sign for a campsite several miles outside of town, she turned the van in that direction. The gruff old man behind the counter took her money and pointed towards a few vacant lots without saying a word. He, like the rest of the world, appeared in shock by the shooting that had occurred in his neck of the world.

They'd spent the night at the campsite. Neither of them had the energy to set up the tent, so they simply slept in the back of the van for another night hugging each other for comfort as well as for warmth.

Now they sat at a twenty-four-hour restaurant a few miles from the campgrounds. Hannah ordered bacon, eggs, toast, and coffee for both of them, then watched as her friend pushed the eggs around on her plate with a slice of toast. Amberlin hadn't spoken ten words since telling Hannah of Kennedy's assassination.

"Please, eat some food," Hannah begged her. "And talk to me. What are you thinking? What should we do now?"

Amberlin looked up from her plate with a glassy stare and shrugged, then resumed pushing the eggs around. Growing more frustrated by the minute, Hannah finally picked up the fork next to Amberlin's plate and stabbed a piece of the egg and held it out to Amberlin.

"Here, eat."

Amberlin moved her gaze from the plate to the end of the fork, and finally, after several seconds opened her mouth so that Hannah could feed her. This continued for several minutes until about half the eggs, and two slices of the bacon were consumed, then Amberlin turned her face away from the next fork of food.

Hannah dropped the fork on the plate with a clatter, then picked up her own fork and took a few bites, washing the food down with the lukewarm coffee. What were they going to do? She'd never seen her friend in such a state of despondency. It's like she's given up all hope, leaving me to make all the decisions, but I don't know what to do now. Do we go back to Austin, or should I call Spooks and ask her to come here? That would mean Spooks would have to find the bus station down in Austin, and I'd need to find where the station was in either Fort Worth or Dallas. No, it made more sense to drive back to Austin. At least that had a map that would give her directions even though she doubted she could depend on Amberlin to help out.

Hannah was still mulling over all this when she felt someone standing over them. Figuring it was their waitress, she looked up to ask for the ticket then stopped with her mouth half open. Rose Gentry stood smiling down at them.

"What in the world? How did you...?"

Rose slipped into the booth next to her granddaughter. "All in good time," she said as she turned to Amberlin. "You've not finished your breakfast. Eat up. You're going to need your strength for what lies ahead."

Already stunned by Rose's sudden, unexpected appearance, Hannah was equally puzzled how little it appeared to affect Amberlin, who continued to stare at her half-finished plate of food. "I had to feed her to get her to eat that much," Hannah explained.

"Really? Well, that's just silly," Rose replied, picking up the fork and placing it in Amberlin's hand. "I know this has been a devastating turn of events, my dear. And I know how you felt about our dearly departed President. But I also know that you know how to eat so do so...Now!"

Amberlin stared at her grandmother for several seconds, then gazed down at the plate before using the fork to scoop up a mouthful of eggs and place it in her mouth. As she did so, tears started streaming down her face, but she continued eating until everything on her plate was gone.

"Well done," Rose said. She waved to the waitress. "Will you bring me a cup of coffee and heat up these girls' coffee as well? Thank you." The waitress brought over a fresh cup and an almost full pot of coffee. When she finished, she asked, "Would you like something to eat?"

"No, I've already eaten," Rose replied. "Thank you very much." Turning back to Amberlin, she said, "Drink a little coffee, dear. It'll make you feel better."

Amberlin picked up the cup, blew across it for a moment then took a couple sips before putting it down.

Hannah watched in amazement until she couldn't stand it any longer. "Please, how did you know where to find us? This is just too spooky."

Rose smiled and reached over to pat her hand. "It's really quite simple. The Gentry women are like a coven of witches. We all have a connection to each other and can find where another is, especially when that one is distressed and in need of assistance. Amberlin's been sending out such signals since early yesterday morning, but it took me until today to finally hone in on the signal."

"Well, I guess that's not any weirder than anything else I've come to know and expect from the Gentrys," Hannah finally replied. "But wait a minute, how about when Amberlin and her mother were separated for all those years?"

"Yeah, well, I think it was a combination of the drugs they were giving Evelyn and her animosity to me gummed up the works. Now that she's no longer taking the drugs and she and I have made up, things are working much better now.

"But enough of that," Rose said, turning back to Amberlin. "We've got to get you back on track and on purpose. This has been a devastating twenty-four hours, and it's not over yet." She reached over and put her arms around Amberlin who sat there for a moment rigid before her shoulders began to shake, and a sob escaped her lips. She then fell into her grandmother's arms and cried for several minutes. When the waitress started over to see what was the matter, Rose waved her away, mouthing, "It's okay. Leave us alone please."

Finally, Amberlin grew quiet, and her breathing came more easily. Rose pulled back a little and, drawing a lace handkerchief from her sleeve, handed it to her granddaughter. "Feeling a little better?" she asked. Amberlin nodded, then wiped her eyes and blew her nose.

"A little. It's just that I was so close. If I'd only figured it out sooner, it all might have been different."

"Yes, dear. I know," Rose replied, "and that's something you'll have to learn to live with, just as I had to learn to deal with my terrible mistakes with your mother. It's all part of life and the evolution of our spirits. Meanwhile, I believe you mentioned that your mystery song referred to two other men. Is that correct?"

Amberlin nodded. "Yes, the other two names are Martin and Bobby."

"So, your mission isn't over yet."

Amberlin nodded again. "Yes, you're right."

"What have you learned from this devastating experience?"

Amberlin paused for a moment considering the question. "Well, two things come to mind. One is that I need to trust myself more and act on my guidance. Lives are at stake. Important lives."

Rose and Hannah nodded together. "And what's the second thing you've learned?" Rose asked.

"Well, I've been looking at what these four men have in common, and it appears that one key thing they share or might share is that someone shot and killed them. Both Abraham Lincoln and John Kennedy were assassinated." As she said this, tears started welling up in her eyes again. She took a corner of the handkerchief and dabbed them away.

"So, if that's true, then...?" Rose paused to let Amberlin consider the question.

"Then, there are two other men out there by the names of Martin and Bobby whose lives are in jeopardy." She looked from Rose to Hannah and back at Rose. "Which means *our* mission isn't over."

"Exactly," Rose replied, and Hannah nodded. The three of them clasped hands over the table. "That includes Evelyn," Rose added, "So we need to get ourselves back to Austin and make plans."

"Will you be coming with us?" Amberlin asked as Hannah waved to the waitress for their check.

"Yes, dear heart, I will. We're in this together against the forces of evil and powerful forces they are."

"But I have a feeling they're no match for the Gentry clan," Hannah added.

"Yes, and that includes you, Hannah dear," Rose said. "As the matron of this coven of witches, I declare you are an honorary member."

"Watch out world. Here we come!" Amberlin shouted.

Epilogue

1

A thin man in an oversized pea jacket with large pockets sat two booths down from where Amberlin, Hannah, and Rose ate their breakfast. He wore a floppy hat that hid much of his clean-shaven face and kept on a pair of sunglasses despite the subdued lighting of the restaurant. A cup of lukewarm coffee sat in front of him. He cocked his head to one side to pick up the conversation coming from the other booth, thankful for his keen hearing despite all the times he'd spent listening to loud music.

When the three women left the restaurant, he slid out of the booth and walked nonchalantly to the men's room where he scrubbed his hands for the fourth time that morning. As he started to leave, he pulled a walkie-talkie out of the pocket of the pea jacket and dropped it into the trashcan. He paused for a moment, considering whether to discard the binoculars as well, then decided to keep them. If nothing else, he could sell them for a few bucks at a pawn shop somewhere. He didn't bother hurrying. The tracker he'd placed on the van formerly owned by his friend, Tattoo, would continue to do its job.

He returned to the booth where he took a final sip of coffee, made a face, then dropped a bill on the table and walked out.

2

As the three of them started home for Austin, they began to brainstorm what they could do to protect Martin and Bobby.

"Are you sure that the song is referring to Martin Luther King and Robert Kennedy?" Rose asked, leaning in from the backseat where she'd insisted on sitting despite Amberlin's invitation that she take the passenger seat. Hannah had insisted on driving.

"You drove all the way up here, so I'll drive back. Besides, it'll be easier for you and your grandmother to talk. I'll listen in and pipe in from time to time."

"Well, I'm pretty sure the Martin in the song is Martin Luther King," Amberlin replied. She pulled a slip of crumpled paper from her jeans pocket and

196

read the lyrics. Again, it referred to a man that had freed a lot of people. Wouldn't that apply to Reverend King as well?

"But it sounds like from the lyrics that he's already dead," Rose pointed out.

"Yeah, I know. I don't understand it completely, but it's like the song is from another time, and it's simply reporting on what happened."

"That could be," Rose agreed. "Dreams and visions can be weird like that, although I don't ever recall one coming to me from the future, but then again, I worked hard for years trying to suppress my abilities."

"There's also the problem that there are two men and we're only four women, including Spooks," Hannah added from the driver's seat. "Does that mean we'll need to split up into two groups?"

The two Gentry women thought about that for a moment.

"No, I don't think so," Rose said.

"I agree. I think we need to stay together. So far, the lyrics have been in order of the assassinations: Abraham first, then John, so I'm praying that will continue. If so, Rev. King will be next."

"Do the lyrics say anything about where or when the next assassination attempt will be?" Hannah asked.

"No." Amberlin frowned. "Unfortunately, it doesn't, though I do appreciate you're calling it only an attempt."

"Hell, yeah. We're on the case now, so this time we've got to find some way to stop it before it happens. Maybe when we do, the lyrics will say something like 'it seems some of the good live a long and happy life.'"

Amberlin chuckled. "That would be nice." Everyone grew quiet as they pondered the tremendous challenge that lay before them.

They pulled into Austin shortly after nightfall and found Spooks outside in a rocking chair waiting for their return. As Amberlin climbed out of the van, she stretched for a moment then walked over to her mother who wrapped her arms around her. "My poor baby. I'm so sorry what happened. I know President Kennedy was very special to you." Amberlin simply nodded and let the tears flow again. She knew someday she'd be able to talk about that fateful day in Dallas without breaking down, but that day felt far off at the moment.

Rose and Hannah walked up, and they all joined in a group hug for several minutes, each of them lost in their own thoughts and grief. Finally, Amberlin pulled herself gently away. "Let's just leave our stuff in the van for now. I'm famished. Do we have anything to eat inside?"

"How about a big bucket of Kentucky Fried Chicken with all the trimmings?" Spooks said.

"Ahh, you're an angel," Amberlin said, and Rose and Hannah agreed.

After everyone had stuffed their face with chicken, mashed potatoes, and coleslaw, Spooks tapped on her ice tea glass. "Now that everyone has finished eating, I have some good news I've been dying to share with you."

"What's that?" Hannah asked. "Did we win the lottery?"

"No, not quite," Spooks replied, "but it's almost as good. I spoke with Al Grossman today, and he has a contract he needs to be signed from Columbia Records."

"You're kidding?" Amberlin exclaimed. "They're huge. What in the world do they want with little ol' me?"

"Well, as Al said, they want to make you a star. The contract starts with a single but with an option to expand that into a full album."

"That's fantastic," Rose said. "My granddaughter is going places."

"Yeah," Amberlin said, trying to sound enthusiastic, but all she could think about was how could she possibly fulfill the contract and also protect Rev. King and Robert Kennedy. She decided to voice her concern to the rest of the group.

"Why should you have to worry about them?" Spooks asked, and the other three took a few minutes to catch her up on their plans.

"Well, that could be a problem, but I'm sure we can figure it out somehow. You can't put your life on hold and simply become a groupie for King," Spooks said.

"Yes," Rose added. "Like it says in the Bible, the Lord never gives us more than we can handle, so we'll just have to work out a way."

"I've been thinking about the fact that we don't know when or where someone might try to harm Rev. King. I noticed as the time began to draw near to this trip to Dallas I started feeling a strong urge to see JFK. I mean, I've always wanted to see him someday, but suddenly that someday had to be soon. Unfortunately, I didn't trust it at first. I think if I had, the outcome might have been different."

"Well, also remember you have the three of us in your corner," Hannah added. "So I say, hang on tight, babe. We're in for a wild ride."

"No kidding," Amberlin said as she reached over and grasped Hannah's and Spooks hands who then completed the circle by grasping Rose's.

3

It was late at night, and Rev. Stover snored away in dreamland next to Missy. She'd tried to sleep, but the activities of the last few days wouldn't leave her alone, so she'd sat up and tried to read from her Bible. It often gave her guidance and peace-of-mind so she could let the troubles go; just turn them over to God.

So far, it hadn't worked. Missy knew her husband had been wrong when he'd said that they were in over their heads. Missy didn't see it that way. She knew God would never give them more than they could handle, though often it would appear that way at first. These were times where God was just testing their faith. No, they could handle what was before them. In fact, Missy knew it was a grand opportunity to further their work for God, perhaps in the greatest game of all: politics. More than just politics, they had an opportunity to play with the big boys, the power brokers who ran the whole world behind the scenes.

Her role was clear. She was to keep her husband on track and in line. Fine. She could do that. Hell, she'd been doing that for most of their married life together. She was still laying out plans when the phone rang, making her jump. Who the hell would be calling this late at night. She reached over to the night table and grabbed the receiver off the hook before it woke her husband.

"Yes?" she said softly. "Who's this?"

"I just heard through the grapevine that Amberlin has gotten a huge record deal with one of the largest recording companies around," Ben Jr. said without bothering to identify himself. The anger in his voice was palpable through the line. "I should have been part of that deal," he continued. "Once again you've managed to ruin my life. I hope you're satisfied. Oh, and by the way, your old friend, Rose Gentry, is still alive." And with that, the phone line went dead.

Missy held the phone out in front of her, studying the receiver. Poor boy, she thought. When would he ever learn not to be such a victim, always blaming others for his problematic life? At the same time, a part of her mind was digesting the new information. So, Amberlin has a big record deal, huh? And her grandmother is back in the picture. I wonder how she managed to escape the fire. Well, it's time—time to take that bitch, Amberlin, down. Hell, while she was at it, she'd take the entire Gentry clan down, ruin their lives, eliminate them from the world.

But how? She didn't have the answer to that question, not yet, but she would. She knew it would all unfold with just a little more prayer time. After all, she'd been part of taking down one of the most powerful men in the world. The Gentry women would be easy.

Did you love *Amberlin: Awakening*? Then you should read *Fantastic Fables of Foster Flat* by Orrin Jason Bradford!

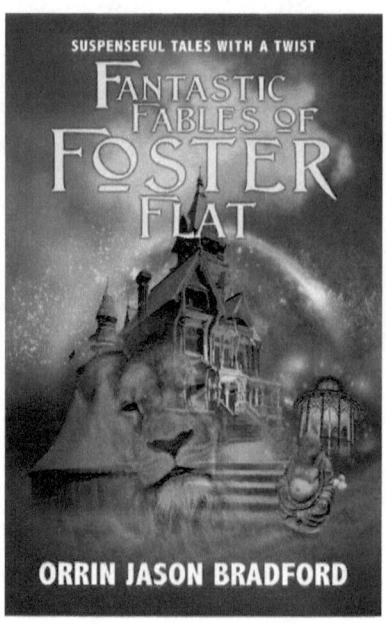

Return to a time of whimsy and wonder in a place unlike any other...

Often as children, we regard the places where we grew up to be the most magical places on Earth. Nostalgia and innocent curiosity tend to paint a picture of incredible wonder and local legend that, as our lives cast their shadows, seem to grow taller with age. Alas, for the most part, these shadows are an illusion--a mere trick that time plays on the mind, one that longs for magic and wonder and adventure. For me, as a lifelong resident of Foster Flat, North Carolina, however, I know this to be untrue. Enchantment is more than just a fairy-tale and not all the strange happenings of a sleepy mountain town are born of the whimsy of children.

I am Mimi Rawlins and I know that magic exists.

Enter the unsuspecting town of Foster Flat and uncover a world of wonder, fantasy, and more. In these incredible tales uncovered by Foster Flat's most beloved sleuthing journalist, the accounts of strange occurrences, magic, and miracle delight a wide array of audiences--from those whose curiosity outweighs their rationale and those that never really stopped believing in magic.

Fantastic Fables of Foster Flat is a collection of suspenseful fantasy tales written in the spirit of Ray Bradbury and The Twilight Zone. Inspired by the Great Smoky Mountains themselves, if you like character-driven stories, southern charm, and twists you won't see coming, you'll love Orrin Jason Bradford's assortment of twisty tales.

Buy *Fantastic Fables* to travel deep into the unique mountain town today! Read more at www.wbradfordswift.com.

Also by W. Bradford Swift

A Life On Purpose Special Report
Clarity of Purpose: Don't Live Life without It

Amberlin Series
Amberlin: Awakening

Standalone
La tua vita con uno Scopo: Sei tappe verso un'esistenza illuminata

About the Publisher

Porpoise Publishing is the imprint of indie author W. Bradford Swift who also writes under the pen name of Orrin Jason Bradford. It is best known for publishing visionary fiction--stories that entertain while also inspiring readers to imagine greater possibilities for their lives.

www.ingramcontent.com/pod-product-compliance
Lightning Source LLC
Chambersburg PA
CBHW020752210626
46807CB00018B/2531